A Nation Destroyed—
a Family Survives

Ted Lopuszynski

PublishAmerica
Baltimore

First printing

ISBN: 1-60703-604-5
PUBLISHED BY PUBLISHAMERICA, LLLP
www.publishamerica.com
Baltimore

Printed in the United States of America

The Russian troopers put my family in a cattle car.
The troopers said to us,
"You have no country.
We own you and your country."

Ted Lopuszynski
September 2008

During family gatherings, family members from Poland spoke about their lives before coming to America. They spoke of the horror and despair they endured for so many years. It seemed that the events they spoke about could not be true but all events proved to be true. Only three members of this family remain alive today who lived through a portion of the horror that beset their country for so many years. These family members find it difficult but also somewhat therapeutic to talk about their feelings. Jan said to me, “I cannot talk about my emotions, you just make them up. You will never even come close to our feelings, for what happened to us was so horrible it cannot be described.” All the events are true.

Acknowledgment is given to Jan Lopuszynski for his help in recalling the many events while I was growing up and to Mary Evans and her husband for all the historical research they did regarding Poland, World War I and World War II. They each gave immense assistance in writing this book, especially Mary by putting the characters’ emotions in the dialogue.

Bibliography/Acknowledgments

Encyclopedia Britannica, Inc. 1969, Volumes 1 through 23 with emphasis on Poland, Volume 18.

Internet site @ amazon.com. "The History Place" World War II in Europe Timeline, for dates of events leading up to WWII.

Internet site @ wikipedia.com. "Poland" for historical dates and events.

Internet site for US Government publications, The World Factbook, Central Intelligence Agency, Map of Europe and World Map.

The Holy Bible, New International Version, containing the Old Testament and the New Testament, Zondervan Bible Publishers.

The Sunday Oregonian, September 26, 2004, Section B4, for elements of the life of Frank Zielony.

Contents

List of Illustrations

Preface

In the year 1770, Poland was a medium-large country of east-central Europe bounded geographically by the Baltic Sea on the north, the Carpathian Mountains and Austria on the south, Russia on the east, and Prussia on the west. Poland's climate provides warm summers and cold winters. The land has forests, clear streams, and a few rivers flow through Poland. Poland has ideal climate conditions for growing a variety of crops. The area of Polish land is approximately 283,204 square miles, and Poland's population is about 11,420,000. The people are predominately Roman Catholic. Polish land is fertile and productive but coveted by Russia, Prussia, and Austria.

In June of 1770, Fredrick II of Prussia draws a military cordon to keep out the so-called cattle plague around the Polish provinces he covets. He has the consent of Catherine II (Catherine the Great) of Russia to do this. Now the Turks, alarmed at Russia's progress into Poland, declare war against Russia.

The courts of Berlin and Vienna decide that to preserve the equilibrium of Europe, it is best to give Polish land to all three powers—Russia, Prussia, and Austria. These three powers write a treaty for the partitioning of Polish lands to keep out a now prevalent cattle plague from their land. Russia, Prussia, and Austria want Poland's rich farmland and they use the cattle plague as a ruse.

On February 17, 1772, the three powers sign a treaty of partition for Polish lands. This is the first partition of Polish lands, and Poland loses half of the country's population and nearly one third of their land. Partitioning their country horrifies the Polish people and they protest strongly. Regardless, the deal for Polish land is a done deal. Russia, Austria, and Prussia mistreat the Polish people hideously.

By May 3, 1791, Polish leaders write a new Polish constitution that helps them and pleases the leaders of France and England. Russia and Prussia oppose the new constitution for it favors the people—the "average person."

When the current war between the Russians and the Turks ends in May of 1792, Russia sends 90,000 troops into eastern Poland, overwhelming the Polish troops. Prussia, alarmed that Russia might take over all of Poland, seizes Great Poland (a large part of western Poland). Prussia does not like Russian advances into Poland and decides to come to an acceptable understanding with Russia. Prussia and Russia invite Austria to be a part of this second partitioning. Austria refuses and does not take part in the second partitioning of Polish lands and abandons her interest in this process.

On September 23, 1793, Russia and Prussia sign the second partitioning of Polish lands. Russia and Prussia have decreased Poland in size to 83,012 square miles with a population of about 4 million. Poland is now one third of her original size and has slightly over one third of her former population. The Polish people want their nation back and in her former size.

Tadeusz Kosciuszko, a Polish patriot, wants to reunite his country to her original size and greatness. He calls the peasants to arms and they respond nobly. On March 23, 1794, Kosciuszko goes to Cracow, proclaims a national revolt, and declares himself the national leader of Poland—of all Poland. Russia and Prussia invade Poland to quell the uprising. At first, Kosciuszko is successful in all his battles.

Figure 1

The Three Partitions of Poland

Nevertheless, on the battlefield at Maciejowice, the overwhelming masses of Russian troops wound and take Kosciuszko prisoner on October 10, 1794.

The greed of victorious Russia soon leads to a rupture in relations between Austria and Prussia but they settle their differences and bring about the third partitioning of Poland. Prussia and Austria do not want Russia to take all of Poland's remaining land and demand a larger share of Polish land.

This third partitioning of Poland wipes Poland off the European map in 1795. Russia takes 63 percent of remaining Polish land, Prussia takes 19.5 percent, and Austria, who still covets Polish land, takes 17.5 percent. All the Polish people now live under three different political, constitutional, and financial regimes as slaves—the Polish people want their freedom and country back.

Before the third partition of Poland, the country had been in a form of regeneration. Poland had growth in their rural economy and the "average person's" condition had improved. This improvement occurred despite interference of Prussia and Russia. Polish grain exports have increased, industrial plants have appeared, trading, banking between towns has increased, education, and wealth is obvious. Russia, Prussia, and Austria do not like seeing Polish power. This evidence of Polish wealth and power is most likely the real reason for the third partitioning of Poland.

Many changes occur in the 1800s, the most notable being the victorious campaign of Napoleon against Prussia. Prussia consolidates many of their holdings of Polish land into a region called the "Duchy of Warsaw." This region included a large portion of Poland that remained after the Second Partition. In April of 1814, Tsar Alexander of Russia defeated Napoleon's armies and laid claim to Warsaw and the surrounding "Duchy."

In the Prussian and Russian sections, the Russians and Prussians treat their former Polish subjects as their slaves. In Austrian Poland, Joseph II, Austria's leader, introduces reforms to protect the Polish peasants from abusive exploitation by Austrian landowners. However, the Austrian people consider the Polish people their slaves.

In all three sections of former Poland, the people work to reunite their country. They work in secret, fearing for their lives while trying to reunite all of Poland. The Polish people meet often to work to reunify Poland. By getting together, they preserve their camaraderie and their common cause—to reunite Poland.

In Prussian Poland and Austrian Poland, the governments treat the people better than the Russian government does in Russian Poland. In Russian Poland, all Polish schools must teach the Russian language. A harsh Russian government imprisons anyone found speaking the Polish language. Russian troopers keep their prisons filled with political offenders—mostly Polish people caught speaking their Polish language.

Poland remains off the European map for 123 years.

Chapter One
Russian Poland

In a small village, east of Warsaw, the Polish people live under Russian domination. The time is March of 1885. Anna and Michat, a married couple, have one child they have named Maciej who is just two years old. Anna, her husband, and their child live in one small room in a wood building that has about fifteen rooms with no running water or electricity. An outhouse is in the back of the building that serves as a bathroom for all the people. Anna and Michat have a small wood-burning stove to keep them warm and to cook food and heat water for tea. They live in constant fear of the Russian troopers.

Today Michat leaves for work just as the sun starts to rise. He quickly notices that three Russian troopers are following him—again. He feels his chest tighten with fear that the troopers plan to arrest him. Michat thinks a Russian trooper may have heard him speak his Polish language to a friend just outside the building where he and his family live. He prays the Russian troopers will not arrest him and send him to prison. Michat knows that no one gets out of a Russian prison alive and that the Russian prisons are full of Polish men arrested with the charge of a counterrevolutionary act—speaking their Polish language.

Michat notices the Russian troopers are the same troopers who followed him yesterday. Michat walks quickly to work and the Russian troopers suddenly disappear. As his workday ends, Michat looks to see if there are any Russian troopers nearby. He does not see any troopers and leaves work, walking quickly to his home.

Suddenly he senses the troopers are following him. He looks back quickly and sees the same troopers following him that followed him yesterday. He fears they plan to arrest him now. He continues to walk quickly home, praying they will not arrest him. Michat fears the troopers will find his plans to leave and the names of Polish people who help a person leave Russian Poland. Michat also knows the Russian troopers prefer to do their arresting in the morning so the Polish people can see the arrests.

Michat enters his room without the troopers arresting him. He sees Anna and tells her about the troopers. They hug each other and Michat tells Anna how much he loves her and his need to leave before the troopers arrest him.

"Tonight, Anna, I will leave in the dead of night and flee to the Baltic coast. Anna, my dearest, I am told there are ships in the harbor getting ready to leave sometime in June. Once I get to the harbor and find a ship, well, Anna, I can work my way to America."

Anna looks with disbelief and horror at Michat. Anna quickly puts her arms around Michat. Tears flow from Anna's eyes as she begs him to stay with her and their child.

Michat looks lovingly at Anna and kisses her passionately. He says no more to Anna, and she slowly releases her hold on him. Little Maciej has started to cry, and Michat goes to him and holds him close to his chest. He rocks his little son to sleep and continues holding his son until almost midnight when he puts him to bed.

Anna looks at Michat and quietly says, "Please don't leave me."

Michat goes to her, kisses, and hugs her fiercely. Now he makes passionate love to Anna. Anna falls asleep thinking, *He loves me and he will not leave our child and me.*

Michat awakens about 3:00 a.m. and quickly puts on his clothes. He looks lovingly at Anna and little Maciej but knows he must leave and now. He quietly leaves their room with just the clothes on his back and one heavy coat. In the pocket of his coat, he has directions to help him find the Baltic port and a list of Polish people who will help him reach his destination. Michat has had these instructions for the past two months and never said a work to Anna.

Michat walks carefully in the dark, making sure no Russian troopers see him. Slowly but cautiously he finds the first house on his list just as the sun begins to rise. He knocks cautiously on the door. Slowly an elderly but kind-looking woman opens the door. Michat quickly says, "My name is Michat and I was told you would help me as I journey to the Baltic port."

The woman quickly grabs Michat's arm and pulls him into her home. "Come in and have some breakfast. I have a bed ready for you to rest before nightfall." Michat enters her home and follows her to the kitchen, where the rest of her family is eating breakfast.

Now the woman's husband greets Michat and tells him to sit in the empty chair next to him and eat. Michat is hungry and eats heartily. As he finishes eating the man takes Michat to a small loft to rest. Michat thanks the man and woman profusely as he lies down on the bed and falls asleep.

As dusk starts to fall, the woman wakens him and says, "Come eat, for it is almost time for you to continue your journey." She points to a basin of water and indicates he should wash before coming to eat.

Michat quickly does as the woman asked him to do.

As Michat sat down at the table, the man asked Michat where his next destination would be. Michat shows the man the map his friend gave him. The man quickly tells Michat, "You can probably make it beyond the next place and stop here." He points to the destination on the map. Michat's eyes light up and he says, "Yes, you are right. This might help me get to the port sooner. I must reach the port before the ships leave."

The man smiles and says, "Yes, we understand and we will pray for you." They do not exchange their names, for it is better they do not know each other's names. Michat eats quickly and then leaves, for now it is dark.

Tonight there is no moon, so Michat must be very careful not to miss the signs that point the way to the port. The signs are simple like a mark on a tree, the ground, or a twig pointing the way. The signs are easy to miss and so normal looking that a Russian trooper would not even think they were signs to help a Polish man find his way to the Baltic port. Michat misses only one sign, but that miss added a whole week of travel for him and two days without food or a place to stay.

The nights are bitter cold to Michat as he walks through the forests and towns, yet he feels a sense of freedom and exhilaration as he walks alone to the Baltic Sea port. Michat seldom sees a Russian trooper and he wonders where they might be hiding. He does not think of his son or wife.

Finally, Michat finds the port city of Gdansk, where he sees a big sign asking workers to work on a ship bound for America. He applies for work. Immediately the man hires Michat, for the ship leaves for America in two days and they need more help. It is now late June and it has taken Michat three months to get to the Baltic port.

Tonight, Michat takes in a deep breath of relief, for he does not have to hide from the Russian troopers. Still, he is careful to say nothing to anyone and is grateful for the food and bed the ship's captain has provided him.

Tonight Michat prays to God, "Please, God, take care of my Anna and little Maciej. Please, God, I have left them to keep them safe, please let no harm come to them." This is the first time Michat has thought of his wife and son since leaving them. Michat barely finishes his prayer when he falls asleep, for he has had little sleep or food during the latter part of his trip to the Baltic port.

The next morning Michat awakens to a lot of noise and a Polish man yells at him to come with him and get some breakfast. He tells Michat, "Today we leave for America, and there is work we must do as the ship leaves the harbor." Michat follows the young Polish man and notices there are many Polish men working on this ship. Michat wonders how many of the Polish men have left wives and children just to get away from the horrid Russians.

Chapter Two
Anna and Maciej

Just after dawn six Russian troopers pound on the door of the room where little Maciej lies sleeping. Anna, awake, is horrified that Michat has gone. She cannot stop sobbing as she answers the door and gasps in horror as she looks at the Russian troopers.

"Woman, where is your husband?" shouts the first trooper who comes into her room.

Immediately she answers in the Russian language, "I know not where he is. He came home last evening for his supper and was gone when I awoke this morning." Tears flow from her eyes as she wrings her hands.

The troopers in the room open drawers, bang, and throw her few clothes and one toy onto the floor. Little Maciej, hearing the noise, starts screaming. Anna runs to him and grabs him from his bedding. She hugs him close to her. She feels the troopers look at her with hate as she sobs.

With Maciej in her arms, Anna speaks in Russian, "I know not where he is. He has left me and our child."

One trooper harshly says, "We should take your child and tear him to pieces."

Anna, horrified, holds her crying child closer and says, "Then you must kill me too." She speaks only in the Russian language and prays they do not ask her anything more for she knows just a few Russian words.

The older Russian trooper, who does not approve of the harsh treatment the Polish people endure, says, "We will find your husband and imprison him but we do not want you or your child." With these words said, the older trooper orders the others to leave her room. He turns to Anna and says, "I hope your husband returns soon." With this said, the trooper leaves.

Quietly, Anna soothes little Maciej and silently prays that her husband makes it to America.

The years pass and Anna hears nothing from her husband. She misses him deeply and fears if he is still in Poland, the authorities will find and kill him. Fearing this, she tells no one where he may have gone. She knows that Michat cannot contact her because that would not be safe for either of them.

Three years pass and Maciej, now five years old, attends the Russian school during the day. In the evening, Anna teaches her son the Polish language and everything about Poland even though this is against Russian law. The only fact she holds back from Maciej is that his father left them to go to America. She also repeats firmly that Maciej must never speak Polish in public. Maciej at the age of five knows if a Russian hears him speak Polish and reports him to the authorities, the Russian troopers will send him and his mother to a Russian prison.

Maciej is bright and learns quickly. He attends the Russian schools and speaks Russian fluently, plus the German and Austrian languages. He advances quickly in school and graduates when he is sixteen years old, in the year of 1899. Poor health overcomes his mother and Maciej fears for her life. The thought that she might die terrifies Maciej, for he loves his mother deeply and he does not want to be alone.

After his graduation from the Russian school, Maciej applies for a job in a Russian store. Because Maciej can speak in Russian, German, and the Austrian languages, the Russian store owner hires Maciej. The man feels proud to have this new employee. Now he has someone who can help him increase his business and profits. Maciej does not tell the owner he speaks Polish.

Immediately after Maciej is hired, he runs home to his mama and tells her about his great fortune. He runs carefully, for he does not want the Russian troopers to stop him and ask him questions. As he arrives at their building, he walks slowly and opens the door to their room. He sees his mama, grabs her, and hugs her hard.

Now he tells her about his new position and the money he will earn. His mama smiles and says, "Oh, Maciej, this is wonderful. Maciej ,be extra careful for you can never trust a Russian, especially your new employer."

Maciej replies, "Yes, Mama, I know. Now you can rest more, and please, Mama, take it easy. I will make enough money for us both to survive. Mama, see a doctor. Perhaps he can help you get your strength back," says Maciej.

"Maciej dear, I am getting old and a doctor cannot help me. Maciej, my dearest son, I will take it easier but, please, Maciej, be careful, extra careful," pleads his mama.

The days turn into months; both mother and son are always careful to speak their Polish language in private. They even have new Polish friends that they can talk to in Polish. Maciej's mama finally tells her son why his father left them and that she hopes he made it to America.

She has had no word from him since he left for America so many years ago.

Maciej feels a sense of relief that his mama has told him about his papa. Despite this revelation about his papa, Maciej feels happy. He feels good that he can take care of his mama. This morning he kisses his mama tenderly and leaves for work. He thinks his mama looks poorly today. Maciej, always concerned about his mother, fails to see a Russian trooper following him to work.

The year is 1903 and Maciej is twenty years old. He has worked at the same store for almost four years. The storekeeper likes Maciej and feels Maciej's skill speaking several languages is the reason his business does so well. Today the storekeeper wonders why Maciej seems worried.

He asks, "Maciej, is something bothering you?"

Maciej replies, "It is just my mama, she is not well and today she seems more pale than usual."

"Oh, Maciej, I am sorry to hear this. I hope she will be better by the end of today. In fact, you can leave a little early if you want," says the storekeeper.

Maciej replies, "Thank you, I will leave a little early but not until I have all my work done." Maciej immediately starts his paperwork and then meets with a customer. He has a busy day and does not see the Russian trooper watching the store. The storekeeper sees the Russian trooper watching his store.

Maciej grabs his coat to leave the shop when the Russian storekeeper calls out, "Maciej, be careful. Have you not noticed the Russian trooper across the street? He has been watching my store since you came to work this morning."

"What?" says Maciej, in a hushed but alarmed voice!

The storekeeper replies in an angry voice, "Maciej, I think the troopers are watching you. You be careful, Maciej. I do not like the troopers arresting your Polish people. It is wrong. What my Russian government has done to you and your people, well, they never should have done such atrocities to your people."

Maciej looks stunned at his boss and thinks, *He cares what happens to me!* Maciej replies, "I will be careful. Thank you for warning me about that trooper."

Maciej leaves the store and does not look at the Russian trooper. He thinks, *That trooper does not need to know that I know he watches me. This is much safer for me, now I have the advantage, for I know the Russians watch my every move.* He walks briskly for a couple of blocks and does not realize the trooper no longer follows him.

Maciej turns the corner to walk to the building where he lives with his mama. Suddenly he feels someone grab his arm; it is his friend Bolek. Bolek speaks softly but firmly, "Maciej, come quickly into the shadows with me."

Maciej does not hear what his friend is saying, for he sees Russian troopers in front of the building where he lives with his mother. Maciej starts to run to his home, but his friend has a firm grip on his arm and prevents him from running to his building.

"Maciej, be still. Those troopers are after someone. We must stay here and watch them. We need to see what they do," says Bolek.

Maciej watches as the Russian troopers shove two of the people that live in the building where he and his mother live into a horse-drawn cage. Maciej's mother is not one of the people shoved into the cage already full of Polish people. Bolek and Maciej remain in the shadows as the horse-drawn cage pulls away from the building.

Slowly Bolek releases his hold on Maciej's arm. Both young men, horrified at what they have seen, look to the other in disbelief. Bolek tells Maciej, "This happens two or three times a week while you are at work. Every day I am grateful it is not my parents. Today I am glad it is not my parents or your mama."

"Bolek, this is wrong. Where do they take those people? What happens to them? Did they do something wrong?" cries Maciej.

"Maciej, some Russian probably heard them speaking in their Polish language or someone told a trooper they spoke in Polish. It makes no difference. Those people go to prison and they die there, for no one gets out alive. However, I have noticed for the past several months the Russian troopers do not come as often to arrest our Polish people," says Bolek rather calmly.

"Maciej, come with me tonight to our Polish meeting where we work to reinstate Poland as a country. Our leader has guards placed at strategic spots to warn us of any Russian troopers that might come and arrest us. You speak several languages and this will help us in our work. Please, Maciej, say you will come," pleads Bolek.

"First, I must go home and check on my mama, for she is not well. If she tells me to go with you tonight, I will meet you at this corner at seven o'clock," says Maciej.

Bolek says firmly, "See you at seven tonight, Maciej!"

Maciej immediately runs home, afraid for his mama. Maciej enters their room and sees his mother standing at their only window. Maciej thinks she looks better tonight. His mother turns and sees her son and quickly walks to him and hugs him fiercely. Maciej hugs his mother fiercely, too. They are each happy to be alive and together.

Maciej says to his mother, “My friend Bolek wants me to meet him at seven tonight and go to a meeting to work to reinstate Poland as a nation. Will this be all right with you if I join Bolek?”

His mother gives him another hug and says, “Yes, Maciej, this is good that we Polish people work for our country. But you must promise me you will be extra careful.”

Maciej replies, “Mama, I will be vigilant. They place guards in special places to warn us if any Russian troopers come nearby, and this gives us enough time to leave our meeting and avoid the Russian troopers.”

Maciej and his mama eat their meager meal of one large potato that they share and a few vegetables and hot tea. They thank God they are still together and pray for their compatriots now in prison.

Maciej meets Bolek at seven, and they walk quickly to their meeting without saying a single word. The meeting is informative and Maciej feels great that he came to this meeting. He feels it is good and right to be working for Poland. He just wishes they could do something now to stop the Russian enslavement of the Polish people.

Tonight’s Polish speaker condemns the Russians for not keeping records of whom they throw in prison and whom they kill.

The speaker states, “The Russian troopers throw our Polish people into prisons without a trial or any evidence of criminal acts. Then the Russian troopers put large numbers of Polish prisoners in the courtyard and shoot the prisoners until all are dead. This is wrong, for they do not even know the names of the Polish men and women they kill.”

The speaker calmly reports a new statistic, “We have noticed the Russians do not shoot as many Polish citizens today. The number of Polish people killed in the prisons this past week has decreased. We wonder why, but hope this trend continues."

Maciej, horrified at the brutality of the Russians, thinks this could happen to his mama, even himself. He tells Bolek he is glad he came to the meeting. After the meeting ends, Bolek introduces Maciej to Gwid. Gwid is just a year younger than Maciej, and the three young men become close friends.

Gwid tells Maciej the Russians arrested his grandparents and he does not know if they are dead or alive. The three young men talk for a short while, and then leave for their homes. They each agree to meet at the next meeting. Bolek tells them the next meeting will be at a different location and as soon as he knows the location, he will contact them.

When Maciej returns home, his mama is waiting for him with hot tea. His mama says, "Maciej, tell me everything that happened at your meeting?"

"Mama, I learned a lot. Especially what happens to our Polish people when the Russians take them out of their homes and put them in prison. No prisoner ever leaves the prisons alive. My friends and I hope to help those that are still in prison, and maybe we will get them out alive. We are working with other groups of Polish citizens to reinstate Poland as a country. Mama, we will have our country back someday, I feel it," says twenty-year-old Maciej.

Mother and son talk long into the night. Finally, tired, they each retire to their mats and fall asleep. All they have in their room are their mats for sleeping, some cooking utensils, a little food, a few dishes, a table and two chairs, plus a small wood-burning stove. In 1903, there is still no indoor plumbing or electricity in their village of Russian Poland.

Several years pass; it is now January of 1910. Maciej is twenty-seven years old. Today he notices his mama does not eat her food and looks paler than usual. Maciej asks, "Mama, why are you not eating?"

Anna replies, "I am not hungry, and you, Maciej, are not to worry. Now you go to work, Son." She gives him a big hug and several big kisses and gently pushes him out the door. His mama is ill but does not want Maciej to worry. However, Maciej thinks his mama might die. He fears for his mama yet he reluctantly leaves for work.

Maciej, concerned about his mama, asks the storekeeper if he can leave early. The storekeeper says, "Yes, you can leave as soon as you finish your work. Remember, Maciej, you have an Austrian merchant coming at three o'clock today and you are the only person that speaks his language."

Maciej replies, "Yes, I know, but the meeting will not take long and it will be profitable for you."

Maciej gets his work done and meets with the Austrian merchant. Everything goes just as Maciej said. As soon as the merchant left the store, Maciej leaves for home.

When Maciej arrives home, he finds his mama on her mat. His mama does not look right, something is very wrong. Immediately, he goes to the room next to their room and knocks on the door. A woman answers the door and Maciej quickly says, "Please come, I think my mama needs help," cries a sobbing Maciej.

The woman looks at Maciej and sadly says, "Yes, I will come."

She goes with Maciej and when she sees his mama, she goes to her and puts her hand over his mama's heart. She feels nothing and she realizes Maciej's mama is dead. She turns to Maciej and says, "Maciej, she has gone to a better place. I am so sorry."

Maciej begins to sob, for his heart has broken. Then he says, "I will not let them take her body and dump her somewhere. I must get my friends and we will bury her properly."

The custom for a dead Polish person is a Russian comes by in a horse-drawn wagon and picks up the dead people. Then the Russian takes the dead bodies and dumps them in a pit with other dead bodies. When the pit becomes almost full, a Russian comes with a huge pile of dirt and dumps the dirt on top of the dead bodies.

Maciej asks, "Can you stay here for just a little, until I find my friends? It will not take long."

The woman says, "Maciej, I will stay with your mama until you return, but do not take a longtime, for my husband returns in about an hour from his work and I must be home when he returns."

Maciej says through his tears, "Thank you." Maciej runs out of his room to find Bolek. He quickly finds Bolek and tells him about his mama. Bolek tell his brother that he needs his help. Maciej, Bolek and his brother with his big toolbox go to Gwid and tell him they must bury Maciej's mother tonight.

Gwid tells Maciej how sorry he is about the death of his mother. The four young men return to Maciej's room. The woman is glad to see them and quickly leaves because her husband will arrive home soon.

Bolek, his brother, and Gwid help Maciej take his mama to a field where the Polish people bury their loved ones whenever possible. Bolek's brother empties his big toolbox into a bag he brought with him and they use the toolbox as a casket to bury Anna.

The four young men dig into the hard but not frozen earth an area big enough to hold the wood box and deep enough to keep the animals from smelling the body in the box. They place the wooden casket in the hole and pile the dirt on top. Bolek says a prayer for Maciej's mama. In deep sadness, the four young men leave her grave. It is late January of 1910.

Bolek looks at Maciej and says, "Maciej, you come spend the night at my home. My mama will be mad at me if you refuse."

Maciej replies, "Thank you, I accept your kindness for tonight, but just for tonight."

Gwid hugs Maciej and says, "So long for now, Maciej. I will see you at the next Polish meeting, and if I can do anything for you, please let me know. Maciej, you are my dearest friend."

After the three young men return to Bolek's place, Bolek's mama puts her arms around Maciej and says to him, "You know, Maciej, your mama no longer suffers. She rests in the hands of our Lord. We will all miss her and we will all work to see Poland a nation again. She will see from the heavens above our nation—Poland—and she will smile on us."

Bolek's mama says, "Bolek, show Maciej where he will sleep tonight. Gwid, you best get home or your mama will be worried and frantic with fear for your life.

Gwid quickly hugs Maciej, says a quick goodbye to everyone, and leaves for his home.

Maciej does not sleep well, but he remembers every word that Bolek's mama said to him. He prays his mama is in a better place and promises God he will continue to work for Poland and the freedom of all Polish citizens. Maciej thinks of his papa for the first time in years and wonders if he made it to America. He also wonders if his papa is alive or dead.

The next day Maciej returns to the room he and his mama shared. He looks at everything in the room and realizes there is not much in their room. He leaves and goes to work.

When Maciej walks into the store, the storekeeper knows something bad has happened, for Maciej looks extremely pale and death like. Maciej tells the Russian storekeeper, "My mother died yesterday, and I feel a need to get out of that room where my mama died. I have this need to find another place to live."

Immediately the storekeeper tells Maciej, "You take the day off. No one is coming that I cannot handle. Maciej, I am so sorry."

Maciej leaves the store but does not immediately look for a place to live. He just wanders around in despair. No one stops him. He wonders why no Russian trooper has stopped him. Maciej looks around and sees no troopers. He wonders why he sees no Russian troopers, for they are always visible.

After many minutes of doing nothing, Maciej starts looking for another place to live. He finds a place near where he works that he likes and rent two rooms from the owner of the building.

The next morning, he moves his few belongings into his new place and leaves for work. Just before he leaves, he looks at his place with the sun streaming into the room from his two windows. Maciej feels good about the sun and his two windows. *This is a fine place and I think Mama would like it too if she had only lived.* Then Maciej remembers his mama always refused to move whenever he suggested getting a better place. *Perhaps she thought my papa would come back to her,* thinks Maciej. Now he leaves his new place and walks to work. He enters the store, greets his boss, and immediately begins working.

At the end of his workday, Maciej, tired and lonely, does not want to go back to his new place. Not knowing what else to do, Maciej walks into the Polish meeting room where the Polish citizens work to reinstate Poland. He takes a seat at the back of the room and sits down.

Many Polish citizens have already taken their seats, and many are smiling and laughing. More people arrive, and some smile at him, but he does not smile back.

Maciej does not hear what the speaker says, for he cannot get his mind off his mother's death. When the meeting takes a break, Maciej leaves. Maciej does not attend another meeting until May of 1910.

It is late May of 1910 when twenty-seven-year-old Maciej walks into the Polish meeting room. Maciej looks around at the Polish people as they arrive at the meeting. He notices some are smiling and laughing. He wonders why he came to this meeting tonight. He mumbles to himself, "The way I feel, I do not care whether Poland becomes a nation or not. I am alone except for my two friends, Bolek and Gwid, and my friends are not here tonight."

Chapter Three
Maciej and Maria

Maria, twenty-seven years old, decides to attend the Polish party meeting tonight even though she must attend alone. She arrives early, takes her seat, and looks around at the people arriving. Suddenly she sees the saddest young man sitting in the back row. She watches him and sees him wipe tears from his eyes. She wonders why he looks so sad. Why is he alone? Without thinking, she gets up, walks over and takes a seat next to the sad-looking young man.

Maciej does not even realize a young beautiful woman has sat down next to him. She places her hand on his arm and says, "You look so sad, is there anything I can do to help you?"

Maciej turns and looks at her. Her eyes and beautiful face overwhelm him and he cannot speak—*Who can this gorgeous creature be and why does she talk to me?* he wonders.

Maria's beauty captivates Maciej. He notices her brown hair that frames her face and glistens when she moves. Her brown eyes sparkle—she has kind and caring eyes, thinks Maciej. As she smiles at Maciej, he thinks, *She has the smile of an angel and she reminds me of my mama.*

Finally, Maciej gets his voice to work and asks her, "Why are you looking at me with such concern? Is something wrong, do you need some help?"

Maria responds, "You look so sad: I thought perhaps you are ill. I feel a need to comfort you. Please tell me how I can help you?"

Maciej, astounded, can barely speak. He takes a couple of deep breaths to gain his composure. He tells her, "I am just sad. My mama died a few months ago."

Maria replies, "Oh, I am so sorry but glad you are not ill. My name is Maria. What is your name?"

Maciej replies, "What a beautiful name, Maria." Maciej pauses a moment then says, "Maria, my name is Maciej."

The speaker starts to talk, and Maria moves back to sit with her friend who has just arrived. When the speaker takes his break, Maciej moves over to Maria and asks, "Maria, may I walk you home after this meeting?"

She replies, "Yes, and I would like you to meet my family. I will meet you outside after our meeting ends." The speaker starts the meeting and Maciej moves back to sit with his friends Bolek and Gwid who have just arrived.

After the meeting ends, Maciej tells his friends he will walk Maria home. Bolek and Gwid look with astonishment at Maciej and ask, "Who are you walking home?"

Maciej points to Maria and says, "That beautiful young woman over their sitting next to that other woman with the black hair."

Bolek and Gwid say in unison, "Wow, Maciej, you are lucky; we know her."

Bolek states, "She does not let many young men get to know her. She is a remarkable, kind, and caring person. You treat her right, Maciej."

Gwid tells Maciej, "You behave yourself with her; I know her, too, and she is a fine woman. I sure would not mind her paying attention to me."

Maciej looks at his friends and says, "Of course, I always mind my manners with other people." Maciej moves away from his friends and goes to the door to walk Maria home. Bolek and Gwid look stunned as Maciej walks out of the meeting room with the lovely young woman they each genuinely admire.

Maciej walks Maria home, and they talk about their wish to see Poland a nation again. Maria becomes aware of her need to know this young man better. She wants to see him again. All too soon, they arrive at Maria's door. Maciej knows he must be with Maria again and suggests that he walk with her to the next "All Polish Party" meeting. Maria says "Yes" to Maciej.

Without even thinking, Maciej kisses Maria goodnight. Maria, surprised by his kiss, thinks what a wonderful young man this Maciej is. She enjoys his rather long kiss and feels sad as Maciej walks away from her.

Whenever a Polish meeting is held, Maciej walks with Maria to every one of the Polish Party meetings. They even walk every evening after their work just to be together. Maciej takes Maria to his room one evening, and she notices that he has little in his room, just a bed, a table, and two chairs. She also notices there is no food in his room. Concerned, Maria decides to invite Maciej to dinner at her parents' home. Maria looks at Maciej and thinks he needs to eat more food.

"Maciej, please come to my place for our evening meal tomorrow," pleads Maria.

Surprised but pleased, Maciej replies, "Yes, Maria, I will come. What time do you want me to be at your place?"

Maria quickly answers, "Will you be able to make it at seven tomorrow?"

Maciej replies, "I will see you at seven tomorrow, and thanks for inviting me." Maria and Maciej leave his place and he walks her to her parents' place. Again, Maciej gives Maria a long kiss before he leaves her.

Maria has a job cleaning for several Russian couples and makes a little money. She spends her money carefully, for she does not make a lot of money. Many Russian families do not pay their young Polish workers, for they consider them their slaves. Maria, a bright young woman and intelligent, has never had the opportunity to learn to read or write. Many bright young Polish children never have the opportunity to go to school because of the Russian rules. All Polish children do learn the Russian language. Russian rule demands all Polish children and adults speak only the Russian language.

Today, after doing her cleaning chores and receiving her pay, Maria goes to market and buys extra food plus some sweets. Maria has learned how to count money and spend money wisely. Tonight will be special, she thinks, and it is wonderful the weather is warm. Maria likes the warm weather because she and Maciej can walk outside and kiss in the shadows. Maria hungers for Maciej's kisses. She believes Maciej will enjoy the food and sweets.

At seven o'clock, Maciej arrives at Maria's home. He knocks on the door, and Maria's sister greets him with pleasure. The wonderful smell of the cooking food pleases Maciej and he realizes he is hungry. Maria's parents tell Maciej, "Maciej, Maria has cooked all this food herself."

Maria cooks the food to just the right temperature, and the smells from the little stove make Maciej hungry. Tonight, Maciej cannot eat enough food. Maria looks at Maciej as he eats her food and wonders where he got such a ravenous appetite. At the end of the meal, Maria's parents and her sister excuse themselves and leave to visit friends.

This pleases Maria and Maciej. Now they can have a few minutes alone. Even though they have known each other a only a few months, Maria hopes Maciej might propose marriage, but he does not. Still, these two young people enjoy their private time together and their many kisses as they clean up the dishes after their wonderful meal.

Maciej does not see Bolek and Gwid as he now spends more time with Maria. Both Bolek and Gwid have met young women they like and they spend more time with them.

Several months pass when Bolek and Gwid meet Maciej as he leaves work. Bolek tells Maciej, "I have met the most wonderful woman, Maciej. I have known her for many years, but now that she has become a woman, I have different feelings. Maciej, I am going to surprise you with what I have to tell you. We plan to marry two weeks from this Saturday, and I want you to stand up for me at my wedding. Please say yes, Maciej?"

Maciej astounded, replies, "Yes, Bolek, of course I will stand up for you." Maciej and Bolek hug and slap each other on their backs before parting for their homes.

Several days later, Gwid tells Bolek and Maciej his startling news that he plans to marry his sweetheart and move to Warsaw. Gwid tells them that he leaves next week and is sorry he will not be able to join Bolek at his wedding. Suddenly Gwid says, "Maciej, when do you plan to propose to Maria?"

Maciej replies, “Oh, I am thinking about asking her, but perhaps later. She sure is a wonderful, kind, and caring woman. I think I am in love with her!”

Gwid says, “It is with regret that I leave you both, but I have the offer of a great position in Warsaw. My sweetheart and I plan to marry there. Her family already lives in Warsaw, and gosh, you know, it is a big exciting city.”

Gwid tells Bolek and Maciej, “You two guys are my best friends, and there are no words to say how sorry I am that I leave for Warsaw next week. Bolek, you have a great marriage and a wonderful life. You, Maciej, you ask Maria to marry you. I will miss you both. If you, Bolek and Maciej, ever get to Warsaw, you must promise me you will visit me.”

Both Bolek and Maciej reply firmly, “Yes, Gwid, we will visit you if we ever get to Warsaw.” Bolek says, “Gwid, you have a great life and I hope you find happiness, for you deserve the best.”

Maciej too says, “Gwid, that goes for me, too.”

Gwid and Bolek look at Maciej and tell him, “Do not take too long to propose to Maria. She has many admirers who want to marry her.”

Maciej replies, “I know she has admirers, but how could she possibly care for me?”

Bolek sternly says to Maciej, “Don’t be a fool, Maciej, she cares for you. You ask her soon or someone else might win her heart and marry her.”

The following week Gwid goes off to Warsaw to work at a new factory and marry his sweetheart.

The next two weeks pass quickly, and Maciej stands up for Bolek at his wedding in late fall of 1910. Both Gwid and Bolek’s weddings are small but held in the Catholic Church. The families place guards on the streets near the churches in hopes of learning if any Russian troopers are nearby. During a Catholic wedding, the priest speaks the vows in the Polish language. The Russian government forbids this even for a wedding.

At Bolek's wedding Maciej is his best man. Maciej hears the wedding vows and watches Bolek and his bride become husband and wife. He thinks, *This getting married is right. Perhaps tonight I will ask Maria to be my wife.*

Two months after Bolek's marriage, Bolek tells Maciej that he and his new wife will leave for a small town in Austria Poland. Bolek tells Maciej, "Living in Austria Poland seems better than here in Russian Poland." Bolek throws out his chest and says, "Maciej, I am going to be a father in about seven months from now."

Maciej slaps Bolek on his back, "Hey, that news is great. You will make a great dad. Bolek, I sure hope life will be better in Austria Poland."

Bolek asks Maciej, "How are you and Maria getting along? You spend many hours together every day. I wonder if you will marry soon, Maciej?"

Maciej, suddenly speechless, says, "I keep planning to ask Maria to marry me, but I have not done the asking yet." He tells Bolek, "I am deeply in love with Maria, but I am not sure she will say yes."

Bolek says, "Just ask her, Maciej. I think she will say yes."

Maciej waits another week, a week of utter loneliness. He does not even see Maria during this week as he tries to get up the courage to ask her to marry him. He knows she will refuse him. *After all, why should she say yes? I am penniless and can never own my own land, home, or anything living under these horrible Russian rules.*

Russian rule states no Polish person can ever own anything, and many Russian people consider the Polish men and women and their children as their slaves.

After almost ten days of not seeing Maria, Maciej can no longer stay away form Maria. His loneliness becomes unbearable and he misses Maria. He realizes he needs and loves Maria deeply. He worries that something bad might happen to her and feels a strong need to protect her. Tonight after work, he runs but carefully to her place.

When he arrives at Maria's apartment, he pounds on her door. He wants desperately to see Maria, but her mother answers the door. Maria's mother says, "Maciej, I am so glad you have come to see us. I have missed you." Maciej appears shocked and disappointed that Maria did not answer his knock.

Maciej stammers, "Aaaahhh, is Maria here?"

Maria's mother says, "Maciej, she will be back in about an hour. Would you like to come in and wait for her? I just made some dinner and I have plenty. Please come in and join us."

Maciej, always hungry, smells the food and replies, "Thanks, I'd love to join you."

Maciej sits down in the chair offered him when suddenly Maria and her papa arrive home. Immediately Maciej jumps up, grabs Maria, and hugs her fiercely. Maria's parents look at their daughter and this young man. Maria's parents smile and leave the room. They know how their daughter feels about Maciej.

Five minutes later, Maria's mother announces, "My dinner is ready to be eaten. Maciej, you and Maria come eat dinner with us."

Maciej tells Maria her mother has invited him to stay for dinner.

"Maria, do you mind if I eat dinner with you?"

Before Maria can answer Maciej, Maria's sister comes rushing through the door into the room crying out, "Is dinner ready?"

Maria gives Maciej a big hug and says, "I am so glad you will eat with us." Maria looks at her sister and simply laughs and says, "Yes, little sister, dinner is ready."

Maciej eats heartily, for it has been a while since he has eaten any good food. The last time was when Maria invited him to the dinner she cooked for him. Maria and her family notice that Maciej eats heartily. They feel pleased, for they know he does not eat often and even forgets to eat.

After dinner, Maria's parents invite Maria and Maciej to walk to the Polish Party meeting with them. Maria replies, "You go to the meeting, and Maciej and I will clean up. Is that all right with you?"

Maria's parents and sister immediately reply, "Yes, that will be fine with us. When we get back we will tell you both about the meeting."

After Maria's parents and her sister leave, Maciej and Maria clean the dishes and put them in the small pantry. They have not talked, nor has Maciej said a single word to her. She wants Maciej to propose marriage to her, but he has not done that yet.

Maciej suddenly puts his arms around Maria and gives her a long kiss. Maria responds to Maciej's kiss but wonders if he really cares about her.

Unexpectedly Maciej says, "Maria, will you marry me?" Maciej, surprised at what he has said, realizes he feels glad he has proposed to Maria.

Maria, stunned, does not hesitate to reply, "Yes, oh yes, my dear Maciej." Maciej, hearing the word "yes," grabs Maria. He hugs and kisses her for several minutes before releasing his hold on her. Maciej feels elated that he has finally asked for Maria's hand in marriage and she said "Yes." Maciej tells Maria he wants to wait until her parents return to ask her father for her hand in marriage. Maciej remembers Bolek's words that he must ask Maria's father for her hand in marriage.

When Maria's parents and sister return, Maciej quickly stands and walks over to Maria's father. He quickly asks her father for Maria's hand in marriage. Suddenly Maciej feels very nervous. When Maria's papa does not answer him immediately, Maciej feels terrified her father will refuse to let him marry Maria.

Maria's papa speaks to Maciej as a father would speak to his son and says in a slightly stern voice, "Maciej, just how do you feel about my daughter and how do you plan to support a wife?"

Maciej answers carefully. He tells Maria's father that he loves Maria deeply. "I do have a good position with the Russian storekeeper and I make enough money to provide for Maria, myself, and even children if we have some. I just hope Maria will give up her job waiting on that Russian family. I can and will be able to provide for us rather well," says Maciej.

Maria's papa walks to Maciej and gives him a big hug and shakes his hand. "Well said, Maciej. You have my blessings and all of our blessings. When do you plan to marry?"

Maciej replies, "We have not yet decided. I hope it will be soon."

"Maciej, you and my daughter talk this over and let me know as soon as you decide. My wife and I want Maria married in church, and we hope that is what you want," replies Maria's papa.

Maciej feels thrilled that her parents have given their consent to their marriage. Maciej says to Maria, "Tomorrow I will take you to the

Polish meeting and we will talk." It is now the end of March in 1911.

Maria tells Maciej, "I will meet you at the meeting, for I must work a little late tomorrow."

Maciej says to Maria, "I hope you will tell your Russian family that you are going to quit when you marry me."

Maciej and Maria talk a little before Maciej leaves for his place. Maciej can hardly believe he has asked Maria's father for her hand in marriage and they both said yes. He wonders when would be a good time to marry. Maciej is now twenty-eight years old. In early April of 1911, Maria will also be twenty-eight years old.

The following evening Maria and Maciej meet at the Polish meeting. They fly into each other's arms and kiss for a long time. Maciej pulls away from Maria and asks if she has picked a date for their wedding.

Maria suggests several dates. Maciej does not reply to any of the dates. Suddenly Maria says to Maciej, "How about the last Saturday in May? The weather will be much nicer in May."

Maciej thinks for a few moments and tells Maria that day is fine with him. The speaker calls the meeting to order as they both sit down. Tonight they do not hear what the speaker says as their thoughts remain on their future wedding the last Saturday in May of 1911.

A few weeks later, Maciej learns that Maria cannot read or write. This bothers him, but just a little. Maciej feels only love and a deep tenderness for Maria. He decides he will teach her to read and write.

The days pass quickly and soon May arrives. Their ceremony is simple with just a few friends of Maria, her sister, her parents, and Maciej's Russian boss attends this event.

Their wedding is simple. Maria wears a beautiful wedding gown that her mother wore when she married many years ago. Maciej looks stunning in his new suit. He sent Maria a beautiful bouquet of flowers just before the wedding ceremony. When Maciej sees Maria walk down the aisle of their church, he feels love and believes he is marrying the most wonderful and beautiful woman in this world. Their Polish priest marries them, speaking the Polish language in their Polish Catholic Church in May of 1911. Maria's father does not post guards on the streets to let them know if Russian troopers might interrupt their wedding.

The Russian government has made a new law stating the Polish priests can perform the Polish marriage ceremony in their Polish language. The Russian troopers do not disturb the wedding of Maria and Maciej as they did to other weddings in the past.

In April of 1911, gestures of agreement and harmony come from the Russian government. A few high-ranking Russian officials talk seriously of uniting the Polish people within the Russian empire. Maria and Maciej are proud of their work in the Polish Party. They believe their work has helped change the Russian government's treatment of the Polish people.

The Russian treatment of the Polish people continues to be harsh, but the murders and imprisonment of the Polish people have significantly declined. However, the Polish people cannot own land or have their own homes or farms. Treatment of the civilian Polish population by the three occupying countries remains cruel.

Maciej finds a small two-room apartment for them to move into after their wedding. He takes his new bride to their own place after all the festivities. In 1911, there is no indoor plumbing (no bathroom) or electricity. Out back is a small outhouse that everyone uses as a bathroom. The Polish people keep the outhouse clean and in good repair.

As a wedding present, the Russian storekeeper gives Maciej a modest raise. Maria still works as a housekeeper for the Russian family. Maciej, happy with all they have, wants much more. He dreams of owning his own home and farmland where he can grow their own food.

Maciej says nothing to Maria about his hopes and dreams for their future. Maciej knows he can never own anything in Russian-controlled Poland. *Someday,* Maciej thinks, *I will be a landowner with wealth.* Maciej has just one problem; how to do all this in Russian-controlled Poland. Maciej is not alone in having this wish for wealth. The Polish people want their country reinstated and to have the right to own their own property—have their own wealth.

In August of 1911, Maria says, "Maciej my dear, next year we are going to have a baby." Maciej, stunned and speechless, feels proud. He thinks, *I will be a father just like Bolek.* Maciej hugs and kisses Maria as if she created this baby all by herself.

Several months pass and Maciej worries about their expenses. He attends a meeting of their Polish Party and learns that America needs workers to work in the coal mines in Pennsylvania. He hears the American companies pay their workers well. Maciej thinks this just might be the answer for him to become wealthy. He remembers his papa left him and his mother to go to America because the Russians threatened his life. Maciej and his mother never heard from him. Maciej believes his father never made it to America because the Russians were after him. He believes his father is dead but hopes he is alive.

How to tell Maria he plans to go to America is a huge problem for Maciej. He loves Maria and does not want to be without her, but he knows he cannot take her with him. He decides to tell Maria about his plan after she gives birth to their child. Meanwhile, Maciej looks into how to get to America and makes some firm plans to leave Russian-controlled Poland.

In late April of 1912, Maria delivers a healthy baby boy. Maciej stays with her and takes care of her and their baby. He does this until the doctor tells him Maria can take care of herself and the baby alone. Maria feels loved and safe having Maciej home with her and their new son. They name their new son Michal. Maria and her parents experience many new feelings after the birth of little Michal. Maria feels a love for her son that grows every time she looks at her baby son.

Maciej returns to work at the Russian shop. He is no longer happy to work for this Russian and completes his plans to go to America. Tonight he must tell Maria about his plan.

It is late August of 1912 when Maciej tells Maria of his plans. Little Michal is just four months old. Maria, horrified, cries out, "NO, Maciej, NO."

Maciej explains to sobbing Maria that he will be home soon with loads of money so they can move to another country and have their own farmland and home.

"Maria," says Maciej, "I can never make enough money here in this Russian-controlled country to buy anything. I want you and our son to have our own home and land. Oh, Maria, our own land to farm and grow our own food," says Maciej passionately.

Maria cries, "No, Maciej, no—please don't leave me. How will I survive? I have our son to care for, I need you." Maria now sobs uncontrollably. She cannot believe what Maciej has just told her.

Maciej tries to soothe Maria, but nothing works. Maria tells Maciej he cannot go to America. Maria cries inconsolably to Maciej, "No, no, I need you here. I cannot go on without you." Maciej decides to talk to Maria's father and enlist his help in making Maria understand his need to go to America.

Maria's father does not approve of Maciej's plans to go to America. He does understand how Maciej feels, but to leave Maria and his newborn son to go to America puzzles Maria's father.

Maria's father tells Maciej that he plans to move his family near the small town of Lwow that lies in the eastern part of Russian Poland. He suggests to Maciej that he change his plans to go to America until the spring of 1913. Maciej thinks carefully about this and asks Maria's father if she and the baby could live with them. Maria's father says, "Yes, but you must stay here until the spring of 1913."

Maciej contacts the man who booked him to work on the ship to America. He learns that it would be better to leave for America in 1913 and preferably in May. His contact tells him there has been a huge disturbance at the port of Gdansk that has closed the port. Maciej does not get all the details but realizes he must wait to make his trip to America.

When Maciej tells Maria his plans to stay, her joy knows no bounds. Maria believes Maciej will not leave her. Maciej enjoys being with Maria and his son, but he wants to make lots of money. He views going to America as his only way to make lots of money

The time passes quickly for Maria but slowly for Maciej. Spring finally arrives and Maciej makes definite plans to travel to the Baltic Sea and work on a ship going to America in early June. Maciej tells his boss he plans to leave the end of next week. His boss understands and wishes Maciej a safe trip to America. Maciej is surprised at his boss's pleasant reply. Maciej hopes Maria will be just as understanding.

When Maciej returns to his home and tells Maria of his plans, she screams "NO, NO."

Maciej quickly replies, "Maria, I can never make enough money here in Russian-controlled Poland to buy anything. I want you and our son to have our own home and land. Oh, Maria, to own our own home, land to grow our own food, and raise our children. This is what I want for you, our children, and our family." Maciej puts his arms around Maria, tells her how much he loves her, and promises her that he will return. Maria, stunned, cannot comprehend everything Maciej is saying.

Maciej helps Maria and her parents move to Lwow in early May of 1913. This move takes about two weeks to complete. Maria firmly believes Maciej will not leave her and their son.

Several days after their move is completed, Maciej learns he must be at the port of Gdansk by the last weekend of May. Tonight Maciej makes love to Maria and she falls into a blissful and contented sleep. She knows Maciej could never leave her and their child.

Maciej does not fall asleep after making love to Maria, for he plans to leave tonight. He looks at his sleeping wife and kisses Maria gently on her forehead. Carefully Maciej leaves their bed and dresses quietly. He picks up his small bag of clothes that he has kept hidden from Maria and leaves the house. Maciej feels elated and excited as he leaves and heads for the Baltic Sea on foot. First, he must stop in the town of Lwow and pick up the horse he bought a week ago.

Maciej walks and runs to the town of Lwow and goes to the livery stable. He picks up his horse and rides his horse the rest of the way to the port of Gdansk. This trip takes several weeks, but the ship Maciej is to work on will not leave for America until mid June.

The morning after Maciej left, Maria awoke alone in their bed. She knew immediately that Maciej left her for America. Maria's mother and father try to comfort their daughter, but today they cannot comfort Maria.

Maria's father is furious with Maciej but realizes he can do nothing. He cannot bring Maciej back. He wishes he had never given his consent to this marriage between his daughter and Maciej.

Chapter Four
The Coal Mines

Maciej travels quickly to the Baltic port and marvels at the huge ship he will work on during his trip to America. He feels a huge thrill and excitement as he climbs aboard the ship.

This trip will take many months, but Maciej does not think about the time. He signs up for work and waits eagerly for the ship to leave for America. The ship leaves port just a few days before mid June for America.

The work proves physically hard, but Maciej enjoys every moment on the ship and does not think about the hard work. When the ship docks in New York harbor, Maciej knows he was right to come to America.

Although he misses Maria, he loves being on his own with no Russian troopers to stop him. One of the ship's workers tells Maciej how to get to the train station and what train to take to get to the coal mines in Pennsylvania. Maciej and several other men join together to find their way to the coal mines.

On the ship to America, Maciej learns English rather quickly. When the ship docks in America, Maciej knows and speaks English clearly with just a heavy Polish accent. He has no problem following the directions given to him to find the train station. He and the other workers find the right train and are soon on their way to the coal mines.

He gets off at the designated stop without any problems. A man from the coal mine meets Maciej and several other men who have signed on to work in the coal mine. This man takes the men to his office to sign more papers. At the coal mine office, some of the men feel tired, but not Maciej.

The man introduces the men to their boss and gives the men some needed equipment. Next, this man gives brief instructions on how to use the equipment. Now the man tells the new workers to report for work at 5:00 a.m. tomorrow. The men look at each other, and Maciej asks the man, "Where will we spend the night and where do we get food?"

The man from the coal mine says, "I will show you now where to sleep and get food. The man takes the men to a boardinghouse where they each get a room with a bed. The man tells the men that their supper meal is on the house. Maciej wonders what does that mean.

A woman knocks on his door and announces, "Dinner is served." Maciej, always hungry, is glad to have some food. Maciej opens his door and follows the woman down a flight of stairs to the dinning room where his new friends are seated. After the men have eaten, the boss (man from the coal mine) tells the men, "This room is where you eat all your meals." The boss speaks quickly, and Maciej has some trouble understanding everything he says. Some of the other men understand nothing he says and keep asking Maciej to repeat what the man has said. Maciej's skill with different languages endears him to the other men.

Maciej does his best to understand what the man says and repeats what has been said it to his coworkers the best he can. His coworkers now depend on Maciej to interpret what the man says. Maciej decides he must teach these men English.

After breakfast the next day, Maciej and his coworkers meet their other boss. This boss tells the men his name is Jerry. He takes them down into the mine and shows them what they need to do to extract the coal and how to use their new equipment.

The men spend long hours down in the coal mine breathing the coal dust with no thought of what the coal dust is doing to their lungs.

The work in the coal mine is a lot harder and the money not as good as Maciej imagined. Still, he enjoys the company of his coworkers while working deep in the mine. Most enjoyable for Maciej is drinking beer with his coworkers at the end of a long workday in the coal mine.

Maciej works extra hours for more money, but when he has a day off, he looks for his father. After two years of working in the coal mine, Maciej gets a day off and goes to his favorite bar. Today he is alone and starts a conversation with the bartender, who is an older man.

He tells the bartender, "My father came to America from Poland many years ago to work in the coal mines. At least that is what my mother told me."

Maciej also tells the bartender, "My father never came back to Poland. He left Poland because the Russians wanted to either kill him or put him in prison."

The bartender looks at Maciej strangely and says, "I knew a man who talked about his wife and a small child. His story was a sad tale. Occasionally that man comes to my bar, but he has not been here lately. I do have his address if you want it?"

Maciej can hardly believe what he is hearing. "Yes, please, perhaps this man is my father?" The bartender writes the address on a piece of paper and writes directions to get to the man's home. It is late summer of 1915.

Maciej immediately leaves the bar without finishing his beer and heads for the address on the paper. He finds the house, goes to the door, and pushes the doorbell. An old man opens the door and looks at Maciej with a puzzled expression. He says, "Is there something I can do for you?"

Maciej, stunned, cannot speak. Suddenly Maciej finds his voice and says his name and that he came from Poland. The man recognizes the name, Maciej.

The man gasps, "You, you, are you my little Maciej?"

"Well, not so little anymore," replies Maciej. "Are you my father? I need to know. I always thought you were dead. My mother told me you were a wonderful man and we wondered if you made it to America. I see you made it to America." Now Maciej asks, "Why did you not get word to us that you were alive?"

His father replies, "To get word to you that I was alive would have caused you and your mother great harm, and I could not do that to her or you. Maciej, I keep in touch with other Polish people here in America and they tell me Poland remains under Russian, Prussian, and Austrian rule. I know that many Polish people work to make Poland a nation, but that has not happened to my knowledge."

Maciej listens to his father and suddenly throws his arms around him. "I am so glad to have found you, Father." Maciej pulls away from his father and tells him, "Mother died several years ago. I found her dead when I came to our room after my workday was over. My friends and I gave her a burial and we said a few words over her grave. Today the Russian troopers do not bother us Polish people as much as they did in the past."

"Maciej, I am so glad she had a decent burial. Thank you. I always worried about both of you and missed the life we might have had together under different rulers. I prayed every day that your mother and you would be safe from the Russian troopers. I knew they wanted me but I was still afraid they might harm you and your mother," said his father.

Maciej begins to cough and his father, alarmed, says to Maciej, "Maciej, are you working in the coal mine?"

Maciej replies, "Yes, and the work is hard and the pay not as good as I thought it would be. Father, I am married now and I have a baby son back in Poland. My wife and son live with her parents in a town near Lwow. I came to America to make money so I could buy my own home and farm. The day will come when Poland becomes a nation again. I truly believe this."

Maciej's father looks at his son and understands what he says but is sad his son left his wife and child. Maciej's father says to his son. "Maciej, it is not good to work too long down in the coal mine. Men who work in those mines often get sick with a lung disease that doctors cannot cure. I have bad lungs from working in the coal mine, and several of my friends have died with this lung disease. You must be careful and not spend long days or many days in a row down in the coal mine."

Maciej looks at his father and sees a tired old man who has the saddest expression on his face. His father says, "You are too much like me. Maciej, do you know there is a war going on in Europe? It began in June of 1914, just last year. This war probably involves Poland because the war involves Russia. I just hope it does not involve your town of Lwow."

Maciej, stunned, replies, "No, I know nothing of this war or if it involves Lwow. I spend almost all my time down in the mines." Maciej finds it hard to believe a war might involve his family.

Father and son have a long visit. Maciej accepts his father's invitation to move in with him until he is ready to return to Poland and his family. For the first time in months, Maciej feels a need to return to Maria and his child. He wonders, *How big has my Michal grown and does he look like me?*

Maciej returns to work at the coal mine and spends days working deep in the mine. Soon his cough becomes severe and his boss sends him home. Maciej returns to his father's place, and his father immediately calls for the doctor to come and see Maciej.

The doctor tells Maciej he cannot return to work in the coal mine. He tells him his lungs are bad. Maciej stays in bed for several weeks, and when he feels better he stubbornly goes back to work in the coal mine. Maciej feels he needs more money and then he will return to Maria and his child. He feels a vast and unexpected need to return to Maria. He says, "I need the fresh air of Poland, and I need and want Maria's arms around me." He wonders about his baby son and feels a need to see his son.

Three months after Maciej returned to work his father dies. Maciej feels a huge loss. His father's last words to Maciej were, "Return to your wife and son, NOW, Maciej."

After Maciej sees his father buried, he continues to work in the coal mine. He still feels he needs more money before he returns to Poland.

Chapter Five
Maciej Returns Home

In June of 1914 after the murder of Archduke Francis Ferdinand at Sarajevo, WWI erupts. July of 1914, Austria and Hungary declare war against Serbia. August 1, 1914, Russia and Germany are at war and Russia invades East Prussia.

The three partitioning powers of Poland are at war. The outbreak of war finds the Polish people bitterly divided about their loyalty to their occupying country.

With the deliberate sinking of American ships and the German plot to have Mexico attack America, President Wilson enters the war to fight against Germany in early April of 1917. Regardless, the German leaders expect to win the war, and in early 1918, it looks as if the Germans will be victorious.

After intense fighting in Europe, the Allies defeat the Germans, and on November 11, 1918, World War I ends. November 18, 1918, Josef Pilsudski returns to Poland and becomes chief of state. On June 28, 1919, Paderewski and Dmowski sign the Treaty of Versailles supported by Poland. However, this treaty leaves the major part of Poland's boundaries undefined, especially in eastern Poland. A major part of the treaty of Versailles states that Germany cannot build any weapons or ammunition.

Poland is not a joyous country, for it is a ruined country with a starved population. The countries that took over Poland destroyed Poland's assets. Polish leaders realize that Poland remains in a difficult position after WWI. The three partitioning powers destroyed Poland's farmland, industrial plants, and banking is nonexistent. There is no education of the young anywhere in Poland. Poland's livestock is gone, and only a small portion of arable land remains under cultivation. Poland's army is almost nonexistent and provides little security for the people of Poland.

All the nations involved sign the treaty of peace—the Versailles treaty. This treaty gives to Poland direct access to the Baltic Sea and strips Germany of its military power. Germany starts violating this treaty even before all the countries sign it.

The war left Germany devastated; the people cannot believe they lost the war. Germany needs a new leader, and Adolf Hitler believes he is the man to lead Germany back to greater success and wealth.

In 1919, Hitler joins the German Workers' Party with his close adviser Heiden, a working journalist in Munich. Heiden introduces Hitler to Rudolf Hess and Alfred Rosenberg. Hitler admires and listens to Dietrich Eckart, a poet, usually drunk. These men soon shape a formidable political party in Germany—National Socialism.

Early December of 1918, Maciej and his coworkers drink to Poland—now an independent nation following the end of WWI. Maciej gets down on his knees and thanks God for this Miracle of Miracles. The men raise their beer and drink to the end of WWI and to Maciej's Poland now a nation—again

Tonight Maciej enjoys the company of other females. This time he does not forget Maria and their child. After all the celebrating ends,

Maciej feels a strong need to return to Maria and his son. His need for Maria grows greater each day as his cough gets worse. He does not spend the night with a woman this time as he did many nights in the past.

Maciej becomes ill with pneumonia and cannot work. The doctor tells Maciej, "If you want to live you must leave these coal mines and it is best that you return to Poland, to your wife, and child. Maciej, coal dust kills, and you either leave or you die."

Maciej counts his money and believes he has enough. He says to the heavens, "This will be enough; Oh, God, let it be enough." Instead of going home to Maria, Maciej becomes doubtful that the money he has will be enough and he returns to the coal mine. He works for another seven months. The need to return to Maria grows stronger and this need finally becomes unbearable. Now he wonders, *Will she be waiting for me when I return. Has she have found another man? What will my son look like? How big has my Michal grown?*

Maciej makes definite plans to work on a ship soon to leave for Poland. He knows he needs the fresh air of Poland and Maria's arms around him and, *Perhaps then, I will get well,* he thinks. He wonders how his baby son, now nine years old, will feel about him.

Maciej tells his boss at the coal mine he will leave for Poland in ten days. His boss is sorry to release Maciej from his work but understands his need to return to Poland and regain his health. He knows the coal-mine dust has hurt Maciej's lungs. The trip back to Poland will take several months.

Maciej's coworkers tell him to be careful with his money. They warn Maciej there are many thieves ready to relieve you of your money.

Maciej heeds his coworkers' warning and makes a money holder to hide his money and prevent thieves from stealing it. However, he does not appear wealthy, for he wears ragged clothes and he looks poorly. Perhaps this is why no one bothers Maciej on the voyage back to Poland.

In October of 1921, Maciej, now thirty-eight years old, returns to Maria and his son at her father's home in Lwow. This part of Russian Poland, now part of the nation Poland, remains the same, for the war missed this section of Russian Poland and the land remains beautiful and fertile.

The reunion between Maciej and Maria knows only joy. Maria cannot stop hugging and kissing her husband. Maciej cannot take his eyes off Maria, for she looks more beautiful today than he remembered. He never wants her to stop hugging him. She never expected to see him again, and her joy knows no bounds.

When Maria finally releases her arms around Maciej, her parents say a guarded "Hello" to Maciej.

Suddenly Maciej senses someone else is in the room. He turns and looks at a young boy standing in the doorway. Michal has come home and looks at the stranger with his mother. Maria sees Michal and says, "This is your father, Michal."

Michal looks at his father for the first time and says, "My father—hardly."

Maciej, shocked, looks at his son. Young Michal looks to his grandfather and feels a bond with him. He feels nothing for "this strange-looking man" who says he is his father.

Michal, a bright and smart nine-year-old, had to drop out of school and help his grandfather with his business. Even though Michal has only a third-grade education, he handles complicated business matters for his grandfather without help from any adults.

When Maciej learns that Michal does not go to school, he is furious and wants to know, "WHY NOT? Tomorrow Michal goes to school." Michal looks at his father and thinks, *This man is crazy in his head. I am working and learning a lot with my grandfather, I do not need to go to school,* thinks young Michal

Ten months after Maciej returns to Poland, Maria gives birth to a second son in 1922. They name their new son Szczepan. Maciej, thrilled to have another son, wants his own land and home more than ever now that he has a second son. Maciej does not want to stay with Maria's parents any longer than necessary.

Maciej has been looking around and finally finds a 250-acre farm with a large house that he feels is just perfect for his family. The farm and house are about five miles outside the village of Dmytrow. Maciej, thrilled with his find and the low price, cannot wait to show the farmland and house to Maria.

After Maciej completes the negotiations for ownership of their home and farmland, he tells Maria what he has accomplished.

Maciej says to Maria, "Now I want to show you our new home and farmland." Maciej does not mention his half ownership in a brickyard he purchased when he tells Maria about their home and farmland.

Maciej takes Maria to their new home. This trip takes several hours, for their new home and farmland lies about thirty to forty miles from the town of Lwow. On this trip, Maciej and Maria pass through the village of Dmytrow where Maciej has half ownership in the brickyard. While in Dmytrow, Maciej tells Maria about the brickyard. He explains to Maria, "The farmland, house, and brickyard are in the county of Radziechow, a province of Tarnopol, and everything is paid—we owe nothing. Most important, our land lies inside Poland."

Maria looks at Maciej with a bewildered look on her face. Maciej sees Maria's strange look and tries to explain. Maria does not understand what Maciej tells her. Maciej now tells Maria, "My darling, we have our own home. I will take you to our home now."

Maria looks at Maciej with understanding and says, "Please take me to our new home."

Maciej and Maria are unaware the boundaries of eastern Poland remain undefined. Maciej believes his home, land, and business are located in Poland. The Polish government believes they now have the land in eastern Poland. However, the Russian government believes they own all of eastern Poland.

The land in eastern Poland is flat without mountains, but there are hills that break up the flat land. Forests and crystal-clear streams run through this fertile land. There are fruit trees that produce abundant fruit. The land grows many kinds of food. Cows, goats, and other animals live on the land, for the land produces food in abundance.

Maria, stunned at the beauty of the land, becomes speechless. When she can talk, she says to Maciej, "Is this land really ours?"

Maciej replies, "Yes, my dearest Maria, all this land is ours, a full 250 acres. Up there," Maciej points to the top of a small knoll, "is our home, Maria."

Maciej takes Maria into their house, and she falls in love with the house. She turns to Maciej and says, "Maciej, this house is just what I have always wanted. Oh, Maciej, I love you. When can we move into our home?"

Maciej replies, "Soon, Maria, soon."

Maciej knows he has not signed all the papers. Next week Maciej will sign the papers, and then Maciej plans to move into their home that very day.

Several hours later, Maciej and Maria head back to Lwow. When they arrive back in Lwow, Maria immediately tells her parents about the home that Maciej has found for them.

Her father looks at Maciej and says harshly, "You, Maciej, take good care of my Maria and my grandchildren." Maria's father never forgives Maciej for leaving his daughter and his grandson.

Maciej can hardly believe his great fortune. He never thought he could buy so much so quickly, a home, farmland, and a business. By the end of the week, Maciej has all the papers signed and the house, farmland, and half ownership in the brickyard belong to Maciej and Maria. They plan to move immediately into their own home.

This will not take a long time, for they have nothing to move, just themselves and their two children. Maciej and Maria shop in Lwow for two beds for the children and a bed for themselves plus some bedding. Then they buy a table with several chairs. Maciej pays for everything with his money. By the end of the month, he hopes to be making money from the brickyard.

The house is several years old but new to Maria and Maciej. They both feel wealthy. It is so wonderful to be in their own home with just their sons. Although Maciej and Maria got along well with her parents, there was the lack of privacy. Maciej felt Maria's father bossed him a lot, always telling him what he should do or not do. Maciej sensed Maria's father did not approve of him because he left Maria and went to America.

Maciej's half ownership in the brickyard starts making money and the farm produces all the food the family can eat. The only problem for

Maciej is that Michal still helps Maria's parents with their business. Maciej wants Michal to return to school.

Although Maciej wants Michal in school, he quickly learns he also needs Michal's help with the work on the farm. Michal tells his dad, "I think you need my help, Dad. Your cough gets worse every day and I can make your life easier."

Maciej is surprised that Michal is so observant. He knows he does need Michal's help with the farm chores. Yet Michal continues to help his grandparents with their business, and this bothers Maciej.

It has been a harsh winter in late February of 1925. Today Maria's parents set out in a small horse-drawn carriage to visit Maria and help her with the coming birth of her third child. While on the road, a storm sets in and they become blinded by the snow. They cannot see the road. At a bend in the road, their carriage runs off an embankment. This accident kills Maria's parents.

An employee at the brickyard on his way to work had been following behind them when their carriage suddenly disappeared. When he realized what happened, he rode his horse to Maria and Maciej's home and told them of the horrible accident. Maria immediately starts crying and says, "NO, OOOH NO, they cannot be dead."

Maciej immediately tries to calm Maria, but she pushes him away. Maria, now hysterical, cannot stop sobbing. Her cries frighten Maciej, for her whole body shakes with grief.

Maciej worries that Maria's extreme grief might cause her to go into labor. Maria, now in her ninth month of pregnancy, needs to remain calm, believes Maciej. Maciej wants her to get control of her grief for the sake of their unborn child.

Maciej's employee tries to calm Maria with some success. This particular employee has experienced many misfortunes in the past and understands Maria's grief. Slowly, he calms Maria and she stops crying. It takes Maria many months before she begins to accept that her parents have died.

Maria asks the man who told them the news of her parents' death, "What is your name?"

He tells Maria, "My name is Frank. I am so glad I could help you. I know how getting bad news can be." Frank stays for just a few more minutes and then he leaves.

Maciej and Maria bury her parents in a small plot on their property that they have set aside for burials. They never thought they would use their land for her parents.

His grandparents' deaths deeply sadden young Michal, for he enjoyed his grandfather's companionship. Michal misses his grandfather and wonders how to go on without his grandfather's wisdom. Young Michal feels bitter over the death of his grandparents.

Michal hears his father coughing again while they bury his grandmother and grandfather. Michal wonders why his father has a cough that shakes his whole body. He thinks that perhaps his father will die, too. Young Michal realizes he does not want his father to die.

Three weeks after they bury Maria's parents, Maria gives birth to their third child, a son. They name their new son Tomasz. Maciej cannot believe that his son can be so happy. It seems that Tomasz was born with a smile on his face.

Michal has begun to understand his father, and he feels some love for him. He worries about his father and wants to know why he has such a horrible cough. Michal once saw his father cough up blood, and this frightened him. He believes that working in the coal mines did something to his dad's health. Now Michal does more and more of his dad's chores without even asking his father for permission.

Maria also has become more concerned about Maciej's "gut-wrenching" cough and difficulty breathing. Maria encourages Maciej to see their local doctor. Maciej visits the doctor and he tells Maciej, "You must take it easier and delegate more responsibility to your young Michal. You are a lucky man, Maciej, to have such a bright, strong, and healthy son. You can go home now, but take it easy."

Maciej wanted the doctor to tell him how to get better. Maciej wonders if he has the lung disease his father died of in America. Maciej, today, wishes he had quit the coal mine when his father told him about the lung problems you get while working in the coal mine.

Realizing how hard it has become to do any farm work, Maciej shows Michal how to plant and harvest the crops and how to take care of their few animals, a cow, several chickens, and two horses. Soon, Michal does everything that a farm needs done to run smoothly and get a good harvest without any help from his dad. Michal goes with his dad to the brickyard and learns how to run the brickyard, deal with customers, and the workers. Michal does all the necessary work on the farm and runs the brickyard business at the age of fifteen. Michal can read and write quite well even though he has only a third-grade education.

One rule Maciej repeats many times to Michal is "Always treat your workers with respect and give them fair pay for their work—especially the Russian workers." Maciej still has a deep-seated fear of the Russians.

Michal and his father get along well, and rarely does Michal disagree with his father on handling problems that do keep coming up. Maciej is grateful for Michal's help and realizes his son is intelligent and capable of running the farm and brickyard. Michal has a unique skill to learn quickly and apply what he learns to everyday problems.

Michal knows everything about running the brickyard and the farm. Rarely does Michal ask his father for any help with the farm or brickyard problems. Michal notices his father's cough has become much worse and that he has more difficulty breathing.

Maciej no longer accompanies Michal to help with the needed work on his farm. However, Maciej enjoys visiting the brickyard and talking with the workers and customers, but he does NO work. Most of the time, he goes into his office and sits in his chair consumed with coughing and the effort to inhale oxygen from the air.

A year passes and one day Maciej cannot even get out of bed, for his breathing difficulties have become worse. Maria, alarmed, notices Maciej's cough has worsened and his face looks—like death.

Maria, frantic with worry, screams at Michal, "Go get the doctor—NOW, Michal."

Michal quickly leaves the house, jumps on his horse, and rides to the doctor's home. Breathlessly, Michal tells the doctor, "You must come quickly; my father coughs up blood and makes a rattling sound when he breathes."

Without saying a word, the doctor grabs his bag and follows Michal in his horse-drawn wagon. The doctor knows Maciej has had another episode of breathing problems and believes Maciej may do more work than he should.

When they arrive at Maciej's home, the doctor immediately enters the house and walks into Maciej's room. The doctor examines

Maciej's chest with his stethoscope and tells Maciej, "You must stay in bed; you cannot get out of bed. You must do nothing. Do you understand me, Maciej? You cannot even get out of bed to use the outside latrine. You must use the can."

(In the Polish countryside, there is no indoor plumbing nor is there electricity in the homes.)

Maciej looks at the doctor and replies with a simple "Yes."

Now the doctor asks Maciej, "How much blood are you coughing up each day?"

"Oh, Doc, I don't cough up much blood. No, I don't even think it is blood."

The doctor looks at Maciej and realizes Maciej cannot face the truth about his illness.

The doctor says to Maciej, "You let young Michal handle the farm and the brickyard. I think he has been doing just that for several years now." The doctor packs up his supplies and puts them back into his bag.

Now he tells Maria and Maciej, "You follow my orders and send Michal to me if necessary. I think, Maciej, if you stay in bed, you will be all right for a while. You know, Maciej, those years you spent working for money in those coal mines, well Maciej, that coal dust destroyed your lungs. I wish, oh, how I wish I could do more for you, but I cannot. You are lucky to have such a smart, bright son in Michal. Your Michal can handle your businesses without your help."

This is a long speech for the doctor. Now he turns and walks out of Maciej's room and leaves the house. A deep sadness comes over the doctor, for he admires Maciej and wants to help him but knows that coal dust did Maciej a harm he cannot cure.

The doctor is also concerned about Maria, whom he admires for all her help with his other patients in Dmytrow. Whenever the doctor needed help he would send for Maria and she always came to help the person in need. Maria is well liked by the people in the village of Dmytrow.

Maria, stunned and devastated by the doctor's words, falls into a chair and starts crying, "Oh, Michal, what are we going to do? Michal, how are we going to survive? You cannot possibly do everything without your father's help," she says through her tears.

Szczepan and Tomasz are standing in the kitchen looking at their sobbing mother wondering what has happened. Michal looks at his mother and says firmly, "Mama, please stop crying. I can run all of Dad's businesses without help. Mama, I have been running everything for the past two years without any help from Dad. Mama, the harvests have been great and I have made money from the brickyard, more than Dad ever made."

Sixteen-year-old Michal turns to Szczepan and Tomasz and says, "I will always look after you and keep you safe. I can do this, for I have been doing this for the past two years."

Polish tradition states the oldest son assumes the responsibility of the family when the father dies. Michal's father is still alive but bedridden and unable to work. Now Michal must meet the needs of his family for food, warmth, love, and run the family businesses. Michal is both father and brother to his siblings.

Several days later, Maciej grabs Maria's hand, pulls her to him, and kisses her. Maria, startled and pleased at Maciej's wish to kiss her, returns the kiss. Maciej does not have a coughing attack and Maria thinks that perhaps he will get better. Then she remembers the last spell he had and what the doctor said. Maria, pregnant, expects she will have another child in just a few months. She wonders how they will manage.

Four months after Maciej's severe coughing spell, Maria gives birth to a daughter in 1927. Maciej cannot believe he has a daughter after three sons. They name their new daughter Aniela.

Aniela soon becomes the darling of their family. Michal, Szczepan, and Tomasz love to play with little Aniela. Aniela seems to resemble Maria, thinks Maciej.

Chapter Six
Michal and Hanka

In the fall of 1928, sixteen-year-old Michal walks to Dmytrow to meet with some friends at the local tavern. The evenings are now cool and the leaves on the trees are turning many colors of red. Michal has grown into a very handsome young man. He is tall and strong, for his muscles have fully developed from working on the farm. His eyes glisten with laughter, for Michal is a happy person.

On the road to Dmytrow, Michal sees a lovely young girl walking towards him. Michal, stunned by her beauty, does not recognize the young girl. There is something familiar about her, but he cannot place who she is. She does not appear tall or short. He notes her blond hair glistens in the early evening sunlight. He also notices her figure. Michal feels his heart beating faster. *Who is she, I know her but*…this beautiful creature sees him and says, "Hi, Michal."

Michal cannot believe his eyes. She looks familiar. Suddenly he remembers her name, "Hi, Hanka," shouts Michal.

Michal realizes he has been so busy running his father's businesses he has lost track of his friends. Michal thinks, *I used to play with her brother Frank, I even went to school with Hanka in third grade, and I see her almost every Sunday at church. Gosh, she is gorgeous.* Hanka has grown into a lovely young woman at the age of sixteen.

Michal and Hanka start talking and Michal forgets to visit the tavern. Michal and Hanka have a long conversation and enjoy each other's company. Michal believes he has just met the most beautiful, the most intelligent young woman in the whole world.

Michal tells Hanka he is sixteen years old. Hanka, surprised that Michal is only sixteen, tells him that she too is sixteen. They now exchange birthdays and they learn that Michal is almost two months older than Hanka. All too soon, Hanka's father calls for her to return home. Michal walks her to her door and impulsively plants a quick kiss on her lips.

Hanka, suddenly shy, turns away from Michal and quickly opens the door to her home. She turns to Michal, gives him a big smile, then enters her home and shuts the door.

Michal cannot believe he kissed her. Now he smiles and knows he wants to kiss her some more. *What are these strange feelings I am feeling?* wonders young Michal.

The next day Michal gets all the farm work taken care of so he can call on Hanka. At the last minute, his father asks for his help at the brickyard and it is a whole week before Michal has enough time to visit Hanka.

This evening he walks to her home feeling somewhat uneasy. He wonders will she want to see me. Michal prays he was not too bold kissing her. Suddenly he remembers how Hanka responded to his kiss. He quickens his pace to Hanka's home. Hanka's home lies just inside the town of Dmytrow about five miles from Michal's home.

Michal shyly walks to the door of Hanka's home and knocks. Hanka opens the door and steps outside as she closes the door. She says, "Hi, Michal. Good to see you."

Michal says, "Hanka, please, can you take a walk with me?" Hanka simply nods her head yes. She even has her sweater over her arm, as it is now fall and the weather cools in the evenings.

Michal takes Hanka's hand in his and they walk and talk for over an hour. They also spend more time kissing this evening, and Michal knows immediately that he loves Hanka. Tonight he does not want to leave her but knows he must take her home and he must return to his home. He does not want his mother to worry about him.

Now every moment that Michal has to spare, he spends with Hanka. They get along well and both Hanka and Michal feel their love for each other and a need for a deeper relationship. Tonight when they kiss, they never want the kiss to end. Michal wants much more than kisses, and Hanka feels the same.

Three days later Michal tells Hanka he loves her, and Hanka tells Michal she loves him. Michal and Hanka have feelings they have never experienced. They know they want and need—to be together now and forever.

Maria is aware that Michal spends almost every evening with Hanka. Tonight when Michal arrives home, Maria decides to talk to Michal.

Maria decides she must talk to him and waits for him to return home. When Michal finally arrives home, she immediately says to him, "Michal, I want to talk to you."

Michal, alarmed and thinking the worst, asks, "What's wrong with Dad?"

Maria replies, "Your father does better now that he does nothing. Michal, I know you are seeing Hanka, and I must ask you to go slow, do not see her so often. Give yourself time to see other young women.

Michal, do not rush into anything right now. You need time to grow and to see more of the world."

Immediately, Michal says, "Mother, no way. I am in love with Hanka and I plan to marry her soon."

Maria, shocked, says, "Michal, take your time, please do not rush into anything, especially marriage," pleads Maria. She continues to explain to Michal all the responsibilities of marriage, that he is young and should take time to have fun.

Michal just replies, "Mama, don't worry. I will take a little time for fun, but it will be with Hanka. Don't you worry, Mama, I know what is best for me."

Michal does not plan to wait to propose to Hanka. In early January of 1929, Michal asks Hanka to marry him. Hanka accepts Michal's proposal with a joyous "Yes, Michal, yes." They hug, kiss, and almost do more, but Hanka's dad calls her to return home and the evening ends. Tonight, Hanka does not tell her parents that Michal has proposed to her.

The following Saturday, Hanka and Michal spend hours kissing and talking about their wedding. After much kissing and talking, Hanka tells Michal, "I must return home and tell my parents, please come with me." Michal agrees.

They both return to Hanka's home and tell her parents their news. Hanka's mother and father cannot believe that these two want to marry. They say to Michal and Hanka, "Perhaps you should wait a year or two until you are older."

Hanka and Michal tell her parents they plan to marry soon and tomorrow they will see their priest about getting married. Hanka's father immediately says, "I see we cannot talk you out of getting married. Therefore, we will have a big celebration. When do you plan to marry?"

Hanka replies, "First, we must learn when our priest can marry us. We see him tomorrow, and as soon as we know we will tell you."

Michal says, "We hope it will be in late May. I will have done all the spring planting and business at the brickyard is not busy then. May is a good time, but we must find out when our priest can marry us."

Chapter Seven
Germany's Power Grows

After the defeat of Germany in 1918, and while Maciej and Maria were raising their children in the 1920s, a political revolution unfolds within Germany. The intensity of this movement will forever change Michal and Hanka's lives. The following account of these events serves to foretell the challenges that will fall upon Michal and Hanka after their simple wedding in Poland. The movements begin while the victorious nations of WWI put sanctions on Germany. The German people cannot believe they have lost the war.

Adolf Hitler fought in WWI, and after the war ended, he moved to Munich with the German army in 1919. Hitler does everything possible to enter politics. He believes a good politician must have great oratorical skills. Here in Munich he tries out his oratorical skills with some success.

In 1920 Hitler leaves the army and the "German Workers' Party" invite him to join them. This party does not interest Hitler, yet he joins the party with other misfits. Hitler's goal is to create his own party. It will take over ten years for the German Workers' Party to become a major party in Germany.

Hitler, an unknown, takes the lead in building this party. In 1920, Hitler begins organizing the party and influencing public opinion. His biggest contribution is his design for an emblem and a flag that he feels will appeal to everyone. He designs the black swastika with a red background, and this design becomes Germany's flag.

Hitler and the people admire the new design. The Third Reich grows and money flows into this party. The German Worker's Party becomes the National Socialist German Worker's Party that gives birth to the word "Nazi." Hitler devotes all his time to his Nazi Party.

By 1921, the victorious countries of WWI present to Germany the bill for reparations for WWI—132 billion gold marks, or in American money, 33 billion dollars. The German government says they cannot pay this bill.

Germany's economy has not recovered from World War I, and the falling value of the German mark influences the general population unfavorably. This presents the opportunity for Hitler to present himself to the people as a leader. In November of 1923, Hitler tries to force the German leaders to join him in taking over the government by jumping onto a table in a beer garden and holding the German leaders hostage with his pistol. He is unsuccessful, and the police arrest him and send him to prison to await his trial.

Hitler thinks, *This trial can provide me with a new platform and make my name known to all Germans.* In February of 1924, Hitler transforms his defeat into triumph. His name is on every front page of newspapers around the world. Hitler's unsuccessful try to take over the government has made him a national figure.

At his trial, the judges sentence Hitler to five years in prison. In prison, the guards treat Hitler as an honored guest. Then the judges release him from prison after he has served only nine months of his sentence. However, during Hitler's imprisonment his Nazi Party falls apart.

While in prison, Hitler uses his time to write some of his book, *Mein Kampf*, which will become the model of the Third Reich. He also gathers some of the Nazi leaders to aid him in his writing and to gain greater power in their party.

Hitler forms his ideas in his early twenties—he despises the Jews and believes all Jews are evil. He equates democracy and Jews as his greatest enemies—the Jews more than democracy. He firmly believes God gave him the foresight to make Aryans (Germans) the rulers of the world.

At first, many Germans in government feel Hitler is no threat. They consider him just a crude joke. Yet, Hitler offers a vision to many of the German people that points to a glorious German destiny. The people like what Hitler says.

During the depression in Germany, which lasts until 1929, the German government borrows heavily from other countries, especially from America. The German government needs to pay reparations to those victorious countries and needs to increase social services to their own people. The German people, severely hurt by the falling German mark, have no buying power. The German government accepts the heavy load of financial reparations but never considers paying the bill.

Mass agitation of the German people, unrelenting propaganda, and the failure of the government to achieve success creates the atmosphere for the rise of the Nazi party with Hitler their leader. Before 1927, the government forbade Hitler to speak in public. During 1927, Hitler's oratory powers grow and the people like what he says. The German people believe Hitler is the one man to take them to greatness. Hitler knows he is the one man chosen by God to take the Aryan (German) race to world power.

Hitler is a good organizer. By 1929, Hitler has increased the membership in his party to almost 200,000 paying members. However, by June of 1930, Germany has plunged into a deeper depression and the people are hurting.

In this atmosphere, Hitler promises the millions of discontented Germans real hope. The election in 1930 is a resounding success for the Nazi party. Hitler's power grows.

Hitler is now a shrewd calculating politician. In 1933, Hindenburg invites Hitler to be chancellor of Germany. This appointment makes Hitler's life more stable and comfortable. Most important, the German party is now successful.

With success, Hitler accepts some material comforts but remains indifferent to clothes and food. He never smokes and drinks alcohol rarely. He prefers tea or coffee.

Hitler sets up a dictatorship while chancellor of Germany and becomes involved with Eva Braun. Hitler likes female companionship. Hitler finds Eva warm hearted, loyal and not smart in politics.

As the German economy recovers, unemployment decreases. Hitler takes full credit for this. Hitler's rise to power moves slowly but firmly.

He presents himself to other countries as a man of peace. Then in 1933, Hitler withdraws from the League of Nations. He signs a treaty of nonaggression with Poland. In 1935, Hitler starts to build up his military forces. This alarms England, France, and Italy, but Hitler manages to allay their fears about his goals. He even negotiates a treaty with England that does away with the Versailles treaty. The Versailles treaty stated Hitler could not build any weapons. Hitler's propaganda works.

Now Hitler gives the orders to his factories to build ammunition, tanks, and planes. Germany's factories build huge amounts of weapons—enough to last for several years of war. Hitler's goal is to rid Europe of all Jews and make himself the ruler of most or all of Europe. For Hitler believes, God chose him to rule Europe and the world.

England and France become alarmed when Hitler makes an alliance with Italy. Soon England and France impose sanctions against Italy. In 1936 Hitler and Japan join in an alliance.

Hitler's goal is to start an invasion of Poland on September 1, 1939. Hitler feels he needs Stalin on his side (Hitler plans to conquer Russia too). Hitler makes a desirable offer of the Baltic countries and Poland's seaport, Gdansk, to Stalin if he joins him. Hitler does not want Stalin to join with England and France. Stalin does confer with England and France, but they offer him nothing. Hitler offers the Baltic countries, and Stalin wants those countries, especially Poland's seaport, Gdansk.

Hitler does not hear from Stalin. He decides to attack Poland on September 1, 1939, without Stalin's help. A week before Hitler has planned his attack on Poland, he receives a telegram stating Stalin will join him in the partitioning of Poland.

Stalin states he is pleased to be Hitler's partner, not even considering that Hitler might attack his country, Russia. Stalin wants the Baltic countries and Poland's seaport, Gdansk, and he can think of nothing else.

Poland does have firm treaties with England and France that they will aid Poland if Germany attacks Poland. The treaty with France states that Poland must be able to last at least fifteen days of fighting before France will help Poland.

Chapter Eight
A Polish Wedding

It is 1929 and the brickyard that Michal runs does well and provides money for Michal and his family to buy those items he cannot grow on the farm. The family feels wealthy and prosperous. The people of Dmytrow consider Michal and his family wealthy, not because of their farm, but because Michal runs a business.

Although Maciej remains ill, he and Maria continue to have sexual relations. In May of 1929, Maria suspects she is with child again and thinks this birth will occur in late December or early January of 1930. Maria hopes Michal listens to her words and does not rush into marriage. Maria likes Hanka but feels Michal and Hanka are much too young for marriage.

Michal heard everything Maria said about being too young to marry. He feels his mother is wrong, and he does not follow her instructions. Michal has not told his mother that he and Hanka plan to marry in May. Nor does Michal tell Maria that he and Hanka will see their priest about marrying them in May of 1929.

The next day Michal leaves his home early and meets Hanka. He does not tell Maria why he is leaving, and she suspects nothing, for Michal often leaves early to go to the brickyard.

Michal meets Hanka and they walk to their local Catholic church.

There they meet with their priest. They tell him of their wish to marry, for they are deeply in love. They ask the priest, "When can you marry us?"

Their priest asks Michal if the last weekend in May would be a good time for him. Michal says, "That is a fine weekend, for I will have done all the spring planting and the work at the brickyard is not heavy." Hanka agrees this is a good time for her and her family.

Now the priest asks Michal and Hanka, "Have you told your parents about your plans?"

Michal and Hanka say in unison, "No, we have not told them everything yet, but we will tell them today."

Hanka says, "We told my parents that we plan to marry but first we had to see you."

The priest says, "That is good, for I will need to talk your parents, Hanka, and your mother, Michal." The priest knows Michal's father, Maciej, is too ill to visit him. The priest states, "Michal and Hanka, you must come and see me again after you tell your parents."

Michal and Hanka immediately say, "Yes, Father, we will come back to talk with you."

Now the two young people leave their priest and Michal says to Hanka, "I will go with you to your home first."

Hanka and Michal enter her home with Hanka shouting, "I am going to marry Michal the last weekend of May, Mama." Hanka's mother is at first shocked. It is noontime and Hanka's father has returned for his noon meal. He hears Hanka shouting she will marry Michal and he wants to know when this wedding will happen.

She tells her parents, "I love Michal and he loves me. Mama, we saw our priest today, and he says he can marry us the last weekend of May.

I hope you can see how happy I am to marry Michal."

Hanka's parents look at their daughter and Michal in shock. Suddenly Hanka's mother, who is crying, says, "Oh, my Hanka, you are so young. My precious daughter, I want your happiness, but marriage… I thought, when you first told us of your plans that you did not mean what you said. I guess I hoped that."

Michal asks Hanka's father for her hand in marriage. Stunned, her father does nothing at first. As he gains some composure, he says to Michal, "Yes, you have my consent if my daughter wants to marry you."

Hanka's father walks over to Hanka and hugs her, saying, "Honey, if this is what you want then we will make this wedding a real festive occasion. Your Michal is a fine young man and a hard worker. I am pleased you and he want to marry."

Hanka's mother stops crying and tells Hanka, "Yes, my darling daughter, we will make this wedding a festivity to remember."

Hanka goes to her mother and hugs her. She tells her parents, "I am grateful you feel this way. I do love Michal. Now we must leave and tell his parents."

Her father says, "Hanka, I think it would be best if Michal tells his parents alone. I think his mother will have some difficulty understanding your and Michal's wish to marry."

Michal says, "Yes, sir, I think it best that I tell my parents alone. Hanka, I will see you tomorrow evening and tell you everything."

Hanka replies, "I do understand, Michal and I look forward to seeing you tomorrow."

Michal leaves for his home. He remembers his mother's words about waiting to marry. He thinks, *I will just have to make my mother understand.* He does not even consider waiting to marry Hanka.

When Michal arrives home, he burst into his home shouting, "Mama, Hanka has accepted my proposal of marriage. Mama, we saw our priest today and he has consented to marry us."

Maria looks at Michal and sits down on the nearest chair and says, "Are you sure, Michal?" Maria goes into shock and cannot move or speak for a few minutes.

Michal sits next to his mama and says, "Mama, I love Hanka and I want to marry her. She is so wonderful, Mama. I know I am young, but I do more work than most grown men do. Please, Mama, try to understand how much I love Hanka. Mama, I will have all the spring planting done before our wedding, and the time is just right for us to marry. Mama, I will always take care of you, Papa, Szczepan, Tomasz, and Aniela." After this long speech, Michal takes a breather.

"Mama, Hanka and I plan to live here, and you will have some help with all your chores. Hanka likes you, Mama." Michal never stops smiling while telling his mama his wonderful news.

Maria realizes she cannot change his mind and does believe that Michal genuinely loves Hanka. She is sad her little boy has grown up but proud that he has become such a fine man. Maria wonders silently why they chose the last weekend in May, for that was when she and Maciej married.

Hanka and Michal are both devout Roman Catholics, as is everyone in the village of Dmytrow. There is no thought of having sex without the bond of marriage. The next day Hanka's mother talks to Maria about their wedding plans. Maria feels pleased that Hanka's parents have included her in the festivities before and after the marriage ceremony. She thinks perhaps that it will be all right for her Michal and Hanka to marry.

With a big smile on her face, Hanka's mother says, "Hanka, this wedding is coming much too soon. I need more time, for there is so much to do." Now Hanka's mother brings out her wedding dress for Hanka to try on. The dress needs just a few changes. Hanka's mother is surprised when she sees her daughter in her dress looking so beautiful. The dress needs only a few changes that Hanka's mother does herself.

Two days after telling their parents their plan to marry, Hanka and Michal visit their priest again as he requested them to do. Today the priest talks to them about the sanctity of marriage and their duties to each other. This visit takes almost two hours. Before the priest dismisses Michal and Hanka he proudly says, "I am so proud that I can marry you two." Michal and Hanka are surprised their priest is happy to marry them but thrilled that soon they will marry.

Finally, for Hanka and Michal their wedding day arrives. It is a beautiful day. The flowers on the fruit trees are many and beautiful. May flowers show their gorgeous blooms. The weather is warm but not hot as it often gets in Dmytrow. The sun shines and no clouds have appeared in the sky. *The day is just perfect for my wedding,* thinks Hanka.

It has been a while since anyone has married with such promise for happiness in the village of Dmytrow. Poland's farmland now produces enough food for almost everyone, but the country has not regained the status it had before the death of Poland.

Poland remains backward when one compares Poland to other countries. The people do not have telephones, radios, or electricity in their homes. Communication between villages remains limited. There is only one telephone and one radio in Dmytrow, and often the telephone and radio do not work.

Dmytrow is a small town, and some people consider it just a village.

The village has just one church with a priest. The only doctor provides care for the villagers in his home. The town mayor has a large home with a radio and telephone that often does not work. Dmytrow is a beautiful village with many big trees and many fruit trees. The people get around on horseback and there are no stores. The brickyard lies about a mile outside the village of Dmytrow. The villagers shop in the small city of Lwow just a few miles north of Dmytrow.

The people of Dmytrow and in the surrounding areas view the marriage of Hanka and Michal as a day of promise for a better life for all the people in Poland.

Hanka's father proudly walks his daughter down the aisle toward Michal and their priest. The wedding vows remind many of the people of their wedding day. For many their wedding day was bleak. Today the guests all feel like their priest is marrying them again, only properly this time—no fear of Russian troopers. Maciej and Maria hold hands during the wedding ceremony and leave for their home immediately after the ceremony. Somehow, Maciej manages not to have a coughing spell during the ceremony but knows he will have another coughing spell soon.

When Maria and Maciej arrive home, Maria helps Maciej get comfortable in his room and then leaves to join her son and his new bride in the festivities after their wedding.

Michal and Hanka's wedding is a beautiful Polish wedding with family and friends. Everyone has fun, and the people feel real hope for the future. Both families are happy that Michal and Hanka married in a proper Polish wedding. In 1929 Poland, seventeen is not too young to marry. Maria and Hanka's parents feel pleased their children wed in a proper Polish wedding and no Russian troopers disturbed their wedding.

After the ceremony, everyone walks to Hanka's home, where all the guests eat, drink, and dance the day away. Dmytrow has a group of local musicians that play their musical instruments for Michal and Hanka after their wedding ceremony. This group of musicians just plays for the pure joy of making music. Hanka and Michal greet all their guests and thank everyone from near and far who have come to their wedding. All the guests wish Hanka and Michal a happy life filled with many children. The celebration ends after everyone can eat no more, drink no more, and dance no more. Michal only wished his dad could be with them during the festivities.

Before the end of the wedding celebration, Maria found Michal and said, "Michal, I have fixed up the room your father and I once shared. I want you and Hanka to have that room as your own. Michal, my son, be happy and never leave your family." Maria gives Michal a big hug and quickly walks away so Michal will not see her tears. Maria finds her children and takes them with her back to their home. She prays silently that Michal will never leave his family as Maciej left her once so long ago.

Michal, stunned and thrilled that his mama gave her room to him and Hanka, can hardly wait to tell Hanka. He knows their life will be happy and without problems. This is how Michal feels and thinks this day in May of 1929.

After all the guests have gone, Michal and Hanka say "Good-bye" to Hanka's parents, her brother, Frank, and her sisters. Michal gets his horse and wagon and with Hanka at his side, he allows the horse to find the way home.

The sky is dark with stars, for the moon is not yet visible in the sky. Michal and Hanka take time to kiss a lot on the way to Michal's home.

Between kisses, Michal tells Hanka that his mother has fixed a room just for them.

Hanka cries out, "Oh, Michal, how wonderful! I think perhaps your mama likes me." Hanka is starting to get a little nervous as she and Michal ride to his home.

When Michal and Hanka arrive at his home, Maria greets them and introduces Hanka to Michal's siblings. Szczepanm now eight years old, Tomasz, four years old, and little Aniela, two years old, they each say, "We wish you much happiness, Hanka, and you too, Michal."

Maciej returned to his home immediately after the ceremony and is asleep but breathing heavily and irregularly with an occasional deep coughing spell. He enjoyed the church service but afterwards felt so tired he simply returned home.

Michal and Hanka take her belongings into the room Maria fixed for them. Hanka notes the room is large and away from the kitchen where Maciej and Maria sleep. Hanka and Michal will hear only faint sounds of Maciej's coughing.

Hanka looks at Michal and says, "Michal, what a lovely room your mama has fixed for us." Michal puts his arms around his lovely bride and whispers in her ear how much he loves her. Suddenly Michal feels just a little nervous.

It is now almost midnight but Michal and Hanka do not feel tired, just nervous. Hanka knows she is ready for this night because her mother had a long talk with her about what Michal would expect from her. Hanka feels she will not have a problem, for she wants to express her feelings of love for Michal—now.

Michal has never been with a woman, and he does feel nervous. He thinks to himself, *I will just let my body tell me what to do and how to please Hanka.* Maciej tried to tell Michal about the first night with a woman but a severe coughing spell prevented his father-son talk.

Michal's partner at the brickyard talked with Michal about how to please a woman. He told Michal, "It is not hard, just follow your instincts." Then he described some important details to help Michal on this special night.

Michal starts kissing Hanka and whispers how much he loves her. Now he removes her clothes, all the while kissing her lips, neck, and then her breasts. Both Hanka and Michal become nervous but their passion and need overcome their nervousness.

Michal and Hanka are saying "I love you" in unison when Michal realizes he is ready and gently he enters Hanka, breaking her membrane. Without warning, Michal explodes, thrusting deeply; he wanted to wait but he could not. Hanka is crying out and responding to him. Amazed at their passion and depth of feeling they have just experienced, they fall into a blissful sleep.

In the morning, Hanka awakens first; she looks at her new husband and feels a joy she cannot express. Michal wakes and looks at Hanka, and he too feels a great joy. They make love again, only a little slower but just as powerfully.

Faint noises come from the kitchen and Michal says, "I must get up and help Mama. I wonder why she has not called me?" Michal, surprised that his Mama has not called him, hopes nothing bad has happened to his father. Hanka agrees, and they both get out of their bed and dress quickly. Now they walk hand in hand to the kitchen.

Maria sees them and says, "I believe you two are hungry, and I have fixed a special breakfast for you both." Michal and Hanka look in amazement at the special breakfast Maria has prepared for them.

Maria says, "You two sit here and eat this breakfast I have prepared for you." Hanka and Michal devour the delicious breakfast Maria prepared for them.

Michal says, "Mama, your breakfast is wonderful, but you need to rest now. Hanka and I will clean up and do the rest of the chores. I am not going to the brickyard today, for I have some farm chores to do."

Maria looks at her son and knows that Michal knows she is with child again.

Maria looks at Hanka and says, "Hanka, I will show you around this big house and how I keep this home running smoothly and where we wash our dirty clothes."

Maria shows Hanka the well where they get their water. Now she shows Hanka how to work the well for water. Michal has devised a way that makes it easier to get their water. Maria likes Hanka and wants Hanka to feel welcome here in Michal's home. Maria shows Hanka where she keeps all the cooking utensils and how to work the stove. Maria now takes Hanka outside and shows her where they keep the wood they use in their stove. Maria tries not to overwhelm Hanka but Hanka understands everything Maria tells her. Hanka's mother runs her home almost the same as Maria runs her home.

Maria comes to adore Hanka, and this large family gets along well together. As the days pass, Hanka takes over more of Maria's chores. Hanka believes Maria should not do such strenuous work and has concern for Maria and her unborn baby. Maria assures Hanka everything is going as it should and she must not worry about her.

Just three months later, Maria believes Hanka is with child. Hanka does not understand why she feels so tired all the time and sickly in the morning. Hanka usually eats a good breakfast but now eats nothing at breakfast.

Maria tells Hanka, “I believe you are with child, Hanka.” Hanka cannot believe what Maria tells her but feels pleased about this news. Maria says, “Hanka, I believe your baby's birth will be in late March or early April.”

Tonight, Hanka tells Michal her news about their coming baby next year. Michal cannot believe what Hanka tells him. He hugs and kisses Hanka every chance he gets. He treats Hanka as if she created this miracle all by herself.

The love that grows between Michal and Hanka astounds Maria. She realizes their love is a rare and beautiful love. She hopes nothing happens to hurt their love. She remembers that she and Maciej almost had something similar in the early days of their marriage. Then the magic of their love disappeared when Maciej left her for America and stayed away for so many years. When he returned she knew she felt different about him. Yes, she loves him, but her love has changed. She knows the coal-mine dust took his health, and most of the work falls on her. Michal does more work than he should, thinks Maria. Maria feels a deep resentment that Maciej returned to her in poor health.

Maria finds it hard to believe that she will have another baby. She expects this baby to be born late December of this year or January of next year. She does not know for sure.

In spite of Maciej's illness, he has continued to make love to Maria as often as he is physically able. Lately, Maciej has not attempted lovemaking, and Maria wonders if his illness has become much worse. Today she does not care.

Chapter Nine
Children and Rumors of War

In early January of 1930, Maria gives birth to a daughter. Maciej chooses the name of Jadzia for his daughter. Maria wonders why he picked this name, but she does not ask him. Maciej, now gravely ill, can barely breathe.

Late March of 1930, Hanka gives birth to a baby boy in their home. Maria helps Hanka with the delivery and fortunately, her delivery is not difficult.

Michal, thrilled and amazed, treats Hanka like a queen. They name their baby son Josef. Michal does all his chores plus helps his mother with hers and does many of Hanka's chores, too.

Several months later, life returns to a more normal pattern for Michal. Spring has arrived and Michal plows and plants his land for food. He continues his work at the brickyard, keeping his customers and conducting business satisfactorily. His partner at the brickyard cannot believe all the work Michal does so well and happily.

Each member of the family does their chores happily and there is little fighting between the children. However, Maciej's health grows worse and Maria wonders why "God" would allow a person to suffer as Maciej suffers.

In midsummer of 1931, Hanka realizes she is with child. Michal, thrilled, finds it hard to believe his great fortune. In early 1932, Hanka gives birth to another son. They name their new son Jan. Their happiness knows no bounds and they feel they have a wonderful life.

Maciej, gravely ill, knows only the struggle to keep living. The family can hear him coughing and his struggle to stay alive. They pray for Maciej, and Maria prays that God will accept him into heaven. She tells God, "Please, God, everything Maciej has done was to help me. Please accept my Maciej into your heaven."

Maciej dies in early 1934. The entire family feels a deep sadness at Maciej's death. Still, they feel relieved that he no longer suffers. The family buries Maciej on their land near the forest. Their priest comes and says a final farewell for Maciej.

Hanka is pregnant and expects to deliver her baby in the fall of 1934. She does not feel well and wonders why. This pregnancy seems different from her other two pregnancies. Hanka tells Michal she has a deep concern for this baby.

In the fall of 1934, Hanka delivers a baby daughter. Hanka and Michal believe it is a special gift to have a daughter. Hanka and Maria have concern about the baby, for this baby does not appear healthy. Within a week of their baby daughter's birth, their baby dies.

Michal and Hanka feel utter devastation as they bury their infant daughter near Maciej's grave. Two deaths in the same year deeply sadden Michal and Hanka. However, Maciej's death was more of a relief for the family as he suffered horribly before he died. No one could help Maciej get better, and the family had to watch him slowly die until finally he rested peacefully in death.

Michal comforts Hanka as best he can. He feels a deep pain seeing her tears over the death of their daughter. He desperately wants to see

Hanka smile and laugh again. The death of his father and baby daughter have only deepened his love for Hanka. Each day Michal helps Hanka with her chores and then he does his work on the farm and at the brickyard. Slowly Hanka and Michal become grateful for what they have and stop grieving over their daughter's death.

Two years later, Hanka wonders why she has not become pregnant again. She wonders if she will ever have another baby. Michal tells Hanka, he believes they will have more children. Michal's customers at the brickyard tell Michal horrible stories about this Adolf Hitler, Germany's leader.

More than one customer has told Michal that Hitler has built big buildings. "Hundreds, maybe more, walk into the buildings, men, women, and children, but no one comes out. At night, a big machine hauls bodies out and dumps the bodies in a big pit. At night, there is fire and lots of smoke coming from the pit. We are not sure but we think that somehow the people died in that building." How, they do not know.

Life remains quiet in the countryside surrounding Dmytrow. Michal continues to hear war rumors but now pays little attention to the rumors. Hanka has told him next year they will have another baby. Michal feels joy, for Hanka now smiles and laughs again. Michal feels a deep happiness.

At the brickyard, Michal learns that homes in the larger cities have running water inside. In addition, they have electricity that gives people light to read after dark. One customer gives Michal written instructions on how to put in plumbing from a well to a house.

Although Michal has only a third-grade education, he learned to read on his own and as he reads the plumbing instructions, he knows he can get water into his home. Michal, with his son Josef's help, puts in the needed plumbing from his well to his house. Water now comes into their kitchen. Hanka, Maria, and the children can hardly believe their eyes. The plumbing is crude, and one must pump the water into the kitchen by a crude handle. However, it allows them to get water inside their kitchen. Michal feels great that he succeeded in doing this task.

Michal would like to have a radio and telephone but has no idea how to perform this feat. The village mayor in Dmytrow has a radio and telephone. The radio has static that makes it difficult to understand what the person says on the radio. The telephone does not work most of the time.

In February of 1937, Hanka delivers another son. Maria and Michal feel a deep happiness, for this baby appears healthy. Michal and Hanka name their baby son Tadeusz.

Tadeusz, a healthy baby, constantly nurses at his mother's breast. When baby Tadeusz is not nursing, he laughs and smiles at whoever holds him. Even the other children enjoy holding and playing with him, for he is a happy baby who smiles and laughs easily.

Some of Michal's customers at the brickyard tell Michal war will come, and soon. Poland's economy has improved, and the people in eastern Poland have the sense that their lives will remain the same.

Everyone in the countryside knows Germany is hostile to Poland and that Russia would like to enslave the Polish people in eastern Poland. The people of eastern Poland have faith in the treaties their leaders have made with England and France that will keep the peace. The Polish people do not want war.

Despite the war talk, the sun comes up each day and the people of Dmytrow see and hear no signs of war. The Polish people who live in and near Dmytrow think that perhaps the war rumors are untrue.

One week before Hitler has scheduled his attack on Poland, Stalin sends Hitler a message that he will join Hitler in his attack. Hitler wants Stalin to attack eastern Poland, and Stalin agrees. Yet Stalin does not attack eastern Poland for several weeks. Stalin begins his attack of eastern Poland in northeastern Poland.

England and France do not want war, but their inaction allows war to occur. The main reason for the war is the deep support the German people give Hitler. The German people have no knowledge about what Hitler plans to do.

On September 1 of 1939, Hitler launches his massive forces against Poland. He orders his army to wipe out all Polish Jews, make slaves of ethnic Poles, and destroy their culture and any sense of nationality the people might have. Hitler talks to the German people, justifying the attack against Poland. Hitler has become a great spellbinder.

Hitler issues one odd order that commands the army to capture all blond, blue-eyed Polish children five years old and younger. The army must take these children back to Germany to a camp. Here the officials put the children in a German orphanage. The people who manage the orphanage raise the children as Germans. The German soldiers capture roughly 200,000 young Polish children that have blond hair and blue eyes and return these children to Germany.

When Hitler attacks western Poland, the people in Dmytrow do not know of the attack. Dmytrow lies in eastern Poland, and it is months before the people in Dmytrow learn of this attack.

In war, it is not the number of soldiers a country has but the strength a country has in weapons. A country's aircraft, tanks, and gun power make the biggest difference in wining a war in 1939.

The French had promised Poland some French bombers, but they never arrive. The Germans have over 3,000 aircraft, mostly new. The Polish air force consists of approximately 300 fighter planes. However the Polish fighter planes are outdated and no match for the modern German bombers and fighter aircraft. Poland has a few tanks and the Germans thousands. The Polish army, although well trained, still relied on their cavalry and their artillery pieces that are still towed by horses. The German army is fully modernized with the latest equipment to fight a war.

When the war occurs, the German soldiers ride in trucks to the battlefield, but the Polish soldiers must walk long distances before joining the main troops.. Within just a few days the Germans bombed and destroyed most of the Polish planes. Next the Germans bombed Poland's rail and road routes. In just a week the Polish army was almost annihilated. This vicious attack by the German military forces caught the Polish military forces by surprise.

On September 3, 1939, Britain, France, Australia, and New Zealand declare war on Germany.

Chapter Ten
World War II Begins

September 3, 1939, Britain, France, Australia, and New Zealand declare war on Germany.

September 4, 1939, British Royal Air Force attacks the German Navy.

September 5, 1939, the United States proclaims neutrality. The German troops cross the Vistula River in Poland.

September 17, 1939, Soviets invade Poland, but not in the southeastern section.

September 27, 1939, Warsaw surrenders to the Nazis.

September 29, 1939, the Nazis and Soviets partition Poland again.

Poland is no longer a nation.

In the town of Dmytrow in southeastern Poland, all is quiet and the people in this area have no knowledge of what is happening in other parts of Poland.

Not all the Polish people know what has happened to their country. The people in the town of Dmytrow have no way of knowing what is happening in other parts of Poland. The town's telephone and radio rarely work.

Chapter Eleven
Fear Grows

Late in October of 1939, Hanka gives birth to twin boys. Michal cannot believe he has two beautiful baby boys. He cradles Hanka in his arms, gently kisses her, and tells her how deeply he loves her. Hanka feels a deep apathy after the birth of her twins. A woman in the village who knows about multiple births came to help Hanka during this birth. This woman tells Michal that Hanka must get several days of rest and if he needs help to send one of the children to fetch her. Giving birth to the twins has left Hanka so tired she can barely move. Maria takes over all of Hanka's chores plus the care of all their children.

Michal tells Hanka she must rest and he and the other children will do her chores. Now Maria tells Hanka, "Dear Hanka, I can handle everything with the help of all our children. Hanka, they all want to help. Now, you take it easy; just ring this bell if you need something." Maria puts a large bell in Hanka's hand for her to ring if she needs anything. Maria feels delighted to be taking care of babies again.

Michal and Hanka name their twins Genek and Edek. Michal is a proud and happy man. His only concern is the continuing rumors of war.

So far, every day is the same as yesterday. Michal prays those war rumors are just rumors. The one persistent rumor is Hitler is coming with a mighty army and Hitler has made a deal with Stalin. That Hitler made a deal with Stalin terrifies Michal. Whenever he thinks of Stalin, he feels a bitter cold grip him, and this fear is sheer terror that immobilizes Michal until he gets better control of himself. He prays that what he hears is not true. "God, do not let these rumors be true. Please keep us safe, keep Stalin and Hitler away from us. Oh, God, no, NOT AGAIN, please," prays Michal repeatedly.

Michal and Hanka's family has grown and they are happy and contented. Michal's brother Tomasz is thirteen yeas old and helps Michal with the farm chores and with the animals. Szczepan, Michal's oldest brother, is fifteen and helps Michal at the brickyard. His sister Aniela is fourteen and his youngest sister, Jadzia, is nine years old.

Hanka and Michal's first child, Josef, is nine years old and their second son, Jan, is seven years old. Little Tadeusz is almost three years old. In January of 1940, their twin boys are only three months old.

Michal, Szczepan, and Tomasz work the farm and brickyard. Every month Michal earns money from his brickyard business. Michal has a contract with the Polish government to provide twelve horses a year to the Polish cavalry. This contract provides the family with a large cash flow. This large family has a big home and they feel wealthy. Most important, they are a happy family who care deeply about each other.

The children and Maria are unaware of the war clouds that will soon destroy their way of life. The adults know war might come but they hear only rumors. In a nearby town where some residents have radios, a man rides his horse to Dmytrow to tell the people about the impending war. Yet, each day the sun comes up and the people do their work without hearing any gunfire. All seems peaceful and quiet to the people of Dmytrow in eastern Poland.

In western Poland the German army bombs the Polish cities with their mighty Luftwaffe (German air force), destroying communication routes in all of Poland. The Polish general wanted to activate his reserves two weeks before the Germans attacked, but Britain and France told Poland that such an act would be a pretext for Hitler to attack.

Poland does not activate their reserves, and Hitler attacks. Hitler needs no pretext, for he planned to attack Poland. After the Germans attack and destroy communications routes, it is impossible for Poland to activate their reserves.

In 1935, France signed a military agreement in Warsaw with Poland's leader. The agreement states if the Germans attack Poland and the Polish army can hold out for fifteen days, and then on the fifteenth day France would send troops to help Poland.

The Polish army fights bravely but has no chance of winning against the well-equipped German army. The Polish soldiers rely on cavalry and horse-drawn artillery while the Germans throw at the Poles their *pantzen* (armored) divisions and run over the Polish army.

The Germans use two- to three-year-old bomber planes. Poland has just a few planes and they are much older. In the south of Poland, the Poles are able to reverse the German advance for only a short time. The Polish military is unable to last fifteen days against the Germans.

All hope dies for the Polish people on September 17, 1939, when the Soviet Union troops attack Poland from the east as part of the strategic agreement between Hitler and Stalin.

The Polish army has retreated to the Vistula River and has formed a second line of resistance. The Polish general and his staff decide to try to save as much of the army as possible by ordering some units to go south and cross over into Romania. The remaining troops perform with great bravery. Regardless, the Soviet troops capture most of the remaining Polish troops and imprison them in soviet POW camps. In Dmytrow, the people continue to have no knowledge of these events—just war is coming.

The Polish generals keep hoping to get help from France and England, but no help comes. Without help, Warsaw falls and surrenders to the Germans. Now, for the fourth time in Poland's history, the Soviet Union and Germany partition Poland. Poland no longer exists as an independent nation—AGAIN.

Back on the farm in Dmytrow, Michal and Hanka know nothing about what has happened in their country or the world. They do not know that their country no longer exists. No planes drop bombs on them, and the countryside remains quiet. The people feel uneasy but continue their daily chores. Under this cloud of doubt, the people continue their normal routines for a few weeks. Nevertheless, all the continuing rumors of war disturb the people—they feel fear consume their bodies.

For several weeks, Michal has put off going to Lwow to take care of some pressing business matters. He feels he must leave for Lwow now and take care of this business. Michal knows nothing of Stalin's attack in northeastern Poland. It is now early February of 1940.

Michal thinks everything will be all right. He decides to leave for Lwow around 3:30 a.m. so he can arrive in Lwow that night and be ready to get his business done the next day. He must also purchase much-needed supplies and warm coats for his brothers and his children, for the children are growing out of their clothes quite fast.

On February 9, 1940, the weather is cold with a mild wind when

Michal awakens to leave for Lwow. He looks down at his beautiful sleeping wife and feels desire for Hanka stir within him.

Michal genuinely loves his wife deeply and passionately. He feels thankful for his beautiful wife and children plus his home and business. He has so much to be thankful for; he thanks God for his many blessings, his lovely wife, his children, Josef, Jan, Tadeusz and his twin sons. He starts to worry as he thinks of his twin boys only a few months old, and a hint of fear for his family starts to grow in his mind.

No signs of war have appeared, and Michal believes he can take care of his business and return before anything happens. Michal knows he must leave and take care of his business matters in Lwow. Michal does not want his family to suffer any financial problems because of his not taking care of this business. He has put off taking this trip because of the war rumors but nothing has happened. He tells himself again, everything will be all right.

Michal is hopeful the pact that Poland signed with Britain long ago (the Mutual Assistance Treaty) will prevent war. Now he must leave for Lwow, the provincial capital in the southeast part of Poland. Michal has concern about this trip because of the long distance involved and his slow mode of transportation—via horse and sleigh. It is bitter cold and snow falls as Michal leaves his home in early February of 1940.

The snow, frozen solid, makes the road safe for traveling quickly. Michal notes there are no Russian troopers anywhere that he can see. All seems quiet and normal.

When Michal reaches Lwow it is now nighttime and he rents a room in a local tavern to get some rest. The first day he takes care of his business. The next day, he purchases all the necessary items for Hanka and his mother per their requests. Michal has now been gone from his home three days.

At the tavern, two men tell Michal that deportation is occurring now in Dmytrow. Michal hopes that is not true, for he feels a need to get a little sleep before heading home.

Michal goes up to his room and lies down on the bed. However, sleep does not come to Michal. He tosses and turns constantly thinking about the rumors of deportation back home in his village. He gets up and puts on his clothes and goes outside to see if it is snowing. A stranger comes up to Michal and tells him the Russians are deporting the people in his village of Dmytrow right now. Michal does not believe this man, for there were no signs of Russians when he left home.

Michal goes back to his room but realizes he cannot sleep. Michal thinks, What if that man told him the truth? He quickly runs back outside and gets his horse, wagon, and races for home. It is about 1:00 a.m. It will take him about twelve hours to reach Dmytrow. Michal makes it back to Dmytrow in ten hours. Michal arrives back in Dmytrow at about 11:00 a.m.

However, the day after Michal left home, ten Soviet troopers and the Ukrainian militia, all fully armed, storm into Michal's family home about 4:00 a.m. They yell in loud voices, "Everyone get up, you are under arrest." Maria and Hanka awaken and get out of bed and move into the room where the troopers wait for them with their guns pointed at them.

One trooper rudely yells at Maria and Hanka, "You must all leave this house within thirty minutes."

The grandmother, Maria, and Hanka cry, "NO, NO, we cannot leave. We have babies to feed and children to care for."

The other trooper yells, "Thirty minutes and we take you out, so prepare for a long journey."

Maria and Hanka panic; confusion and fear take over. All the loud yelling awakens the children. They get up, walk into the room next to the kitchen, and see their grandmother and mother crying and wringing their hands. The children start to cry. The older children try to comfort the younger children but NO ONE prepares to leave the house. *Surely,* thinks Maria, *these troopers will not force us out into the bitter cold with babies and little children.*

The children cry, Maria and Hanka just stand around wringing there hands. Maria and Hanka do nothing about planning for this trip and do not put warm clothes on the children. Michal's brothers, Szczepan and Tomasz, are just teenagers, and his two sisters, Aniela and Jadzia, are just fifteen and ten years old. Hanka, who is caring for five young ones, panics, goes into shock, crying "OH NO," all the time wringing her hands. The birth of the twins has left Hanka physically weak. The grandmother, Maria, cannot grasp what is happening and just tries to comfort the children.

The two Soviet troopers physically search the older boys, Szczepan and Tomasz. Thus, when the thirty minutes are up, the Soviet troops force the family from their home out into the bitter cold with nothing on them but the clothes on their backs.

The Soviet troops force them onto a sleigh and take the family to the railway station in the village of Dmytrow, five miles from their home. At the station the troopers, at gunpoint, force the family onto a cattle car with other Polish people from neighboring villages. Unknown to Hanka, the Russian troopers already put her mother, father, sisters and her brother, Frank, in another cattle car on this train. Hanka never sees them again.

Everyone in this bitter-cold cattle car huddles together from both fear and the cold weather. Inadequately dressed for the cold weather, Maria, Hanka, and the children huddle together. Jan feels his feet turn to ice and he jumps up and down to keep his feet warm.

A Soviet trooper sees him jumping up and down and yells at Jan, "YOU STOP THAT JUMPING—KEEP STILL." Jan stops jumping until the trooper moves away. Then he continues jumping up and down trying to keep warm.

Out of shock and fear, few families on this train prepare themselves for what lies ahead. The Soviets fill about twelve cattle cars with men, women, and children from various Polish villages. Fortunately for all of them on the cattle car with Hanka and her family, this train does not leave immediately.

Michal returns to Dmytrow about 11:00 a.m. three days after his family was put in the cattle car. Outside the village, some of Michal's Ukrainian friends intercept him and tell him about what has happened to his family. They tell Michal, "The Soviets will send everyone in the cattle cars to Archangel in northern Russia, and that includes your family."

The Russians send many trains with cattle cars full of Polish citizens to the Ural Mountains and Archangel in Russia. The Russians pick only families who appear wealthy. They do not want the poor.

Michal immediately heads toward the train station in Dmytrow to find his family. One Ukrainian soldier (this Polish man joined the Soviets to aid the Soviets) calls to Michal and says, "Hey, Michal, you should join us and be free." Michal just looks at him in shocked horror. Michal could never consider abandoning HIS family.

As fast as he can Michal urges his horse pulling his wagon to race to the train station where he finds his family huddled together in the cattle car crying and shivering in the bitter cold. Michal looks at his family in disbelief, for they have no warm coats on to protect themselves from the bitter cold. Anger and fear take a firm hold on Michal, for he learns his family has been on this cattle car for three days.

Michal cannot believe his family took nothing with them when they boarded the cattle car. He knows he must return to his home and get food and clothing for everyone—not just his family but for the others in the cattle car with his family. This will not be an easy task to do. Before Michal leaves the cattle car, he gives to Maria the new coats he bought for her, Hanka, and the children. Now Michal leaves for his home.

When Michal reaches his home, two Ukrainian guards prevent him from entering his home. Both guards look vaguely familiar to Michal but he simply cannot remember ever seeing them. One guard harshly tells Michal, "This property is now the property of the Soviet Union and YOU MAY NOT ENTER."

Michal knows he must get the necessary supplies for his family or they will perish.

Out of despair, Michal grabs an ax, firmly holds it above his shoulder ready to strike, and says to the guards, "I do not care whether I live or die, for without supplies I and my whole family will perish. Now, you let me in for my supplies," demands Michal in a firm strong voice.

Both guards had worked for Michal in the past at his brickyard and respect him. Now the two guards out of respect and admiration for Michal's treatment of them in the past allow him to enter his home and take what he needs. The guards even make sure no one sees what Michal takes from his house.

Michal gathers all the warm clothes and blankets he can find. Next, he collects all the jewelry that he sees and money that is in the house and hides these items in his clothing. Then he turns his attention to food. He puts together a pile of food—two big bags of potatoes, a bag of flour, fresh eggs, and dried vegetables and fruit. He kills two chickens, chops off their heads, and puts them in a bag. Then he milks the cows and brings a couple of gallon jugs of milk for the twins, only a few months old. Michal remembers Hanka's milk has been drying up sooner than she expected.

Michal gathers so much of what he needs, the guards must help Michal put all the items onto his wagon. Both guards escort Michal to the train and help him unload everything onto the cattle car. The other guards at the train are so busy with the screaming terrified people in the other cars that they do not notice what Michal and the guards with him are doing.

As Michal enters the cattle car he notices some of the people are already dead. He checks each person to make sure they are dead. Now he calls the guards and tells them to remove the dead people. The guards just look at Michal and miraculously they remove the dead people. As the two guards leave the cattle car they close and lock the door.

Chapter Twelve
War Has Arrived

When the imprisoned family sees Michal and the lifesaving supplies he has with him, they all cry with joy and some relief. Michal's family and neighbors greet him with pleasure for bringing so many needed supplies. Michal has a little wood stove on his wagon, and he takes the stove with him onto the cattle car, plus a pile of wood. After Michal has everything from his wagon in the cattle car, the guard now locks everyone in the cattle car and walks away.

Immediately Michal checks to make sure his children and Hanka plus his mother, Maria, and his brothers and sisters have their warm coats on. Now he wraps the twins, each one, in a warm wool blanket. Hanka hugs Michal fiercely, all the while crying in fear. "Why, oh why, did those Russians take us from our home, why, Michal?"

Michal just hugs his wife. Tenderly, he says to her, "Hanka, war has found us, but I will do everything in my power to protect all of us." Michal believes he will be able to do this—he prays he can.

The small wood stove is full of wood, and Michal starts a fire in the stove, for the cattle car is freezing cold. Michal makes sure that everyone has a chance to be near the heat for a while to thaw out and to get his or her clothes warm.

No toilet exists on any of the cattle cars. Therefore, Michal cuts a

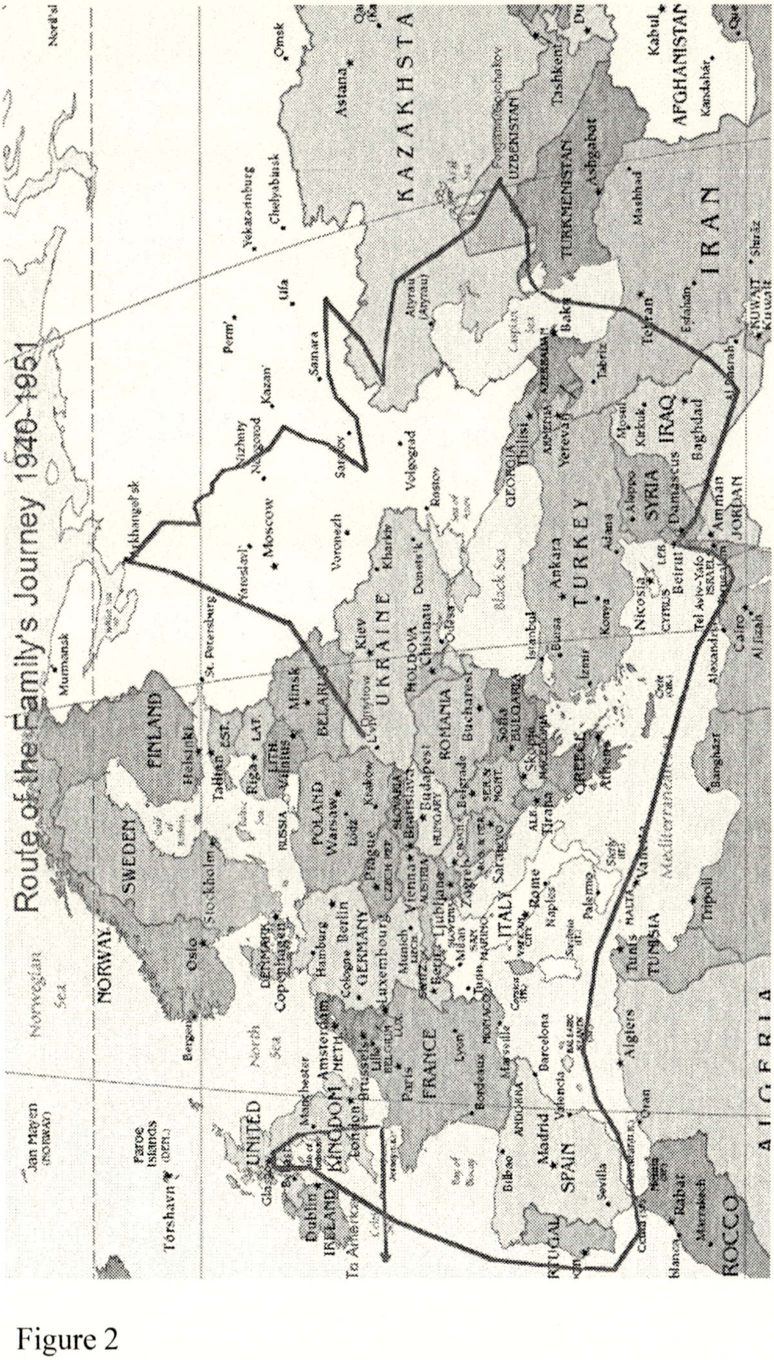

Figure 2

Route of the Family's Journey 1940–1951

hole in the floor of the cattle car for everyone to use so the other areas of the car can remain clean. Michal and two of the other men hang a blanket around the hole for privacy. Early the next day at about 3:00 a.m. the train leaves the station for Archangel in northern Russia.

No one knew that Stalin's plan is to deport all the Poles from eastern Poland, so after the war when the Russians hold an election to decide the future of the region there will be only Russians, Ukrainians, and a few minorities to vote. Stalin's order to the Russian troops is to take all the wealthy and educated Polish people and put them on the cattle car train.

Historians have written various accounts about the number of Poles exiled under this plan. All the Poles taken from their homes are ethnic Poles of the Catholic religion. There are no Polish Jews on this train. The number of ethnic Poles the Soviets uprooted and exiled under his plan was between 1.5 million and 2 million. The impact on all involved remains the same. They have no country. Stalin abuses and mistreats the ethnic Poles. The Polish people do not realize they are at Stalin's mercy—Stalin has no mercy, nor do many of the Russian troopers.

The train hauling the cattle cars full of Polish citizens begins the trip to Archangel in northern Russia. The trip will take over three weeks. The cold gets severe and colder as the train heads north.

When the train stops at a station, the Soviets allow their prisoners to get off and receive a meager portion of food. Most of the adults and teenagers form a long single line to wait for soup that is mostly warm water and one or two slices of thick, vile-tasting dark bread. The bread does not taste good, but it does take away the hunger pangs.

The twin baby named Edek is not doing well. Maria holds Genek, and Hanka holds Edek, trying to keep them warm. Hanka tries to nurse

Edek. Hanka looks at Michal sobbing, "Oh why, why, Michal, why did those troops remove us from our home? Michal, my babies need a warm home. My milk is drying up and soon I won't be able to feed my babies." The tears flow from her eyes as she sobs in fear. Michal cradles his wife and son in his arms and wonders how to save his family from this appalling ordeal.

The tiny baby falls asleep, and Michal takes little Edek from his mother and says to Hanka, "I will keep him warm. Hanka, you try to get a little rest." Michal looks at his baby son and says, "Oh, my son, how can I keep you alive, my precious son? This is no place for a baby or anyone; my God, this is a cold, disgusting cattle car." Michal feels deep hate form within him toward the Russians.

The twin boys, three months old, drink all the milk in just a few days. Michal worries where or when he will find more milk. Hanka's breasts produce little milk. Michal shares everything he has with the other people on the car. There are about thirty or more people in this cattle car including the children. The cattle car has many places where the wind blows the bitter cold inside. Everyone is grateful for the food, warm clothing, and wood stove Michal brought onto the cattle car.

One cold night the little baby, Edek, dies in Hanka's arms. Hanka cries out, "NO, OH NO." Michal quickly goes to Hanka and takes the tiny baby from his mother. He checks for breathing, a heartbeat—there is none. Michal gasps in horror and hugs Edek to his breast. The other people in the car start crying. Several of the women go to Hanka and put their arms around her. They try in vain to comfort Hanka, but there is no comforting her.

Michal keeps little Edek next to him, constantly checking to see if little Edek is alive. Michal knows little Edek is dead but does not want to admit this fact. Adults and children cry fiercely for the death of little Edek. Edek's death is the first death in this cattle car.

When the train stops and the guards unlock the cattle cars, Michal and two other men leave the car. Michal carries little Edek and one man carries a shovel. Michal puts little Edek on the ground and the men take turns digging Edek's grave. Here on Russian soil Michal buries his baby son, Edek, under a tree near the train tracks. The Russian troopers do not interfere in this burial. There is no priest to say a prayer or give last rites. Michal speaks a few words as tears flow from his eyes and he places a cross on his son's grave site. The women sob loudly. The death of baby Edek makes everyone feel vulnerable to death.

The train is about to leave, and the Soviet troopers force everyone back onto the cattle cars. Little Genek, three months old, and little Tadeusz, just three years old, are now the youngest children in this cattle car.

The train begins to move and Michal looks back at the tree where he buried his baby son, Edek. Suddenly he sees a Russian trooper kick the cross off his son's grave. Michal and two of the other men saw what the Russian trooper did and they cursed that Russian trooper.

The Soviet troops provide only one or two slices of bread with a watery soup to each person on the train and only when the train stops. Sometimes when the train stops, they provide nothing.

The food Michal brought with him is soon gone. Michal constantly wonders how to get more food for his family and the others on the cattle car before someone else dies.

The train is slowing down when Michal sees a big dog at the edge of the forest chasing the train. Michal speaks to the other men, pointing to the dog. Michal tells the men he wants to kill the dog and bring it back to the cattle car. The other men agree. When the train stops, Michal leaves the cattle car while the other men on the cattle car block the guards so they cannot see Michal enter the forest.

Cautiously Michal stalks the dog, then attacks the dog with just a big tree branch, and kills the dog. Michal puts the dog in an empty sack he has with him. Now he picks up several large pieces of wood, and puts the wood in the bag with the dog. He quickly returns to the cattle car and hides the sack. Then he leaves the cattle car and gets in the food line with the other Polish people.

They all get their ration of a slice of bread and watery soup and return to the cattle car. No one saw what Michal did to the dog. The Russian troopers did not see what Michal did, for they were busy with all the other people.

After the train begins to move fast, Michal and two of the other men butcher and prepare the dog for cooking. The women roast the dog on the little stove. All enjoy the feast as they fill their stomachs with food. After their feast, they drop the bones of the dog through the hole Michal cut in the floor of the cattle car while the train moves. The main goal of each adult on this cattle car is to survive and prevent death from occurring again.

The cold gets colder and more severe as the train moves farther north. It is obvious to all that the clothes and blankets Michal put onto the train are the reason they are still alive. The train is now just one week from reaching Archangel when another misfortune occurs.

Two days later when the train comes to a standstill, Hanka puts a large pot of water on the little stove to boil. She plans to do some cleaning that she feels is necessary in the cattle car that holds twenty-plus people. All the people in the cattle car get off so Hanka can do her cleaning. The weather is cold and Hanka has on a warm sweater but not her heavy coat.

The water comes to a full rolling boil. With a heavy cloth in each hand, Hanka lifts the pot of boiling water off the stove. Suddenly the train lurches forward as the engine restarts. The sudden movement of the train knocks Hanka off balance and the pot of boiling water spills onto her chest, abdomen, arms and hands, and even onto her upper legs. Although Hanka has her clothes on, her clothing could not protect her from the huge amount of boiling water that spills onto her body.

Hanka suffers severe burns but probably only second-degree burns. Hanka cries out loudly, and a few of the women outside the cattle car hear her cries and come running to her. The women do what they can by removing her hot wet clothing, and one woman gets a pail of snow and applies the snow to Hanka's burned skin. The snow melts quickly, and another woman puts some rags over the snow, hoping to keep the snow in place before it melts. Dirty rags or clothing is all that is available on this prison train. The cold rags help a little to relieve Hanka's pain. With minimal care at home, Hanka would have recovered from this accident.

The train whistle goes off and the other people return to the cattle cars quickly with the armed Russian guards yelling at them to get on—NOW.

When Michal looks at Hanka burns, he wonders how to help her. Suddenly Michal feels a deep worry for Hanka—a worry for her life. He wants to help Hanka but does not know how. The train starts to move, and he must wait until it stops to ask for help. Michal wonders if the Russians will provide help for Hanka.

Michal looks up to the roof of the cattle car and prays, "God, show me how to help my Hanka." Michal feels a fear he cannot explain and asks his mother, Maria, "What can we do?"

Maria, crying, says repeatedly, "I cannot believe this. Oh, dear God, why did you let this happen?"

Maria desperately tries to get herself together and stop crying. She turns to Michal and tells him, "Michal, I do not know what we can do. The women are doing all they can for Hanka. Michal, we must get those guards to get her a doctor. Somehow we must get our Hanka medical help."

All too soon, the cold soothing snow turns to warm water. The women tell Michal they will get more snow when the train stops. No one knows when the train will stop.

Each time the train stops, Michal demands help from the Russian guards, but the guards state firmly and harshly, "When the train arrives in Archangel, we might get your wife help. No help until this train reaches Archangel. Understand? Now, you, stop bothering us."

One guard stops Michal as he heads to his cattle car and says, "I will try to get some help for your wife when we reach Archangel." Then the guard walks away. Michal, astounded, memorizes the guard's face.

Finally, the train reaches Archangel in northern Russia, where the train tracks end. The train has taken over three weeks to reach Archangel. When the Russian guard unlocks the gate to Michal's cattle car, Michal immediately asks the guard for medical help for his wife. This guard just ignores him. After everyone is off the cattle car, Michal looks for the guard who offered to get help for Hanka. Michal does not see this guard anywhere and wonders what has happened to him.

The train arrives at Archangel during the nighttime. Clouds hide the stars, and it is snowing and bitter cold. Many horse-drawn sleighs sit at the train station. Michal wonders, *Why so many sleighs? Where will these Russians take us? What do they plan to do to us?*

A new set of Russian troopers arrive and roughly order the people to get onto the sleighs. Michal asks one trooper, "Where are you taking us?"

The trooper laughs and says, "You'll find out," as he walks away from Michal.

Another trooper yells, "All of you get on this sleigh—NOW. You are going to a labor camp near our river, Severnaja Dzwina, WHERE YOU WILL WORK FOR RUSSIA."

Devastated that he cannot get any help for his beloved Hanka, Michal wonders how they can survive. He knows he cannot stand to have another death in his family. He cradles Hanka in his arms, careful not to hurt her burned areas, and tries to keep her warm. Maria holds baby Genek and little Tadeusz in her arms. The other children huddle together with their coats on and blankets wrapped around them trying to keep warm.

CHAPTER THIRTEEN
DISASTER STRIKES

The ride into the forest felt like a bone-chilling cold. The troopers provide no blankets. The men and women on Michal's cattle car did grab every blanket and article of clothing they could to take with them. They did this in spite of the troopers yelling "Get off" while pointing their guns at the people exiting the cattle cars.

Hanka's parents and her siblings get off the train and immediately the Russian troopers take them by sleigh to a work camp. Their work camp is located far from the work camp where the Russians take Hanka, Michal, and his entire family.

Three Russian troopers load the sleigh with the people from the cattle car containing Michal and his family. The sleigh leaves the train station for the work camp in the forest where there are large barracks to house the people. Soon the people are able to see large buildings among the trees, for the sun has begun to rise.

The sleigh stops and the people get off. Several more sleighs arrive, and now there are many people standing in the falling snow and freezing cold in front of a large building.

A Russian trooper leads the people into the building. This building has many rooms, and each room has a small wood stove. The Russian trooper firmly states, "One family in one room." If a family has only two members, they get one room. In Michal's case, there are ten family members and one tiny baby, making eleven people for one room. The rooms are empty, without any supplies except for the wood stove. Outside is an outhouse in shabby condition. The Polish people look at their rooms and wonder what the Russians plan to do with them—*Can we survive?* wonder the Polish people.

Suddenly a loud bugle blares. A Russian trooper shouts loudly, "Everyone outside NOW." The Polish people go outside. As the people congregate outside the building, the Russian lifts his megaphone and yells into it.

"All you kids twelve years old will work in the forest. You, old woman, (he points at Maria holding little Genek) and all you old women will take care of the children younger than twelve."

Michal interrupts the Russian officer and says, "Beg your pardon, my wife needs medical attention."

The Russian looks at Michal and laughs. He yells, "Your wife will work with the rest of you in the forest." The Russian stomps out of the barracks mumbling, "That guy is nuts. Russia does not provide medical care for dumb Polish people."

Suddenly the Russian stops and returns and looks at a young boy and says, "How old are you, boy?"

The boy says, "Ten years old, sir."

The Russian laughs and tells the group of Polish people, "This boy looks twelve, he works in the forest."

No one has papers with them to prove their name, age, or country affiliation. The Polish people brutally taken from their homes are to work in the forest logging trees, trimming, cutting the trunks of trees into specific-size logs. Then they must load the cut logs onto a cart.

Two men take the cart to a boxcar on the train tracks, where they load the logs onto the boxcar for transport elsewhere. The Polish workers must fill about ten boxcars a day. If they do not meet their quota, they do not get food.

The Russians can order the Polish people to do anything they want done. The Polish prisoners do every chore the Russians demand of them.

Many of the workers suffer from frostbite almost immediately. Already many men, women, and children die of exposure to the cold and malnutrition. The cold is so severe it is obvious to all those living that they might not survive this frigid cold. Food is scant and grossly inadequate for the harsh work the Russian troopers demand of the Polish people.

Hanka has only second-degree burns. With proper care, her burns would heal and she would live without any scarring. Living in a dirty, crowded cattle car without any care, Hanka's burns become infected. She develops a fever. Michal and Maria want Hanka to receive medical care. Michal does not want Hanka working in the forests.

Michal and Maria demand the Russian trooper provide medical care for Hanka. In addition, Michal and Maria state strongly that Hanka cannot work. This time they talk to a different Russian and he tells them that he will arrange for some help.

The trooper had noticed Hanka's beautiful face and the pain that she endured from her burns. He feels a deep compassion for Hanka and wants to help her. Before the end of the workday, this Russian tells Michal that early tomorrow morning a boat will take Hanka to the hospital that lies on the other side of the river.

Maria and Michal feel great relief and gratitude toward this Russian.

Michal thinks now Hanka will get help and get better. Maria wonders why this Russian was willing to get help for Hanka.

The next morning Michal accompanies Hanka to the dock where she will take a boat to the hospital. He tells the person at the boat emphatically, "I must go with my wife. She needs me."

A Russian trooper arrives at the dock and tells Michal, "NO. If you want her to get help, she goes alone. You get back to work—now."

Michal does not rush to work. First, he tenderly helps Hanka onto the boat and kisses her good-bye. He watches as the boat leaves the dock and then he rushes back to work. He works furiously to get his assignment done so he can meet Hanka when she returns sometime before night falls. At least, the person rowing the boat told him she would return in his boat before nightfall.

On the boat, the Russian trooper is smitten with lust as he looks at Hanka's beautiful face. Then he sees her hands and notes a foul order about her. Hanka's burns are badly infected. As soon as they reach the other side of the river, another Russian takes Hanka to the hospital by sleigh. This Russian helps Hanka down from the sleigh, leads her to the admitting area, and quickly leaves her.

A woman comes toward Hanka speaking only Russian. Hanka understands some Russian because Michal hired Russians to work in the brickyard and she had contact with them and learned some of their language. Hanka understands this woman wants her to follow her, and Hanka follows the woman. The woman takes Hanka to another room and removes her upper clothing. Then she places a light clean gown over her wounds. Soon the doctor arrives to see Hanka.

The doctor cleans all her wounds with cool water all the while talking to her in Polish. Hanka feels safe and her pain seems relieved after the doctor cleaned her burns. Now the doctor applies a soothing cream and a light dressing on all of Hanka's wounds. Hanka can talk to the doctor, for he understands her Polish language, and this comforts Hanka. It is a wonderful feeling to be able to talk to someone who understands what you say.

Hanka received minimal help for her burns, but she feels better after her treatment. The doctor gives Hanka a large jar of cream and some dressings so she can take care of her burns. The doctor walks Hanka back to the boat dock and tells the trooper firmly, "This woman cannot work in the forest until these wounds become healed—I mean it, she cannot work. Do you understand me?"

The trooper says to the doctor, "Yes, I understand, and I will tell the trooper assigned to her." Now the trooper takes Hanka back to the other side of the river.

Daylight starts to fade when Hanka returns to the other side of the river. Michal finishes his work early and waits for her at the dock. He suddenly sees the boat coming across the river. He says a silent prayer that they helped her.

After the boat docks, Michal helps Hanka out of the boat. Michal tenderly hugs Hanka and gives her a kiss. He asks Hanka, "Did the doctor help you?"

Hanka replies, "Yes, Michal, he helped me. The doctor told the trooper in the boat that I cannot work in the forest." Hanka seems better to Michal, and this pleases him.

Back at the barracks, the trooper tells Hanka, "You will work. You got your doctor care, now you work." Many other Polish workers hear what this trooper says and they just look in horror at the trooper. They talk among themselves and agree that Hanka must not work in the forest.

They tell Michal, "Michal, somehow we will do our work and your wife's workload. To carry out this task without the guards noticing Hanka's absence, she must walk with us into the forest. She does need to look like she is working when the trooper looks at her, but we will make sure she does not do any work." What little work Hanka does prevents her burns from healing and only makes her sicker as the infection spreads throughout her body. She did not receive an antibiotic cream or oral antibiotics.

Lack of proper food, the crowded living conditions, plus being out in the cold, and the recent birth of her twins keep Hanka's health from improving

The cold continues unbearable for everyone. For Hanka the cold relieves some of her pain, but being out in the cold forest prevents Hanka's health from improving. She now runs a high fever and can barely eat what little food her husband brings her. Soon she cannot get up to go to work.

The trooper yells at Michal, "Since your wife cannot work your workload has tripled." Michal just nods his head, agreeing with the trooper. Hanka's skin feels hot to Michal's touch. She has used up all the cream and dressings the doctor gave her, yet her burns remain grossly infected.

Five weeks have now passed since the Polish people arrived at the barracks. Hanka has collapsed, and Michal fears for her life. The thought that Hanka might die terrifies Michal. Michal demands medical care for Hanka. The Russian trooper refuses to send her back to the hospital.

At night, Michal holds Hanka tenderly and in such a way as not to cause her any pain. Michal gets little sleep, but he is unaware of this fact. Michal knows only that he must keep his Hanka alive.

Tonight, Michal holds Hanka as she sleeps. Michal thinks she is a little better, for her skin feels almost normal. Hanka awakens and talks to Michal. She starts to cry while begging Michal to keep their children safe, especially baby Genek.

Michal assures her he will always protect their children. Hanka says, "I love you, Michal," and falls asleep again. Michal hopes his Hanka feels better, but at the same time he senses a real fear for her life. He tells himself, *I think she is a little better.* Then Michal drifts off into a light sleep.

Suddenly Michal awakens and looks at Hanka; she does breathe, thinks Michal. He carefully moves his arms away from her so he can look at her more closely. He suddenly knows his Hanka has gone and he starts to sob uncontrollably.

Michal's sobbing awakens Maria, and she goes over to him and checks Hanka. Michal's grief knows no relief and without realizing it, he cries out, "NO, NO OH, NO," as he hugs Hanka to his breast. Now Tomasz and Szczepan awaken and go to Michal. They look at Hanka and know she has died. Aniela and Jadzia awaken and begin to cry. They all cry together for a short time. They feel horrified that another member of their family has died.

The people in rooms near Michal hear the sobbing and know another death has occurred and that this death must be Hanka. The older men and women go to Michal's room to comfort him. People in this barracks feel deep anger and raging hate toward the Russians who have imprisoned them. Each of them blames the Russians for the deaths that have occurred among their people.

Michal asks Tomasz and Szczepan to help him hide Hanka's body until the end of the workday so he can give her a proper burial. Maria quietly tells her sons, "I will keep Hanka safe from the Russians until you return from work." Michal does not want Hanka's body thrown into the pit with the other dead bodies.

Michal does his work as usual but sets aside enough wood to make a coffin for Hanka. That night Michal, his family, and others from the barracks watch as Michal puts Hanka's body in the coffin he has made. Now quickly and quietly, everyone moves into the forest where Szczepan and Tomasz have dug a grave for Hanka.

Michal says a few words of love over Hanka's coffin. Now Szczepan and Tomasz lower Hanka's coffin into the grave and fill her grave with dirt. Michal puts a cross with Hanka's name on it into the ground to mark her gravesite.

Michal and his family have been in the Russian work camp for two months. Michal feels he cannot go on, but he knows he must, for he gave Hanka his word that he would look after their children and keep them safe. He wonders how to do this task. It is now April of 1940, and he fears that their imprisonment may never end.

Chapter Fourteen
Change Occurs

When the Soviet commander learns that Michal previously owned and managed a brickyard, he decides Michal must reactivate the nearby brickyard and make bricks. The commander orders a trooper to bring Michal to him. The Soviet trooper goes to the forest, orders Michal to follow him, and refuses to tell Michal anything. Michal follows the trooper but becomes fearful about why and where the trooper might take him.

As the trooper walks away from the forest and heads for the building where the commander works, Michal feels absolute terror. *What did I do to make the commander want to see me?* wonders Michal.

The trooper points at Michal and yells, "The commander wants to talk to you."

Michal walks up the few steps to the door and then enters the building. Michal sees the commander and walks toward him. Michal feels his heart pounding as he tries to control his shaking body.

The commander sees Michal and says, "Please sit down, Michal. I want to talk to you about your brickyard experience."

Amazed, Michal sits down in the chair opposite the commander. A large table separates them. The commander says to Michal, "Your papers tell me you once managed a brickyard—is this true?"

Michal replies, "Yes, I was half owner of my brickyard and I did all the maintenance work to keep the brickyard functioning and putting out great bricks. I know everything there is to know about making good bricks."

The commander smiles again at Michal and says, "Good. Michal, I want you to reopen the brickyard that lies just one mile from this camp. I want you to make many bricks."

Michal answers quickly. "I can do what you ask," says Michal.

Michal can hardly believe what the commander has said to him. He knows this means his family will not live in the frigid cold barracks; instead, they will live next to the brickyard that provides heat, and this heat will keep his family warm. They will also have more room than they had in the barracks.

Their new home is a large one-room house with their own outhouse. This outhouse is just a mere fifty feet away from the house. Michal and his family are ecstatic.

Now that Michal does skilled labor, the Russians provide him better rations of food. With the money he has hidden in his clothes, Michal can buy some vegetables from the Russian people in the nearby village. Regardless of this improvement, their diet remains grossly inadequate. The vegetables will improve their health, but they do not receive an adequate amount of food for the size of their family. Their diet contains no fruits.

Maria and Michal's two teenage sisters, Aniela and Jadzia, have looked after Genek since Hanka became ill. Nevertheless, lack of milk and the cold contributes to the child's death. Baby Genek, just ten months old, dies in August of 1940.

Michal makes a coffin for his baby son. He takes the tiny lifeless body of his son and places him in the coffin. Michal buries his tiny son near a cemetery and he says a few words through his tears. He places a small cross over Genek's gravesite. Michal feels as if he has died as he makes a vow—"There will be no more death in my family," he shouts to the heavens above.

Michal becomes concerned about little Tadeusz, now three years old. Tadeusz has survived all the hardships of life in Russia. Michal knows Tadeusz needs food, for he looks like a skeleton, but a hungry and alive skeleton. Soon the day comes when Michal can no longer stand the hungry looks on his children's faces.

After much thought, Michal decides to visit the warehouse where the Russians store their food. Michal takes his second son, Jan, with him. Jan witnesses the unusual altercation between his father and the Russian officer.

After Michal and Jan reach the office of the Russian officer and face him personally, Michal in a polite yet subservient voice says, "My family is starving. We need, NO, we must have more food."

The officer looks at Michal and in a mocking voice replies, "No. You may not have more food."

Michal looks at the officer and pulls out from under his coat a hefty ax handle. With a wild look on his face, Michal firmly and passionately yells at the officer, "I WILL NOT LEAVE HERE WITHOUT MORE FOOD. Do you understand?"

Immediately the officer pulls out a pistol as Michal, raging in anger and desperation, moves toward the officer. Michal raises his ax handle in his hand above his head and yells, "I MUST HAVE MORE FOOD."

Luckily for all of them, the Russian officer, stunned at Michal's behavior, puts down his gun. The officer orders his soldier to give

Michal and Jan several loaves of bread and two large sacks of potatoes. Michal thanks the Russian officer for the food. Jan and his dad take the food and leave. For the size of Michal's family, this food will last only two weeks or less.

All too soon, the need for more food becomes acute—again. Michal tries to provide food for his mother, Maria, his sisters, Aniela and Jadzia, and his brothers, Szczepan and Tomasz, and for his sons, Josef, Jan, Tadeusz, plus himself. Nine people, seven of them children, always hungry. The need for food remains the same—always severe.

Today Michal delivers bricks to a neighboring village when he notices a sheep. The sheep just wanders in the village. It does not belong to anyone, thinks Michal. Remembering the hungry faces of his starving family, Michal decides to take the sheep from the village on his next visit.

Two days later Michal passes through the village again and sees the sheep. He decides to kill this sheep. He looks to see if anyone might see him kill the sheep. Michal sees no one. He is alone with the sheep.

Michal gets close to the sheep, grabs it, and kills it. He puts the dead sheep in a big sack that he brought with him. Quickly he returns home. Now, Michal butchers the sheep and Maria cooks it. The family eats well tonight. After the feast, Michal buries the left-over sheep in the snow for another meal or two.

Obviously, someone saw Michal doing something he or she considered suspicious. The next day two Russian police come into their house demanding to search the house. Maria, consumed with fear, allows the police to search the house. The police search diligently but find nothing. Maria, relived, says a quick prayer, "Thank you, God."

When Michal and his two brothers return home at dusk and learn about the police searching their home, they arm themselves with stout sticks to defy the police if they return. Since the police found nothing, they do not return to search their house.

Maria cooks the rest of the sheep, and everyone eats heartily and with relish, devouring the rest of the sheep. Michal burns all evidence of the sheep in one of the brickyard ovens.

Michal constantly looks for ways to add to his family's food supply and avoid another death and starvation. He learns of a farmer a few miles away who will sell him potatoes.

After a full day of work in the brickyard making bricks, Michal walks several miles to the farmer's home. Michal buys two large sacks of potatoes each weighing two hundred pounds with the money he has kept hidden in his clothes from the Russians.

Michal is a strong man, but he cannot carry four hundred pounds of potatoes at one time without a wagon or wheelbarrow. He is afraid to leave one sack behind while he carries one home because he knows someone would find and take the bag left behind.

Michal solves this problem by carrying one sack about a hundred yards as he watches the sack left behind. Then he walks back and picks up the sack left behind and carries this sack about a hundred yards past the first bag, always keeping the other sack in view. He continues this pattern until he has both sacks in his house. By the time he reaches home, he feels extreme exhaustion.

Maria happily cooks the potatoes and everyone feasts on these potatoes as if they are the finest food in the entire world. Michal looks at his children's satisfied faces and feels the effort getting those potatoes home was well worth it.

Still, hunger remains with them. Yes, occasionally they hit a jackpot and eat reasonably well for a few days, sometimes even a week. Most of the time, the family's diet is inadequate in amount of grains, meats, and vegetables. There is no fruit in their diet. Fruit has not been available to eat for over a year. No dried fruit or fresh fruit exits for Michal and his family or any of the Polish people taken from their homes by the Russians.

One day Maria has enough supplies to bake a half loaf of bread. The smell of the half loaf of bread tantalizes young Tadeusz. Maria tells Tadeusz, now almost four years old, to take this half loaf of bread to his uncle Szczepan and aunt Aniela who are working about a mile from their house. Maria points toward the direction that Tadeusz must walk. The bread is for their lunch.

The smell of the baked bread makes Tadeusz feel deep hunger pangs. Tadeusz thinks, *If I take just a nibble from the end of this bread, well, my aunt and uncle will not notice the missing bread.* One nibble follows another nibble. When Tadeusz gets to his destination, nearly half of the half loaf of bread is gone. Tadeusz feels terrible that he left so little of the loaf of bread for his aunt and uncle. He knows they are hungry, too. Tadeusz's aunt and uncle say nothing to Tadeusz; they just take the bread and eat the remaining bread. They even feel guilty eating the rest of the bread, for little Tadeusz looks as if he is nothing but skin and bones—a living skeleton.

Chapter Fifteen
War Takes a Turn

Unknown to the Polish people enslaved in northern Russia, three countries make an alliance. On September 27, 1940, Germany, Italy, and Japan sign the Tripartite (Axis) Alliance. These three countries plan to conquer the world.

By the spring of 1941, Michal and his family have settled into a routine. The adults feel their horrific enslavement will never end. Some of the older children and even the adults are learning to speak Russian. The Russian language now seems intended to be their new language.

From everything, the Polish people hear the Soviet Union and Germany are going to control most of Europe and a large part of Asia and Africa. In 1941, the thousand-years Reich seems a reality rather than just Hitler's dream. Fortunately for the enslaved Polish people and millions of others, change will occur.

On June 22, 1941, Hitler with his huge victorious armies attacks the Soviet Union as "Operation Barbarossa" begins. When Hitler attacks Russia, events change. The Soviet Union now fights for her life and becomes part of the great alliance fighting the Germans. Russia must pay attention to her allies, especially England and France. More important, Russia must honor Britain's alliance with Poland.

World events occur rapidly and on December 5, 1941, the Germans abandon their attack on Moscow.

On December 7, 1941, Japan bombs Pearl Harbor. December 11, 1941, Germany declares war on the United States of America. Uninitiated and unwelcome, war comes to America.

The Polish government set up an office in London, England, when the Germans attacked Poland. Now the Polish government demands from the Soviet Union an accounting of all their Polish citizens whom Stalin took against their will from their homes and forced into exile within the Soviet Union. In return, the Polish government promises to raise an army to fight the Germans.

Michal has had no contact with Hanka's family since their enslavement by the Russians. Frank has no knowledge of his sister Hanka's death or the death of her baby twin boys.

The Polish army slowly forms in the Republic of Uzbekistan. Other Polish divisions later fight the Germans with their now Soviet allies. Stalin wants the Polish men he captured and enslaved to fight as human fodder in his Russian army under Russian officers. The Polish government flatly refuses. The Polish government tells Stalin he must set the Polish people free and send the men to Uzbekistan to join the Polish army, under Polish commanders. Stalin reluctantly agrees to the Polish command.

General Sikorski becomes prime minister of the exiled Polish government. He also becomes commander in chief of all Polish forces including the soon-to-be-released Polish men held prisoners by the Russians.

General Sikorski refuses to send his troops to war unequipped and improperly trained. General Anders, the commanding general of the

Second Polish Corps, and other Polish officials state positively their men must receive proper training and be given proper equipment to fight the war. These generals also state their Polish troops must gain proper health before they can fight. Stalin does not want to agree to these terms, but he does, for he has no choice.

Of utmost importance, the Polish government states only Polish generals will command the Polish forces. After prolonged and heated arguments with the Soviets, the Polish authorities win the right to command the Second Polish Corps. The Russians refuse to give the Polish officers the right to command their other independent divisions and brigades. Stalin does free all the Polish prisoners and allows the Polish army to form on Soviet territory under the command of General Anders in Soviet Central Asia—the territory of Uzbekistan.

As the Polish army forms, the leaders become overwhelmed with volunteers, none of them officers. Soon it becomes obvious to the Polish leaders that most of their officers captured by the Soviets in September of 1939 no longer exist. In late 1942 and early 1943, the advancing German armies found mass graves in the forest of Katyn, Russia. The number of dead Polish officers varies but may be as many as 15,000.

An English publication reported the Germans and Russians might have killed another 2,000 Polish officers. What the Soviets did was tow a large tugboat full of Polish officers out to sea and then sink the tugboat. Russian gunfire killed many of the officers and the others died in the frigid water of the Baltic Sea.

After weeks of negotiations, Poland demands Stalin free all civilians in various labor camps in Russia. To fortify Polish national pride, Stalin must issue an edict that all Polish men must enlist in the newly formed Polish army. Stalin must also free all the Polish people they enslaved.

The Polish army will bring the Polish men up to proper health, train, and equip the men in the Second Corps but not in the other independent divisions and brigades.

In August of 1941, three Soviet officers march into the Russian labor camp where the Polish people remain enslaved. The Soviet officer demands the Russian troopers gather all the Polish people in front of him. He has several Russian troopers build a platform for him to stand on that will enable him to talk to the large group of Polish people.

When all the Polish people assemble in front of him, the Russian officer makes a startling announcement—"You people are all free and you must leave this place—NOW. All the men must enlist in the Polish army. The Russian government grants all Polish men in this Russian camp amnesty so you can now join the Polish army."

The officer says no more, steps down from the platform, and walks away. The officer does not tell the Polish men where to find the Polish army. Stalin still wants the Polish men fighting in his army as human fodder against the Germans, and, in this way, hinders them from finding the Polish Second Army. The agreement Stalin made with the Allies forbids him using the imprisoned Polish men in his army.

Michal and his family hug one another crying, "WE ARE FREE." Everyone is crying and hugging the person close to them as they jump for joy crying, "We are free, thank you, God." Their joy over their freedom overwhelms all the previously enslaved Polish people.

After all the rejoicing, Michal says, "Szczepan and Tomasz, we can now enlist, NO, we must enlist in the Polish army."

Two Polish men approach Michal and ask, "Michal, where do we find the Polish army and how do we get there?"

Michal thinks for a moment and says, "We must talk to that Russian officer and get answers to our questions. He said nothing except that we are free and we men must join the Polish army. What did he mean we must leave NOW? Leave for where?"

While the women and children are hugging and jumping for joy, the men leave to find the Russian officer and get some answers to their mounting questions. The Polish men decide to demand answers. They want to know exactly what the Russian meant when he said they must leave now. *Leave for where and how?* wonder the men.

One Polish man says, "Michal, I saw that Russian officer go into the building where the officers always get together."

"We should all go over there together," shouts Michal.

Without hesitation, the men run to the officer's quarters. The officer sees the men coming toward his quarters and he immediately goes outside to tell the men they must leave.

The men shout in unison, "Where do we find the Polish army and how do we get there? What happens to our women and children?"

The Russian officer merely says, "You should perhaps head south to find the Polish army. I suggest you follow the river. Your Polish leaders did not tell us exactly where your Polish army is forming!" The Russian officer knows where the men must go to join the Polish army, but he follows Stalin's wishes to not tell the men where or how to get to their Polish army.

Another consideration the Polish government knows, the imprisoned Polish men hate their Russian captors passionately and might even kill them if they had to fight together.

The Russian officer speaks harshly to the men. "You must leave NOW. We are closing the barracks and you and your people are on your own." The officer walks back into his quarters.

The Polish men look stunned. Michal says, "Let us leave together and follow the river. I think the river goes south. First, we must get our families together and collect our few belongings. We will meet back here and leave together as soon as possible."

All the Polish people leave the Russian camp with joy, for they are free. They stay together at first, feeling a certain safety in numbers. The question now in the minds of the free men and women is where to find food and shelter tonight. The children play happily as they and their parents leave the slave labor camp.

While they were prisoners, the Soviet troops fed them and provided shelter (however inadequately). Now as a free people, they must find food and shelter in a war-ravaged country—poor even in the best of times.

A large group of men, women, and children meet to walk south along the banks of the river, Severnaja Dzwina. Other people picked different routes.

Michal, his family, and several other families walk along the riverbank heading south. After two hours of walking near the river's edge, the group decides to stop and rest.

The group, now hungry and tired, wonders where to get food. Michal and several other men say, "Let's catch some fish." Michal and several men catch some large fish for their evening meal. Everyone eats well this night, happy to be free. As night falls the group moves away from the river and closer to the forest. They feel safer with the trees hiding them. Fortunately for the now free Polish people, the weather is warm as they head south in August of 1941.

The next morning, Szczepan goes to look at the river when he sees a big boat coming toward them. He runs back to the group crying, "There is a big boat coming down the river. Come see."

The men run to the river and see a stern-wheeler coming toward them. The ship stops as it reaches the men standing on the shore. The captain's first mate gets off and asks the people if they want to get on his stern-wheeler. Several of the Polish people decide to take the stern-wheeler, for they have some money to pay for their ride and it seems like a faster way to get to the Polish army. Not all the Polish people get aboard the ship. Michal and his family get on the stern-wheeler.

When the ship stops at a small village, Michal and his family along with several other families get off. For the next few weeks, this group becomes smaller and smaller as some groups decide to go in other directions. Soon Michal and his family of nine travel alone.

Michal and his family hitch rides on various trains, always trying to head south. Michal does not want to part with any more of his money. Michal feels a need to keep his money because he does not know what lies ahead or where or when he will find the Polish army. Michal feels he might need money later for more important matters.

There are no train schedules and Michal and his family often do not know where the train is heading when they all get on. They try to get on empty cars, for they do not want anyone to see them and charge them money. They travel alone now and fear strangers, for they remain inside Russia. Occasionally Michal asks someone where a certain train is going. He tells them he must find the Polish army and does not know where the army is forming. Sometimes the person would say, "Don't take that train, take the next one." No one knows exactly how to find the Polish army.

There comes a time when Michal and his family find themselves on a train that moves fast. "We will be at our destination real soon," says Tomasz.

On the second day, Michal learns from a stranger on the train that this train's destination is Kamchatka, Russia, thousands of miles from their destination. Michal tells his family, "We must get off this train."

Szczepan immediately suggests a plan of action to Michal and his family. He states firmly that he and his brother Tomasz must jump off first so they can help the others as they jump off the train. Each member of Michal's family plans to jump off the moving train with all their possessions. Jumping off the moving train will not be easy.

Szczepan and Tomasz jump off the train with their possessions and quickly pick up their possessions and start to run to the women and children that now jump off the train. Michal gets off last and walks back to help those getting off the train before him. They all knew they must get off this fast-moving train.

No one suffers any injuries, and each person picks up their possessions without incident. This leaves the entire family and their possessions strewn over a full mile before they are all off the train. Still, no one knows exactly where the Polish army is forming.

Michal and his family have now been trying to find the Polish army for many days when Michal meets a Polish man who tells them the Polish army is forming in Uzbekistan. He tells Michal there is a train station about ten miles ahead and that train will take them to Uzbekistan.

Another ten miles does not seem far to Michal and his family, and they reach the train station after only a few hours. After riding several days back to the south and west on this new train, they get off somewhere in Uzbekistan. Michal hires a wagon pulled by an ox to take them to the small town of Fergana. Michal believes this is the best way to find the Polish army, but he is not positive where the army forms.

It is late November of 1941 when they arrive in Fergana. The family spends the next few months in a *kolkhoz* (a collective farm). They stay in an old shabby teahouse as their home. This teahouse has little likeness to our present-day teahouses shown in movies. Nevertheless, the teahouse provides the family some shelter from the rain and snow, for winter has arrived. While living in the teahouse, Michal and his family become ill with various diseases due to their constant inadequate diet and total lack of fruit.

Michal, Szczepan, and Tomasz immediately visit the Uzbekistan authorities. The authorities, English supervisors, decide how to handle the children. After Michal, Szczepan, and Tomasz enlist in the Polish army, the authorities put all the children in an orphanage. The authorities decide Maria must work in the orphanage. Maria is pleased to work in the orphanage, for she can keep an eye on her and Michal's children.

The local Polish recruiting officer now tells Michal that he and his brothers must leave Fergana and report to the Polish commander in Gorchakov or face arrest. Gorchakov is the name of the camp where the Polish army trains the Polish men for battle.

Michal cannot believe this order. He and his brothers discuss how to handle this problem. Although Michal, Szczepan, and Tomasz are glad the children are in a safe place, they do not want to leave Maria and the children in Russian-dominated Uzbekistan.

Michal tells Maria that he and his brothers must leave and join the army in Gorchakov or face arrest. Maria cannot believe what Michal tells her. She tells Michal, "We must stay together." Michal, Szczepan, and Tomasz agree.

Michal and Maria go to the orphanage and remove Aniela, Jadzia, Jozef, Jan, and Tadeusz. With the last of his money, Michal hires an Uzbek (a person) with a wagon pulled by a camel to take all of them to Gorchakov, where they can find the Polish Second Corps army. The trip will take about four or five days.

At the end of the second day of their trip, the Uzbek tries to abandon them in the middle of nowhere. Michal uses all his verbal powers of persuasion to get the Uzbek to continue the trip. When Michal's persuasion fails to get the Uzbek to continue the trip, Michal threatens the Uzbek with his heavy ax. This act works again and the Uzbek continues to help them to their final destination, the military camp in Uzbekistan.

Chapter Sixteen
War and Misfortune

Michal, Szczepan, and Tomasz report to the commander of the Polish army forming in camp Gorchakov in Uzbekistan. The Polish commander asks Michal and his brothers, "Why have you taken so long to enlist in your Polish army?"

Michal and his brothers tell the commander their story. The commander merely says, "Yes, I understand." He has heard this story many times, as the formerly enslaved Polish men slowly join the Polish army.

The Polish commander assigns Michal to the artillery regiment, Szczepan to the motor transport battalion, and Tomasz to the infantry regiment.

The Polish army has no permanent barracks available; therefore, the soldiers live in tents. The size of the Second Polish Corps varies in size, but at one time, the army consisted of over 120,000 men. There are two divisions of infantry, several independent brigades and regiments of artillery and some independent battalions. The families of the soldiers live in a separate tent city near the soldiers' camp.

Polish authorities try to classify the people who have no papers that identify them. Since none of the enslaved Polish people has any papers, the Polish authorities issue new ones based on the best information available that may be accurate or inaccurate.

Again, the authorities put Josef, Jan, Tadeusz, and Jadzia in an orphanage because their father and brothers serve in the Polish army. Aniela remains with her mother, Maria, because the authorities consider Aniela an adult at the age of fifteen.

There are two areas of hundreds of tents set up about a half mile apart. One set of tents house the civilians and the other the soldiers. Maria and Aniela have one tent to themselves. Maria takes care of her family and Michal's children plus many other children for Maria works at the orphanage with Aniela at her side.

Food supplies remain meager; only children under five years of age get milk at the orphanage. Maria, the children's grandmother, simply cannot remember Tadeusz's birthday and makes him four years old so he can get milk rations. It is now March of 1942 and Tadeusz is five years old. His papers state that he is four years old.

Jan fears Tadeusz might die because Jan can see every rib, bone, and joint in Tadeusz's body. Jan gives food off his meager plate of food to Tadeusz, hoping his little brother will not die. Jan goes to the doctor's office and demands that the doctor examine Tadeusz.

The doctor, amazed at Jan's concern for his little brother, decides to examine Tadeusz. After his examination of Tadeusz, the doctor finds Jan and tells him, "My examination of your brother shows his diet lacks proper nutrients but nothing else. Jan, your brother is not dying." The doctor feels he should examine Jan. This boy, Jan, does not look well, thinks the doctor.

At mealtime, the soldiers eat first. Then the children receive whatever food the soldiers do not eat. Jan continues to give food off his plate to Tadeusz. Jan risks his health out of fear and love for the life of his younger brother.

Hundreds of tents are set up to house everyone. One area of tents house civilians and their families. The other area of tents is about a half mile from the civilian tents, and these tents are for the soldiers.

In just a few days, Jan collapses and the attendant calls the doctor. On examination, the doctor notes Jan's high fever and bleeding gums. The doctor immediately sends Jan to the hospital.

When Michal and Maria learn that Jan is in the hospital, they go to the hospital immediately. They look at Jan, and fear for his life overcomes them. Jan does not know his dad or grandmother is present as they look at him and talk to him, for Jan is unconscious. Michal asks the nurse to let him talk to the doctor.

The doctor comes quickly to talk to Michal and Maria. He tells them, "Jan needs treatment now or he will probably die. Jan is unconscious most of the time since his admission to the hospital and when he talks, he is delirious. Your son's fever remains high despite all our efforts to lessen his fever," states the doctor.

Maria and Michal look at each other in dismay. Michal tells Maria, "This cannot happen. I must not lose Jan."

Maria hugs her son and quietly says, "What next?" They both leave the hospital in despair.

Michal receives new orders. The Polish commander has ordered Michal's unit to Tehran, Iran, to become part of the British Eighth Army. Michal tells Maria his news. Maria tells Michal they must all stay together, and Michal agrees.

Maria and Michal go to the hospital to get Jan. The doctor says to Michal and Maria, "Jan is gravely ill and to move him will kill him. I refuse to release Jan to you. Michal, I want your Jan to survive. This means Jan must remain in this hospital." Michal looks at the doctor and senses the doctor wants Jan to live.

The doctor remembers that Jan demanded the orphanage nurse have him see little Tadeusz. The doctor also knows that Jan has continued to give some of his food to Tadeusz to keep him from dying. This brief meeting with Jan's love and concern for his little brother has deeply touched the doctor. The doctor decides to use every skill he knows to save Jan's life. He feels the world needs someone like Jan to live. A child who knows how to love must live, believes the doctor.

Michal has no choice. He must leave, and now. He wonders if he will ever see his Jan again. The family wonders if Jan might die. Jan's illness deeply saddens the entire family. Michal loves each of his children dearly and wants them with him. But since the doctor says it is best that Jan remain in the hospital—then that is where Jan must stay.

Negotiations continue between the Soviet Union, the Allies and the Polish government in London. The Americans have now joined the Allies in the war against the Germans. Stalin wants the other countries including Poland to form a second front against the Germans in Russia. Finally, Stalin agrees the Second Polish Corps will be more useful in other endeavors and agrees to allow them to move to become part of the British Eighth Army.

The Polish leaders know the Polish men who have enlisted can never fight the Germans alongside Stalin's soldiers, for the Polish men hate the Russians passionately. Michal wants to kill Russians, as do all the Polish men taken from their homes to work as slaves for the Russians. The Russians brutally harmed every Polish family they took from their homes.

The task of moving a 120,000-man army with all their equipment and supplies plus close to 500,000 dependents during wartime conditions becomes an awesome undertaking. This task takes months to complete. The Polish authorities try furiously to get all the Polish people away from possible Russian domination, for the Polish people hate the Russians. Nor does the Polish government or Polish people trust Stalin, for they know Stalin can change his mind in midstream.

The ability to transport people remains limited. The Polish authorities make priorities regardless of the hardships on individuals, groups, and families. The first and most important priority is to get the soldiers and their equipment to the front lines quickly. The Polish leaders realize that some of the soldiers must stay behind to protect the civilians and keep order.

Chapter Seventeen
War, Accidents, Separations

The authorities have already sent Michal, Szczepan, and Tomasz to Tehran, Iran. They traveled by train to the seaport on the Caspian Sea. There they boarded a ship that took them to the other side of the Caspian Sea. As they left the ship and walked ashore, a military officer greeted them and transported the arriving soldiers in a military truck to their training base.

Before Michal left, he tells Maria she will receive her orders in a day or two telling her when the government plans to send her and the children to Tehran.

Maria, the adult, remains in charge of Michal's sisters and his children. She receives her orders four days after Michal left for Tehran. Maria's orders state she and the children must be at the train station tomorrow by 3:00 p.m. to board the train that will take them to the Caspian Sea port. The train will take them to the seaport and a military man will meet her and many others after they get off the train. The officer who greets them will help Maria and the children get on the right ship to take them to the other side of the Caspian Sea. After Maria and the children get off the ship another officer will guide them to a bus that will take them to Tehran.

On the afternoon of departure, Maria with her two daughters and

Michal's two boys arrive at the train station. The wise authorities now divide and separate Maria from the children.

The person in charge puts Maria and her daughters, Aniela and Jadzia, in one car, which is in the middle of the train. A second man in authority puts Josef in a car toward the end of the train with a group of children his age. Josef, twelve years old, behaves like an adult, for he is wise beyond his years. Another person in charge decides to put Tadeusz in the second car behind the engine. This car has many children four and five years old. When the train has all the passengers aboard, nighttime has arrived.

The train leaves in the dark of night. The authorities scheduled the train to travel at night without lights on because of the wartime blackouts. Traveling at night without lights makes this train an accident waiting to happen. The train tracks go just one way and no one checks to learn if another train might come on the same tracks this particular night.

The train leaves the station and gains full speed. The engineer of the train does not know another train traveling at full speed heads towards him. Tadeusz in the second car behind the engine is alone without any family member.

A head-on collision occurs with disastrous results. The collision smashes the first three cars into pieces and all the other cars become derailed. This horrendous collision kills hundreds of children and injures many children and adults. It takes all night for the workers to clear the tracks and sort out the wounded from the dead. At dawn one of the workers trips over something. The worker tries to pick up this object.

The worker realizes the object is a child's arm, and wonders of wonders he finds a body attached to the arm. Now working frantically the worker calls for help. Other workers respond quickly to clear away the debris to free the body. Quickly they unearth the body of a small little boy alive, although unconscious. Quickly, the authorities send the little boy to the hospital.

No one knows the name of the little boy. Nor does anyone know to whom he belongs. For many days, the little boy remains unconscious and no one comes to claim him. This train accident separates many families for many days.

Josef survives the train accident without any injures, for he was in the car farthest from the engine. Josef gets off the train and asks everyone if they know anything about his little brother. At first, he learns nothing except that many children are dead. Josef never gives up; he keep searching and asking about his brother. Josef feels he must learn what has happened to his little brother Tadeusz.

Several days later, Josef meets one of the workers who tells him about a little boy that someone pulled from the train wreck barely alive—but alive. He tells Josef the authorities sent the boy to a hospital and no one knew him or his name.

The Polish and English authorities must still get all the people and soldiers on the wrecked train to their destination, Tehran. The authorities transport the remaining soldiers first to Tehran. Next, the authorities transport Maria and her daughters, and her grandson Josef, with many other families on another train to Tehran. Josef, furious, tells the authorities that he must stay and find his little brother. The authorities remain firm and Josef must leave with his grandmother. Josef, heartbroken, curses the authorities.

Maria, her daughters, and Josef are distraught over the loss of

Tadeusz. They also remain concerned about Jan, whom they left behind in the hospital. Are the boys alive or dead? Each family member is horrified thinking they might be dead. The thought of another death of one or two of their family devastates each family member alive after the train accident. With fear and heartbreak, they board another train that will take them to a ship to across the Caspian Sea and finally to Tehran.

After the family arrives in Tehran, Josef and Maria immediately go to the authorities asking them the whereabouts of Tadeusz and Jan. The authorities in Tehran cannot tell Josef and Maria anything because they know nothing. To Maria and Josef, the authorities appear stupid. However, the authorities in Tehran have not even heard of the train wreck and have no knowledge of Jan.

Tadeusz, the little boy pulled from the train wreckage, remains in the hospital for many days. When he becomes conscious, he has no memory of what happened to him but he remembers his family. He wants his grandmother.

The little boy is all right except he cannot see anything. He can tell the difference between light and dark shadows, and that is all he can see. The little boy remains scared and lonesome. In fact, he feels more lonely than scared. He wonders if any of his family is alive and thinks maybe they are all dead. He puts his head in his pillow and sobs for his heart feels broken. Time passes and slowly but firmly the little boy gets better.

In the spring of 1943, the doctors tell the authorities the little boy pulled from the train wreck can travel.

Because Tadeusz was on the train where everyone's final destination was Tehran, the authorities put him on another train. This train will take Tadeusz to the Caspian Sea port to board a ship. The ship will cross the Caspian Sea, where Tadeusz will leave the ship. Once he gets off the ship, a man will meet him and transport him to Tehran. The authorities assign an officer to escort the child on his journey to Tehran. On their arrival in Tehran, the officer has orders to take the child to the hospital to continue his recuperation.

The officer admits the child into the hospital after their arrival in Tehran. The little boy remains scared and so lonely. He desperately wants his family nearby and he needs to know he is not alone. The little boy feels terrified he will never see his family again. His sight remains the same; he sees only light and dark shadows. Many days pass while the little boy lies alone in his hospital bed.

In Tehran, the superior officer of Szczepan sends him to get some papers at the hospital where the little boy remains a patient. At the hospital, Szczepan feels an unexplained need to visit the children's ward. He walks into the children's ward where the little boy lies in his bed. Szczepan sees no one looking like Tadeusz. Szczepan realizes he wants to find little Tadeusz and hoped he would be here. Szczepan feels a deep sadness that he has not found little Tadeusz.

He turns to walk out of the children's ward when he hears a noise and turns toward the sound of the noise. Suddenly he sees a little boy in bed. It is Tadeusz. Szczepan runs to Tadeusz and puts his arms around him hugging him fiercely. Tadeusz recognizes his uncle's voice and hugs his uncle in a fierce grasp.

Their reunion is joyful and exhilarating for both Szczepan and little Tadeusz. Tadeusz cannot let go of his grasp on his uncle. They both hug for a long time. Little Tadeusz cannot stop crying. He can see his uncle's face but not clearly.

Without pulling away from Tadeusz, Szczepan tells Tadeusz all the news about their family, but he does not mention Jan. Tadeusz asks about Jan and learns there is still no news about Jan. This deeply saddens Tadeusz.

Tearfully Tadeusz asks his uncle to get him out of this hospital so he can be with his grandmother. Szczepan tells Tadeusz he will go talk to the doctor. Only then does Tadeusz release his grip on his uncle.

Szczepan leaves to talk with the doctor about releasing Tadeusz from the hospital to him. However, the doctor refuses to dismiss Tadeusz now.

Szczepan returns to Tadeusz and says, "Tadeusz, the doctor wants to keep you for a few more days until you see much better. Then I will come and take you out of this hospital. Tadeusz, I will visit you every day and I will bring Josef and everyone to visit you.

Tadeusz replies, "All right, but you come see me every day, please, Uncle Szczepan."

Szczepan replies, "Tadeusz, I will come every day. Now you rest and you get better. See you tomorrow."

Tadeusz sees his uncle wave his hand to him as he left the room. Tadeusz feels a deep sadness overwhelm him. He hopes his uncle returns soon.

The authorities continue to separate families. As the families of the army arrive in Tehran, the British authorities send family members to different locations. The British authorities send Josef (Michal's son) now thirteen years old, to a Polish camp for boys in South Africa. Next, they send Jadzia (Maria's youngest daughter) also thirteen years old, to a British camp somewhere in India. India became a British colony in 1943.

Maria cannot believe the authorities will separate her from her young daughter. Maria furiously shouts at the authorities, "You cannot send my young daughter to India of all places." No matter what Maria says, the authorities refuse to change their minds. Jadzia leaves for India just two days after the authorities told them of their decision. Maria is devastated and furious with the authorities. Maria should never have been separated from her young daughter.

The authorities allow Aniela (now sixteen years old) to remain with her mother in their camp about twenty miles from the hospital where Tadeusz remains a patient.

Szczepan, Maria, and Aniela visit Tadeusz often. They bring him news about the family and they bring food. Maria brings Tadeusz clothes to wear when the hospital discharges him. She puts his clothes in the empty box next to his bed for his personal items.

On the way to visit Tadeusz in the hospital, Szczepan buys a big basket of fresh fruit and chocolate. He knows Tadeusz will enjoy this treat. Szczepan gives this basket of delicacies to Tadeusz and he hugs the basket to his chest.

Szczepan smiles at his nephew and says, "Tadeusz, this basket belongs to just you. Enjoy the food, my precious Tadeusz. I must leave now, but I will return tomorrow."

Little Tadeusz has not fully recovered from the malnutrition that he endured during his time in the Russian camp and the long trip to find the Polish army. Tadeusz has not tasted fresh fruit since leaving Poland. Nor has Tadeusz ever tasted chocolate.

Tadeusz hugs this big basket of fruit and chocolate placed on his bed. Then he starts to eat the fruit and chocolate. Tadeusz cannot stop eating and stuffs himself with everything as quickly as he can until he empties the basket. During the night, Tadeusz becomes ill and remains ill for several days. The Arabs would say Tadeusz has the mother of all bellyaches!

A month later, Tadeusz feels great. His vision has now fully returned and his overall health has improved. Today the doctor does a routine physical on Tadeusz. The nurse puts a mercury thermometer under Tadeusz's tongue and walks away. Suddenly, the thermometer slips out of Tadeusz's mouth and falls onto the floor, breaking into many pieces. The broken thermometer horrifies and terrifies Tadeusz.

No person in authority has ever shown Tadeusz genuine kindness. Tadeusz believes the doctor and nurse will severely punish him for the thermometer breakage. He immediately sweeps up the broken pieces the best he can and hides the evidence under his bed. Tadeusz feels desperate; he must get out of here and find his family.

Tadeusz quickly puts on his clothes from the box next to his bed. With extreme caution, Tadeusz leaves the hospital. He has no idea where his grandmother lives. With firm determination, Tadeusz sets out to find his grandmother.

Outside the hospital, Tadeusz finds a busy street with many people, horses, and horse-drawn carriages. Tadeusz sees two horses pulling a carriage coming toward him. He decides this carriage must be going in the right direction to get him to his grandmother. He has just a moment to think and no time to feel any fear. Quickly he jumps up on the little ledge on the back of the carriage and hangs on for dear life. Tadeusz wonders if the carriage will ever reach a camp. Finally, the carriage passes through a gate and he jumps off and enters the camp, making sure the guard at the gate him does not see him.

Inside the camp, Tadeusz asks some kind-looking women about his grandmother. After talking to many people who have no knowledge of his grandmother, Tadeusz becomes discouraged and thinks that perhaps he is in the wrong camp.

Tadeusz looks forlorn and lost when a woman comes up to him and begins to talk to him. Tadeusz, now in tears, describes to the woman how his grandmother looks and his need to find her.

This woman tells Tadeusz, "You come with me. I know where your grandmother might be." Tadeusz, ecstatic with joy, follows the woman. Suddenly he sees a bench and his grandmother sitting on the bench with his aunt Aniela.

Maria turns her head and sees Tadeusz. She shouts with joy, "Tadeusz, you are here!" Aniela and Maria jump up and hug Tadeusz until he gasps for air. Maria thanks the woman for bringing Tadeusz to them. The woman feels thrilled that she united a young boy with his family.

The woman looks at Tadeusz and Maria and says, "I am sorry. I must leave and meet my husband at the gate." The woman says, "Good-bye," and quickly walks away.

Aniela looks at Tadeusz and says, "Tadeusz, how did you get from the hospital to this camp?"

Quickly, Maria says, "Tadeusz, why did the hospital not tell us that they dismissed you?"

Tadeusz hangs his head and tells his grandmother and Aunt Aniela why he left the hospital and how he came to their camp. Maria and Aniela decide to do nothing unless someone comes looking for Tadeusz.

Before this war, the camp housed several regiments of the Persian cavalry. The camp now houses the displaced Polish people. Even though Russia now fights alongside the allies, the Russian government does not return the land and homes they took from the Polish people. The Polish people remain displaced—no homes, business, or land to return to.

Tadeusz, Maria, and Aniela live in an old huge building that has many small stables inside for the army's horses. There are about 150 to 200 people in a small section of the building. One family gets so many square feet of space to call their space. The space a family gets depends on how many people are in the family. The people, desperate for privacy, hang sheets from one wall to another wall to create "rooms."

Maria feels Tadeusz needs a cot to sleep on. To get a cot for Tadeusz, they must visit the military officer who issues the cots. The family decides to make Tadeusz a bed out of blankets because they do not want to visit the military officer.

Tadeusz says, "Grandma, I like my bed; I do not need a cot." No one, and this includes Tadeusz, wants the military officer to know another person lives in this building.

The old building formerly used as a stable has no lighting. Each family has either a kerosene lantern or candles to help them move about in the dark. In the past, the building had no indoor plumbing. Today the building does have indoor plumbing, but the number of bathrooms does not meet the needs of the many people living in this huge building. Thus, there are long lines of people waiting to use the bathroom all day long and into the night.

Providing food for all the people has become an enormous challenge for the authorities. The army sets up several community kitchens and assigns a specific number of people to each kitchen. The army provides the food and the women cook the food. However, the food provided to the people satisfies only their hunger pangs and prevents starvation—that is all. The food supplied by the military lacks proper nutrition for all the displaced people.

For two or three years, the Polish people have missed their church services. Now that several Polish priests live with them, the people seize the opportunity to create a makeshift church. The Polish people want their spiritual needs met by their Polish priests. Soon the people and their priests have church services available to all who want them. Maria, Aniela, and Tadeusz go to church whenever possible.

As camp life becomes routine, mothers feel the children should be in school. Within this large number of Polish displaced people, there are several teachers. With the help of several volunteers, the teachers set up a school for the Polish children. Maria and Aniela want Tadeusz in school, but the teachers tell them he cannot attend until he is five years old. Maria wonders when Tadeusz will be five, in just a few months or six. She does not know. Tadeusz does not go to school even though he is actually almost six years old in January of 1943.

Near this large stable lies an American army camp. Once a week the soldiers show a film in their camp and they invite the Polish families to watch the movies with them. Even though the movies are in English, the Polish people enjoy the movies. Almost none of the Polish people have ever seen a motion picture film, and the movies seem like a miracle to the Polish people. Their favorite movies are the Western movies with cowboys and Indians.

The American camp also provides jobs for the Polish women. Aniela obtains a job as a server in the enlisted men's club. Aniela's income helps her mother, Maria, immensely. The British government gives each family some money each month to buy necessary items, but this money buys only a few items. Of huge importance, Aniela can bring left-over food from the club to her family. She even brings ice cream, a new treat for all the children. Tadeusz and his family live in this camp for about eighteen months.

After working for several months at the American camp, Aniela meets a young soldier from Georgia, USA. Aniela tells her mother she loves Ed. A few months later, Ed asks Aniela for her hand in marriage. Aniela knows she loves Ed dearly and wants to marry him.

Aniela tells her mother, Maria, Ed has asked her to marry him. Maria feels Aniela should not marry until she becomes older and wiser. Maria tries to talk Aniela into waiting but without success.

Aniela decides to marry Ed, and soon. Marriage to Ed means that Aniela can stay with Ed when the displaced people have to move again. Aniela and Ed know they feel a deep love for each other and refuse to wait.

Three weeks later the Polish priest marries Aniela and Ed. Maria, Tadeusz, and a few friends attend their wedding ceremony. Everyone appears happy, but there is not the celebrating that Michal and Hanka had at their wedding. There are no wedding gifts. This does not matter to Aniela and Ed. Their wish to marry has come true, and this has made them happy, even in wartime.

All too soon in late 1943 the authorities tell the displaced Polish people they must now move to Iraq. Tadeusz and his grandmother, Maria, must leave for another displaced person camp in Iraq. Maria wants to refuse to move. All this moving, well, makes no sense to Maria. Maria and Tadeusz move to Iraq, but Aniela stays behind with her husband, Ed.

Chapter Eighteen

War Ends and the Polish People Have No Place to Return

After the authorities move Tadeusz and his grandmother to Iraq, Maria tells Tadeusz he must attend school. Tadeusz, now six years old, wonders what school means for him.

During the first year of school, Tadeusz learns to read and write. However, Tadeusz's grandmother, Maria, remains illiterate. Maria never had the opportunity to attend any schools while growing up in Russian Poland. Maria can hardly believe that Tadeusz has picked up the ability to read and write after one year. Maria, impressed with Tadeusz's new skills, decides Tadeusz can write for her.

While in second grade, Tadeusz becomes a writing secretary for his grandmother. Maria wants Tadeusz to write letters to all her children and grandchildren who are now on three different continents. Tadeusz writes to Jadzia, Maria's youngest daughter now in India, to her grandson Josef (Tadeusz's oldest brother) now in Africa, and her daughter Aniela, who now lives in America with her husband, Ed.

During the war, Ed sustained severe injuries and the authorities sent Ed and Aniela back to America. Ed spends several months recuperating in the Vancouver, Washington, hospital.

Tadeusz also writes to Maria's sons, Szczepan, Tomasz, and Michal

(Tadeusz's father), who are all fighting in Italy.

Most of the displaced people now living in Iraq have achieved somewhat better health. This includes Tadeusz and his grandmother. They receive regular medical attention and some dental care. Most important, their diet, although plain, is nutritious.

Most important to the adult Polish men and women is their Polish priest that now sees to their spiritual needs. The Polish people consider their priest an important man. Tadeusz, now just six years old, does not consider spiritual needs important at all. However, here in Iraq, Tadeusz does receive his first communion.

As Tadeusz grows older, he discovers the world around him. In the spring of 1944, Tadeusz sees flowers growing out of trees. He has never seen flowers on trees and so he breaks off a few of the flowers and runs home to show them to his grandmother. Maria carefully explains to Tadeusz about the blossoms in spring that later produce delicious fruit for them to eat. She tells Tadeusz fruit is good for him and everyone. Tadeusz just nods his head agreeing, for he remembers the fruit his uncle Szczepan gave him when he was in the hospital—and he got very sick.

Early in 1945, there are rumors the displaced people must move again. This rumor creates deep concern among the Polish people. The people fear the authorities are forcing them into another unknown place when all the people want to do is go home. Yet, the people prepare for another move "into the unknown." Tadeusz is now eight years old, but his papers say he is seven years old.

Maria bakes a dozen or more loaves of bread and packs them into two of her pillowcases. Everyone starts to hoard foods that do not rot. This helps the people face the uncertain future and possibly hunger—

again. Maria wonders when she will be able to return to her home in Poland. She dreams often of being in her own home, cooking in her own kitchen, and sleeping in her own bedroom.

A week later, the authorities tell the people the army will move them to Lebanon in two days. The people try to prepare.

Two days later, the army takes several thousand displaced persons and puts them on military trucks. The authorities tell the people, "You are now civilians." This means nothing to the displaced people.

Once a truck is full, the truck moves toward Lebanon. These trucks transport the people nearly a thousand miles through deserts and mountains to get to Lebanon. The trip takes a week to complete because of frequent stops, equipment breakdowns, rest periods, and food preparation.

All the trucks and people finally reach Lebanon. It is now May of 1945—Victory day in Europe. As the people get off the trucks, a general tells the people of the victory in Europe. He tells the people, "The war is not over, but it cannot last much longer."

The homeless people shout, "Thank you, God. Thank you." Now they shout and ask the general, "When can we go home?"

The general replies sadly, "I do not know. Russia and England are talking. Russia wants your Polish lands. What they will decide, well, I just do not know what Russia will demand and get. I am so sorry to have to tell you this news." The general walks away, for he knows he has no real answers for these people.

In Lebanon, Tadeusz and his grandmother do not live in a camp but rather in a village and in a private home. Two or three families usually live in one house. During the first year, Tadeusz and his grandmother live in a two-room house with two other families. The other families get the rooms and Tadeusz and his grandmother live in the hallway—between the other two families.

Several weeks after arriving in Lebanon, the general visits Maria. He tells her the Germans at Monte Casino, Italy, killed her son, Tomasz. The general tells Maria, "I have some good news for you. Your son Michal and Szczepan are alive and well."

Maria, now sobbing, barely hears what the general says to her.

The general continues to say, "Maria, I am so sorry about your son, Tomasz. Maria, he fought bravely and received a medal for his bravery. If you need anything, Maria, please contact me." The tears flow from Maria's eyes, and the general gives her a small cloth to wipe the tears from her eyes. After a few minutes, the general gives Maria a hug and leaves the house. Tomasz is the only family member to lose his life in the war.

Fortunately for Tadeusz and Maria, Michal visits his family on military leave a few weeks after they arrive in Lebanon. When Michal sees his family living in a hallway, he becomes furious.

Immediately Michal goes to the housing authorities and raises "holy hell" with them. The authorities decide they must move Michal's family.

Michal and his family move to a large house that they share with only one other family. Their new home is only thirty-six miles east of Beirut, Lebanon, in a small valley near the mountains.

A Polish priest lives in this village and attends to the people's spiritual needs in the Catholic Church. Maria attends the church often, and the priest helps Maria deal with her feelings of despair.

Maria wants Tadeusz in school and learns Tadeusz can go to school here in Lebanon. She enrolls Tadeusz in school, and Tadeusz enjoys his new school and does well with his studies.

The only problem for Tadeusz and the other children is the lack of school supplies. The children receive only a few sheets of paper to write out their assignments.

Tadeusz's grandmother believes every space on a sheet of paper, front and back, must have writing on it. She wants Tadeusz to fill in the whole page on both sides with no blank spaces before she would give him another sheet of paper. Tadeusz must hide sheets of paper in order to rewrite his written assignments for the next day. He rewrites his homework after his grandmother goes to sleep, for Tadeusz knows his teacher would not accept the work the way his grandmother wants him to do his homework.

The school in Lebanon wants the children to wear shoes while in school. The children who have been walking barefoot for the past several years do not want to wear shoes. Shoes hurt their feet. To solve this problem, the children carry their shoes until they get near the school. Then they put their shoes on their feet. For the next few hours of school, the children suffer pain from their shoes.

Tadeusz continues to be his grandmother's secretary. He reads to his grandmother all the letters she receives. Then he writes whatever she tells him to write—but not always exactly.

In Ted's young eyes, Maria, now sixty-some years old, has become bitter. She does not understand everything that has happened to her or why. Maria lost her home and everything dear to her. Strange soldiers force her to move from one place to another place. Soldiers force her to live in horrible conditions and make her eat terrible food. Living conditions in Lebanon are good, but for Maria everything remains bad. Maria hungers to return to her home where she gave birth to her children and lived with her husband.

Maria dictates bitter and unpleasant letters to Tadeusz. However, Tadeusz does not think his dad or his other relatives want to hear about his grandmother's bitterness. Therefore, Tadeusz writes positive and happy words on paper to his relatives from his grandmother.

Maria wants to return to her home and farm near Dmytrow. The war has ended, and Maria does not understand why she cannot go home. The war has not ended, for America still fights the Japanese. Russia continues to demand the land where Maria once lived.

Russia and the Polish government have heated arguments about the land in eastern Poland. The Polish leaders believe the Polish people have the right to return to their homes, land, and businesses. Russia says their land and everything on it belongs to Russia. In the end, Russia gets the land. The Polish people refuse to live under Russian domination. The Russian government does not permit the Polish families to return to their homes and businesses at this time.

Chapter Nineteen
Life in Lebanon

The Polish children in Lebanon have never seen or even had a toy since their imprisonment in 1940. The children have the time to make up games to play, and the older children make their own toys.

The children create a game similar to soccer. They wad up fabric into a tight ball and secure the ball with string. The balls do not last long, so the children make a few spare ones to replace a failed ball. The boys nine to thirteen years old enjoy their made-up soccer games.

Another game the boys make up resembles a form of baseball. The boys cut a short stick about an inch in diameter and six inches long. The boys sharpen both ends of the stick to make the end of the stick pointed. This stick they call their "ball." For the bat, they select a longer stick about thirty inches long. With their ball pointing in the direction they want the ball to go, a boy strikes the forward pointed end, causing it to jump up several feet. Now he hits the ball with the bat. If he misses, that is a strike. If he hits it, he runs their makeshift stops (bases). The children made their baseball running stops out of rocks or pieces of wood. The opposing player has to pick up the ball and tag the person running the bases—if he can. Soccer and baseball become the boys' favorite games to play.

The boys and girls learn a form of gambling from watching the soldiers play with their coins. The children have no money so they gamble for buttons. The children assign a value to each button they have in their possession. Large coat buttons are worth three of the little shirt buttons. Standing about eight feet from a wall, a boy or girl tosses a button at the wall. The button must hit the wall for it to count and the button closest to the wall wins. Tadeusz's grandmother complains to Tadeusz about all the missing buttons on her clothes. She asks Tadeusz about her missing buttons. Tadeusz merely replies, "Grandma, I have no idea what is happening to your buttons."

In Lebanon, the children have more freedom, for they no longer fear for their lives. One child has made a most ingenious riding toy that he calls a "hulajnogas." This toy resembles a bicycle. To make this toy several children experiment with brakes, but the brakes rarely work the way the children want them to work. Regardless, the Polish children make several of these hulajnogas and race them against one another or just ride them for the fun of it.

When school is not in session, the Polish children take turns riding the hulajnogas in the street. Finally, it is Tadeusz's turn to ride a hulajnogas. The child riding the hulajnogas gets off the strange bike and leaves it in the street for Tadeusz to go and get it. Tadeusz runs to pick up the bike but a Lebanese driver in his truck races down the street and runs over the hulajnogas, smashing the bike to bits before Tadeusz gets to the bike.

The driver of the truck stops immediately and tells the children he is sorry for smashing their toy. He sees the faces of the children and realizes they do not hear a word he says. Tadeusz just kicks the driver's truck wheel in utter frustration. Tadeusz and the other children go home in tears.

Several days later, the children meet to talk about making another "hulajnogas." They cannot hear what they say because of a sudden loud noise coming from the far end of the street. The noise comes from a procession walking toward the children.

The curious children decide to follow this procession. At the next bend in the road, the procession enters a large beautiful courtyard. One boy next to Tadeusz says, "This is a big wedding procession. I have seen many of them and they are fun. We will get to eat cake, too."

Many people fill the courtyard waiting for the bride and groom. Everyone laughs and appears happy. The mule the groom rides on becomes spooked and bucks the groom off and onto the courtyard-tiled floor. The mule kicks the groom several times before two of the guests are able to pull the bucking mule away from the groom.

One of the guests, a doctor, immediately examines the fallen groom with great care. The groom does not move, nor does he appear to be breathing. The doctor pronounces the groom dead.

In shock, everyone cries and wrings their hands, "Oh NO, this cannot be."

Their crying and wringing of their hands goes on for over an hour. Tadeusz thinks this wailing will never stop when suddenly several men speak. They say in unison, "We must have an immediate funeral, now."

The older men do not like to keep a corpse around long, for that is unhealthy for everyone. The children become fascinated at the turn of events. The adults accept the children as official guests of this wedding party—now a funeral.

Tadeusz leaves the party and heads home to tell his family about these strange events. He walks into his house and immediately Maria yells at him, "Tadeusz, go get me some milk, now." Maria hands him some money. Tadeusz looks at his grandmother and knows he must go for milk. Perhaps later he will tell her about the events at the wedding party.

Tadeusz knows where he must get the milk, for it is an interesting trip. Tadeusz walks by terraced farm fields that look like giant staircases. The farmers have the flat areas at least ten yards wide and the walls no more than a foot high. He marvels at the terraced land where the farmers grow their food. Soon Tadeusz arrives at the farmer's store, buys the milk, and heads home. On the way home, he picks blackberries and eats the berries, for he still feels hungry most of the time. Tadeusz grows taller every day and soon outgrows his clothes. Maria cannot understand why Tadeusz needs new clothes so often.

The authorities continue to consider the Polish people in Lebanon displaced people. They cannot send the people back to eastern Poland. Maria does not understand why she cannot go back to her home. The authorities try to make life better for the Polish people. They feel sad the Polish people have nowhere to call home. The Polish men fought valiantly during the war, and some of the authorities feel these soldiers and their families have the right to return to their homes in their native Polish country, especially eastern Poland.

The authorities now give the Polish people the right to have chickens. This means the Polish people can have fresh eggs, a genuine delicacy that they thoroughly enjoy. Maria likes having these chickens. She wants to know why the authorities took so long to let them have chickens.

The Polish displaced people have not had an adequate supply of food rich in protein for a long time. Their bodies crave protein and even fat.

When Maria has the opportunity to fix a chicken for her family, Tadeusz tastes and eats the chicken and fat ferociously. Tadeusz tells Maria, "This is the greatest food I have ever tasted."

Food remains important in the lives of the displaced people. Now that they feel well fed, the adults look for other interests. Several adults organize a one-day trip to the historic town of Tyre (now called Sur) and take several children with them on this trip. Tadeusz goes with them on this trip.

The trip to Tyre becomes a spectacular trip for everyone. They all ride in a big truck; this excites the children. As the group passes through the beautiful city of Beirut, children and adults shout, "Look at that," many times.

Adults call out, "See that building, see that park, and see those flowers." Everyone points out beautiful places to look at, exclaiming, "Look, look, isn't that beautiful."

Beirut is the largest city most of the displaced people have ever seen. The children cannot believe the beauty they see in this place. They see people walking, talking, and laughing without any soldiers with guns yelling at the people to do this or that.

Soon the truck with the displaced people leaves Beirut. Now the truck passes through the countryside and quickly reaches the historic town of Tyre, once the seaport of ancient Phoenicia. In Roman times, the city became famous for manufacturing silken garments and the color Tyrian purple.

One of the Polish men tells the group, "The Muslims destroyed this city in 1291, and today the city's only claim to fame is its history." He tells the group that Jesus once visited the area around Tyre where he healed a sick child. He tells the group that Jesus' disciples Mark and

Paul spent a week in Tyre. Mark and Paul joined other Christians in prayers on the journey from Ephesus to Jerusalem.

The group of Polish people and children stop and get out of the truck and eat their lunch provided by their various families under a big tree. After lunch, they head back to the parked truck. The adults feel a deep satisfaction that their outing pleased everyone. The children paid close attention when the adults talked about Tyre's history, and this pleased the adults. As the truck starts to move, the children fall asleep on the return trip to their village.

A full two years pass while Europe rebuilds after the end of WWII. Tadeusz's dad, Michal, sends word to his mother, Maria; he is coming home on military leave. The year is 1947. Tadeusz has seen his dad only twice since 1942.

This is the first long leave Michal has received from the army other than a one-day or a two-day pass while fighting in Italy.

When Michal arrives at their home, Tadeusz and Maria cannot take their eyes off him. They just want to keep him all to themselves. However, after a couple of days with his family, Michal wants to have some fun. Michal, now almost thirty-five years old, wants some fun and companionship with men and women his age.

There are only a few single able-bodied young men in the Polish community where the displaced people live. Michal becomes a man in great demand. Polish families invite Michal to all sorts of parties and events. He becomes the center of attention and loves it.

The young women in the camp enjoy having a young, handsome, and single man in their community. Michal has lost that young boyish look and has a mature handsome appearance. Yet, he never forgets his promise to Hanka to take good care of their children.

Today Michal takes Tadeusz to an event but then forgets about him. Michal finds it exciting being with men and women his own age. This lack of attention by his father hurts young Tadeusz. He has hungered for his dad's presence and affection for many years.

Little Tadeusz has grown up. At the age of nine or maybe ten (his actual birth date still being uncertain), Tadeusz has become wise for his age. He realizes his dad has become "somebody" since his return from the war. In the army, Michal was just a private, but here, in Lebanon, he is the war hero. The men and women in this community admire and enjoy being around him. A few young widows want to learn more about this interesting young man, Michal. Tadeusz hungers for his dad's attention.

Michal and a soldier friend, Phil, fought in combat together during the war in Italy. Phil has returned to the same community where Michal lives. Phil asks Michal to be his best man at his wedding and suggests that Michal bring a "lady" friend. Michal chooses not to bring a woman and decides to take Tadeusz to the wedding. Tadeusz can hardly believe his good fortune.

When Michal returned from the war, he began to teach Tadeusz how to dance. Tadeusz asks his dad if there will be dancing at this wedding. "Of course," Michal says "yes, lots of dancing, Tadeusz."

Tadeusz remains unsure about his dancing abilities, for he has never danced with a girl. Every spare minute he has, he now practices the dance steps he learned from his dad. Tadeusz practices alone.

Just five days later, Michal and Tadeusz go to the church where the priest will marry Phil and his bride. Michal takes Tadeusz to the front row seat and tells Tadeusz, "Now be good and I will get you after the wedding. Tadeusz, we will have fun after this ceremony."

Tadeusz watches the wedding ceremony and he likes the ceremony, for it makes him feel good. After the ceremony, Michal takes Tadeusz to the bride's home, where everyone has gone to celebrate. Tadeusz immediately sees a large table with all kinds of food. Instantly Tadeusz feels hungry.

The band starts playing music and Tadeusz sees his dad dancing with a young woman. Immediately Tadeusz forgets about food, walks over to a young girl his age, and asks her to dance.

Tadeusz and the girl start to dance, and they do have a great time dancing. After a few dances, Tadeusz and the girl walk over to the food table and load their plates with food. Between bites of food, they talk about the hardships of their life. Tadeusz learns that she is also a displaced person living in Lebanon. Suddenly, or so it seems to Tadeusz, the festivities end and Michal stands in front of him to take him home. *Darn,* thinks Tadeusz.

Tadeusz wants to talk more with this girl. He says to his dad, "I need to get her name. Dad, I like that girl but I do not even know where she lives."

Michal replies, "Not now, Tadeusz, she has gone home with her family. You may see her again sometime and then you can get her name."

Tadeusz is not sure about this; too many times, he made friends and then they left and he never saw his friends again. For young Tadeusz, the evening was magical. Michal senses his young son has developed an interest in girls. He thinks, NO, he is too young, for he is only nine years old. When Michal and Tadeusz return home, Tadeusz goes to his bed, undresses, and falls asleep almost before his head touches his pillow.

Two weeks later Michal's leave is over and he returns to Italy. One week after he returns to Italy, the British government transfers Michal and the entire Polish Second Corps to Great Britain. The war has now been over for two years and the Italians are eager to get the foreign armies off their soil. The British government remains responsible for the Polish displaced people. The British government continues to pay the soldiers and support the soldiers' families.

The Polish people have a real problem. The Russians have taken over the Polish government in Poland and the Soviet army occupies Polish soil. Few of the exiled Polish people want to return to Poland, for they know their homes do not belong to them. The Russians have their land, homes, and businesses. All of Poland is now under the protection of Stalin—Russia's leader. The Polish people hate and despise Stalin for what he did to them.

The few Polish families who returned to their homes in Poland found conditions so horrible that they had to leave Poland. The Russians do not give back their land, homes, or businesses they so brutally took from the Polish people.

These families write to their friends in Great Britain, tell them of their plight, and tell them—do not return to Poland. The Polish people living in England believe simply this—WE HAVE NO COUNTRY.

Chapter Twenty
Life in England

In the fall of 1947, the British government moves the entire Second Polish Corps to England. The English government settles the soldiers in an abandoned camp the Americans built during WWII. When the soldiers become settled, the government brings the soldiers' dependents to England hoping to reunite families. The war has divided many families for six or more years.

The British government knows this will be a difficult task to perform. It means moving about a half million people from several different continents. Only a few ships are available to move people; therefore, the task will take time to complete. The authorities set up priorities about whom to move and when.

The authorities tell Tadeusz and his grandmother, Maria, they will move to Great Britain. Then the authorities tell her Tadeusz must move first as he is a young dependent child. Maria will move later.

Tadeusz cannot believe his good luck that he will travel alone to Great Britain. He looks forward to this trip with great anticipation and excitement, for he feels he can handle anything. He just wants to know WHEN he leaves. Tadeusz is thrilled Maria will not travel with him.

Maria looks at this move with severe anxiety, especially since Tadeusz will not be with her. Maria depends on Tadeusz to help her get through the day. She still does not understand why she must move again, and she remains angry and confused about those authorities always forcing her to move when she does not want to move.

Tadeusz learns he will start his journey to Great Britain in early July of 1947. Maria immediately goes to the authorities and tells them, "Tadeusz is too young to travel alone. He needs his grandmother with him, and I want to be with him." The authorities listen but ignore Maria's plea to travel with Tadeusz. Instead, one of the authorities tells Maria to have Tadeusz ready to travel on July 5 and have him at the appointed checkpoint in the morning of July 5. The man hands Maria a map showing her exactly where to take Tadeusz for his trip to Great Britain. He goes over the map with Maria several times, hoping she understands where Tadeusz must be on July 5. Maria does understand but wants to go with Tadeusz so she argues with him for a long time.

The day for Maria to take Tadeusz to the checkpoint arrives all too soon for Maria. Tadeusz is ready to leave two minutes after he awakens, for he had everything ready the night before he is to leave. Maria sadly walks Tadeusz to the designated checkpoint.

A big military truck waits for all the people who will travel to Great Britain. Maria hugs Tadeusz and blows him kisses as he gets on the truck. Maria looks so sad and forlorn that Tadeusz waves both hands and blows kisses to Maria until she is out of sight. Tadeusz feels sad for Maria and a little worried about her. Actually, the authorities were wrong to separate Tadeusz from Maria. Tadeusz needs guidance and supervision on this trip and gets very little adult supervision.

Now that Maria is out of his sight, Tadeusz feels the thrill of traveling on his own. Well, he is not on his own, for the military looks after him. Tadeusz feels glad Maria is not with him, mainly because of her bitterness.

The first phase of the trip is by a military truck. Tadeusz wants the driver to go faster, but he goes slowly until he leaves the camp. Once out of the camp, the driver picks up speed until he goes into the mountains of Lebanon. Now he goes slowly again.

A British guard tells the people in the truck, "Once we are outside Palestine we will stop so you can get off and walk a little. No one can get off this or the other trucks until we are outside Palestine. Unfortunately, Palestine has become a terrible place. Many men fight with gunfire."

The Polish people on this truck and the other trucks were unaware of fighting in Palestine. The people look at each other and start praying that they get through Palestine without anyone killed.

Tadeusz becomes excited. Now he will get to see some real action, and he looks forward to seeing the fighting in Palestine. So far, Tadeusz has never seen gunfire or soldiers shooting and killing people.

As the truck approaches the tip of Palestine, several officers stop the convoy of trucks. An officer walks up to the driver of the first truck and tells him the entire convoy must take a detour. The officer points to the direction he wants the driver to take. The convoy of trucks takes the new route.

After a short distance, another guard stops the convoy of trucks again. Tadeusz and the other people on the trucks hear gunfire. After a few minutes, a guard motions the lead truck driver to go down a narrow street. The driver does what the guard tells him to do and the other trucks follow the first truck.

When the convoy of trucks comes to an intersection, Tadeusz and the others on the trucks witness active fighting on a street near the intersection between the Palestinians and Jews who are seeking and independent Israel. Suddenly a Jewish freedom fighter stops the convoy of trucks. One freedom fighter gets on each truck and interrogates everyone. The Jewish fighter wants to know why they are in Palestine.

Soon other Jewish freedom fighters get on the trucks to help in the interrogations. The officer that gets on the truck that Tadeusz rides on tells everyone he once was a member of the Second Polish Corps. This officer deserted the Polish army in 1943 to join the Jewish people who were fighting for their independent state. Now he leads the Jewish freedom fighters. The officer looks at the Polish people and the children on this truck and the other trucks. A Polish man on the truck with Tadeusz recognizes the freedom fighter and soon both men talk in earnest.

After what seemed an eternity to Tadeusz, the Jewish officer gets off their truck and suddenly all the trucks move toward their final destination—the port city of Haifa.

(Author's note: Fighting continues to this day in the Palestine region. The UN has tried to bring about peace in this region but has failed. In 1948, the UN helped to create Israel. This region's history is another story.)

At last, the convoy of trucks reaches the port city of Haifa. Now the British put everyone aboard a ship the government built as a troop carrier. This ship has few creature comforts, but the Polish displaced people expect nothing. The people find the food acceptable. Tadeusz likes the food and especially having his stomach full.

The British move 600 children and 100 adults. Tadeusz and the other children have a ball and do not mind the lack of adult supervision. Tadeusz enjoys the lack of adult supervision.

During the voyage, Tadeusz learns how to play poker and blackjack with the other children. The children have no money. The adults keep the money to themselves, but the money keeps changing hands among the adults. A plentiful supply of cigarettes exists, and the children gamble with the cigarettes. Tadeusz not only learns to gamble but he starts to smoke.

On this ship, a British officer tells the adult men the British authorities have disbanded the Second Polish Corps. In a forceful voice, the British officer tells the men, "Now you can and should enlist in the Polish Resettlement Corps."

The British officer then states, "Since you men are still in uniform you are subject to military discipline and rules. There will be no drilling to get ready for war, but you men must study to prepare for new jobs." The officer adds, "As soon as we get to Great Britain." The officer walks away, leaving the men perplexed.

After a few smooth sailing days in the Mediterranean Sea, the ship enters the Atlantic Ocean. The seas become much rougher and almost everyone gets seasick. The adults and children stop playing their games and no one smokes. It takes Tadeusz three or four days before he feels like he will live.

As the Polish displaced people get over their seasickness, they feel their diet remains satisfactory but the ship's cook serves too much canned spam. Some of the people like the canned spam. However, Tadeusz hates that canned spam.

As everyone's health improves, the adults and children go back to their games of gambling. The adults play with money and the children with cigarettes. Tadeusz and the other children go back to smoking.

The journey ends when the ship docks in Glasgow, Scotland. It takes several days to get everyone's' paperwork completed. One hundred adult men and women and 600 children must have their papers examined and corroborated. Until the authorities complete all the paperwork, everyone stays on the ship to sleep and eat.

The government does not always tell a parent that a member of his family has arrived. After processing Tadeusz through all the paperwork, an officer takes Tadeusz to a military camp where the British government has stationed Michal, Tadeusz's father.

When Michal returns to the camp after working, he cannot believe his eyes. Michal gives Tadeusz a big hug and tells his son, "I am so glad to have you here with me." Michal wants to know why no one told him that Tadeusz was on his way to Scotland.

The reunion between Michal and Tadeusz is joyous. Tadeusz tells his dad everything that happened on the voyage to Scotland, but he does not tell his dad he smokes. Michal has never heard Tadeusz talk so much. Michal looks at Tadeusz and realizes Tadeusz has grown tall. Tadeusz no longer behaves like a child; he has a certain maturity about him. Michal thinks, *My son has grown up and I did not see him grow up.*

With the arrival of adult Polish men, the British authorities have another problem. During the war when most of the men were fighting, the women took up most of the jobs. Now the war is over, the men cannot get jobs. The British have a difficult time finding jobs for their own veterans. Only after all their own veterans have jobs do the authorities consider placing other men into work positions.

Thousands of allied soldiers and Polish displaced people have arrived in the United Kingdom. These men need jobs that provide money for them to support their families and buy necessary items.

Tadeusz lives with his father and the other Polish soldiers in the military barracks. The barracks provides a bad influence for a ten- or eleven-year-old boy. Tadeusz's language becomes salty, and he can now cuss with the best of the men. Michal takes classes, but Tadeusz has no classes to continue his education. More important, Tadeusz has no supervision. Tadeusz loves having no supervision.

The older boys invite Tadeusz to play volleyball whenever they are short of a player. Tadeusz, big for his age, becomes a good volleyball player. This helps keep Tadeusz out of trouble, and he enjoys playing volleyball.

Tadeusz wants money, and he is industrious. He manages to pick up odd jobs and make a little money. He picks walnuts and sells the walnuts to the soldiers. Tadeusz's idea to sell walnuts provides him a profitable enterprise. When blackberries become available, he picks them and sells them for money.

One month later, Michal receives a letter and a package from his sister, Aniela. Aniela married the American, Ed Ledbetter, during the war, and she now lives with him in Vancouver, Washington, USA. Somehow, Aniela learns Michal's address in Great Britain and sends him a letter and a package.

Michal and Tadeusz excitedly tear open the package. In the package, there lies the first store-bought toy Tadeusz has ever seen. The toy, a western cap-shooter, looks like a real gun, and the caps sound grossly loud when he fires the gun.

When Tadeusz fires the gun, the noise makes the soldiers think someone has attacked them and they dive for cover. Two soldiers close to Tadeusz tackle him and take the gun away from him. The soldiers examine the gun and realize it is just a toy gun.

Michal reads Aniela's letter. He feels pleased that Aniela has found happiness in America with her husband. Michal does not think of going to America. He just wants to make a home somehow in Great Britain.

Tadeusz and his dad stay in this camp just a few months. Finally, the employment people find a job for Michal. Once again, Michal's bricklaying skill has paid off for him. Michal is given the job of assistant bricklayer—but he must move to southern England.

The British government moves Michal and Tadeusz to Northwick Park, a camp for displaced Polish people. The camp is near Cheltenham in Gloucestershire in southern England. Again, this is a military camp built by the Americans during the war. The camp can hold up to 1,500 people. When Michal and Tadeusz arrive, there are only 600 to 700 displaced Polish people living in the camp.

Two days after arriving in the camp, Michal goes to the authorities to inquire the whereabouts of his son, Jan. Michal gives the authorities all the information he has, but no one knows anything about Jan's location. They tell him they will get back with him when they know something. Michal never hears from the authorities. Often Michal will look up at the heavens and says, "Hanka, I will find our son. I will never give up."

Like all the other camps, this camp has a common kitchen where everyone cooks and eats. Michal and Tadeusz sleep in a large barrack. Near the camp is a Catholic Church with a Polish priest and a Polish grade school. Michal immediately enrolls Tadeusz in the Polish school. Michal wants Tadeusz in school and learning, for he is now ten years old.

The school principal gives Tadeusz many tests to show him what grade will best suit Tadeusz. After evaluating the tests, the principal places Tadeusz in the fifth grade.

Michal works only three miles from their camp. At 5:00 a.m., Michal gets up and goes to the mess hall. Here he eats his breakfast, packs his lunch and leaves for work. Michal must walk three miles to his work at the brickyard.

To speed up his commuting time and keep a better watch on Tadeusz, Michal buys a used bicycle. The bicycle reduces his commuting time, and Tadeusz has less unsupervised time. Michal has become concerned about Tadeusz's salty language and poor manners. Michal suspects Tadeusz smokes.

Tadeusz gets up each morning and fixes his own breakfast. Then Tadeusz walks to school. After classes, he plays soccer or volleyball with the other children his age. Tadeusz is very good at both of these sports and usually acts as captain when selecting teams. The children play soccer and volleyball in bare feet, for they have no decent shoes. The field they play on is a makeshift field at best.

One day a local English school challenges the Polish displaced kids to a soccer match. The English school came to the Polish displaced kids' school since the Polish school could not financially pay a bus to transport their players to the game.

The English school players arrive on time with their coaches and great equipment. As the players get off their bus, they look baffled when they see the playing field that is different form their field. The English players put on their equipment and listen to their coach's instructions. Now one English player says, "Coach, those kids have no equipment and I do not see their coach. Do they have a coach?"

The English coach replies, "I did not realize till now they do not have proper equipment and they have NO coach. You players go out there and win; this should be an easy win."

When the match starts, the English players are careful not to hurt the Polish players. Suddenly the Polish players are ahead by two goals. The English players realize their opponents know the game and play well. The English players decide to fight to win with fierce determination. The Polish players suffer bloody toes and bruised shins but win the game—5 to 1.

Tadeusz's classmates consider him a great athlete. Tadeusz's teachers view him as a mediocre, failing student. Tadeusz seldom studies. He cuts his classes and goes away from school to smoke his cigarettes without his dad knowing what he does. Tadeusz even skipped school for an entire two weeks. Now one of Tadeusz's teachers takes a sudden and decisive action that shows Tadeusz why he must attend school and quit smoking.

Again, Tadeusz skips a day of school. Today when Tadeusz returns to his barrack after lunch, his teacher waits for him. This teacher, like a biblical shepherd, left his class to look for his one lost sheep. First, the teacher calmly asks Tadeusz if he has been sick or did his dad take him somewhere? Tadeusz has no satisfactory answer for his long absences from school. Now the teacher lectures him about why he, Tadeusz, must get an education. To underline his point, the teacher takes off his belt and beats "the rebellion" out of Tadeusz. The teacher meant for this beating to stick with Tadeusz so he would mend his errant ways. The teacher replaces his belt and reminds Tadeusz what time class begins in the morning.

As the teacher prepares to leave, Tadeusz reaches into his pocket to get his handkerchief so he can wipe up the blood on his leg. As Tadeusz withdraws his hand from his pocket, a pack of cigarettes falls onto the floor. Tadeusz, horrified, looks at his teacher. The teacher's eyes open wide. After a brief lecture on the evils of smoking, the teacher takes off his belt and again beats Tadeusz just as thoroughly as he did the first time.

Tadeusz does not enjoy the beatings, but he does not tell his father about the beatings. He knows if he tells his dad he will receive a thrashing more severe than the one he got from his teacher. Inwardly, Tadeusz feels proud that he never once cried out during the beatings he received from his teacher.

Whatever one says about the merits or demerits of physical punishment, well, Tadeusz has never smoked a cigarette since that day. He returns to school and becomes a good student. He now reads books regularly, and during the balance of his fifth grade he read at least thirty books, most of them classics in Polish literature. In addition, he learns the thrill of playing chess and plays it whenever he can—to this day.

Chapter Twenty-One
Families Reunite and Decide Where to Live

The British government sends Jadzia from India to Lebanon to be with her mother. They did this shortly after Tadeusz left for Great Britain. Although Maria enjoys having her youngest child with her, she remains bitter about everything that has happened to her. Maria sees no reason for all this moving around. Maria wants to return to her home in eastern Poland.

Just two weeks after Jadzia joined Maria, the two women learned they are to leave for England in two weeks. Maria could not believe those stupid authorities expected her and Jadzia to move to England. Maria said "NO" to the officer who brought them the news. The officer just looked at Maria and walked away from her shaking his head.

Jadzia tells her mother quietly and with love, "Well, Mama, I will go to England alone."

Maria says nothing at first. Several days later, Maria says, "Jadzia, when do we leave for England?"

Jadzia smiles and tells her mother, "Mama, just four more days till we leave." Since they have very few belongings between the two of them, Jadzia already has everything packed that they need to take with them. Four days later, they leave Lebanon, and after several days of traveling, they board the ship for England.

Maria continues to say she wants to return to her home in Poland during the entire trip to England. Jadzia decided to let Maria complain. Jadzia finds the ship exciting and the food good. All too soon for Jadzia, the ship arrives in England. As Maria and Jadzia disembarked, Jadzia sees Michal waiting for them.

Maria grabbed Michal, hugged him fiercely, and told him what a terrible trip she had. Jadzia looked at Michal and said, "It was a wonderful trip, Michal. The weather was great and the food very good. My only complaint is my mama and her complaining."

"A bus is waiting to take us to our camp," said Michal. Slowly and reluctantly, Maria follows Michal and Jadzia to the bus. After several hours of riding on the bus they arrive at the camp for the displaced Polish people. Everyone gets off the bus and immediately Maria announces, "I want to go back to my home in Poland." Michal and Jadzia just smile at Maria. They understand her wish to return to their home in Poland, for that is what they would like to do, but they understand Russia has their home and land.

With the increase in the size of Michal's family plus two of them being females, the British authorities put the entire family in one Quonset hut with no other families in their hut. Michal can hardly believe their good luck. The entire family feels as if they are royalty in a castle except for Maria. She complains about everything, for Maria remains scared. Unfamiliar surroundings and people she does not know frighten Maria. She wants to live in her home near Dmytrow, Poland.

Michal hopes that Joe, his oldest son, will join them soon in England. However, Joe, seventeen years old, lives in South Africa. Since Joe will be eighteen in just two months, the authorities consider him an adult. As an adult, Joe has the right to decide where he lives. Joe has a job in South Africa that he likes and he enjoys his life in South Africa. Joe writes his dad he plans to stay in Africa.

Again, Michal goes to the British authorities and demands that they find out where his son Jan lives or if he is dead? A week later, a British man tells Michal they have no knowledge of Jan and can find nothing to say whether Jan is alive or dead. The man asks Michal many questions but still can give Michal no information about Jan. Michal thinks perhaps Jan died, but Michal finds this thought so horrible, he refuses to believe it.

Whenever new groups of people enter the displaced peoples' camp, Michal and his family look for Jan. Now Michal turns to the Red Cross hoping they will find Jan. The family keeps trying to find Jan even though they have lost faith they will ever see him again. However, in the hearts of this family, there is that faint glimmer of hope of finding Jan.

One day on the way to school, Tadeusz sees a group of boys playing volleyball by the camp's front gate. He cannot believe his eyes—one boy looks like Jan. Tadeusz looks at the boy's face and his heart skips a beat. *That is Jan, I have found Jan,* thinks Tadeusz. He runs up to the boy and immediately realizes the boy is not Jan—just another lost Polish boy.

Michal's family continues to grow. Michal's brother Szczepan and Hanka's brother Frank arrive in England. Frank does not yet know that his sister Hanka died in the Russian camp in 1940.

When Michal tells Frank about Hanka's death, Frank just clenches his fingers into a fist and walks away from Michal. He returns later and asks Michal for more details of Hanka's death.

Michal tells Frank the story of their imprisonment and the refusal of the Russians for medical care for Hanka. Frank says he saw the Russians kill his sisters and his parents. Frank firmly states his feelings for the Russians. Both men simply hug each other. They can no longer talk about the Russians and the horror they endured from the Russians. They both know that they must put this part of their lives behind them or they will die with grief.

Frank says, "You know, of course, we have no homes to go back to after fighting this war. I wonder where we will be able to find a home for our families?"

Frank and Szczepan find jobs in nearby cities and visit Michal and his family every weekend and holidays. Michal sees Frank often. One day Frank stops seeing Michal and spends more time with Jadzia. A few months later, Michal and Maria see an obvious romance developing between Jadzia and Frank. Michal and Maria believe they will marry and soon.

Szczepan buys a motorbike and has several accidents on his motorbike. He kills some livestock, and the owners of the livestock want him in jail. In addition, he has suffered some serious injuries from these accidents. Slowly Szczepan recovers from his injuries, and the owners of the livestock settle their differences with Szczepan.

Tadeusz and Szczepan play blackjack a lot together. Tadeusz wins a lot until Szczepan starts to cheat. Normally, Tadeusz and Szczepan play on a bed with their legs crossed. Tadeusz soon discovers that Szczepan has a mirror between his legs that allows him to see all the cards he deals. Tadeusz never confronts his uncle Szczepan that he knows about the cheating. Tadeusz just found reasons not to play blackjack with him.

During the early summer of 1948, Tadeusz and several other boys playing volleyball stop their game when a car pulls up. A Polish man steps out and asks the boys if they would like to go to a Boy Scout camp for two weeks. This Polish man, thinks Tadeusz, represents the Polish government in exile. None of the boys ever heard anything about "Boy Scouts," but they are eager for a new adventure.

The man gives each of the boys a piece of paper that his parent or guardian must sign. When the parent signs this paper, this gives the boy permission to go to the Boy Scout camp. The boys have two hours to get their paper signed. Tadeusz knows his dad is working and will not be home for several hours. Therefore, Tadeusz signs his dad's name to the paper.

Tadeusz tells his grandmother where he is going and that he will return home at the end of summer. Maria pays no attention to what Tadeusz says. She just nods her head as if agreeing. Tadeusz leaves home and meets the Polish man. He gives the man his signed paper. The man looks at the signature with a strange look on his face but does not say anything.

The Boy Scout camp is a great adventure for all the boys. The theme is the summer Olympics. In 1948, the Olympics resumed after their absence because of the war. There are many sports competitions between the various groups present. There are about 300 boys present from all over Great Britain. The camp employees divide the boys into groups that they call troops. Tadeusz is in the troop called Szczecin, named after a German city.

The boys learn many of the tasks that regular scouts do, such as tying knots, starting fires without matches, the Morse code, and many other interesting tasks. Tadeusz enjoys most singing by the campfire and listening to the stories told to the boys by their leaders. Most of the stories are patriotic in nature and Tadeusz becomes an enthusiastic Polish patriot. He cannot get enough of the stories and legends the camp men tell the boys. When the Boy Scout camp ends, all the boys reluctantly return to their homes.

When Tadeusz returns home and tells his dad about his adventure, he realizes he should have told someone other than Maria that he would be gone most of the summer. He loudly yells at his dad that he told Maria what he planned to do.

Michal, beside himself with worries for his son's safety, is angry that Tadeusz did not tell him about this adventure. Michal wants to whip Tadeusz fiercely. Maria quietly tells Michal that Tadeusz told her something but she cannot remember what he said.

After talking with the man from the Boy Scout camp, Michal learns the Boy Scout camp demands honesty and fair play from their boys. Michal senses that perhaps this camp might have taught his son a few of these qualities, especially honesty.

Michal decides to ask Tadeusz if he enjoyed the Boy Scouts. Tadeusz merely said, "Yes."

Tonight, Michal tells Tadeusz he has enrolled him in the Copernicus Gymnasium School near Cambridge. He tells Tadeusz this school enrolls only boys. Michal has done this because Tadeusz's teacher has promoted him to the sixth grade and his current school does not have the higher grades.

This is the first year the Copernicus Gymnasium School opens for teaching young boys. The students live at Camp Cambridge and walk to their new school that is nearby. The school has grades six through twelve, and most of the teachers are professors from the Polish universities. Thus, the quality of instruction for the boys should be excellent, thinks Michal. These professors have been teaching older students whom they call "gentlemen." The professors do not consider boys "motley kids."

The professor that Tadeusz likes the best teaches Polish literature. Before WWII, this professor taught at the University of Krakow, perhaps the oldest and most prestigious school in Poland. He has published several novels and some books of poetry. He has a passion for the subjects he teaches and some of his passion rubs off onto his students.

During one of his lectures, Tadeusz read his book. The professor sees one of his students reading and not paying attention to him so the professor stops his lecture. Tadeusz realizes what he has done and expects the professor to punish him. The professor walks up to Tadeusz and grabs the book out of Tadeusz's hands.

The professor looks at the book, turns to the class, and says, "This is my favorite Book, *Pan Tadeusz*, by Adam Mickiewicz, and once one of my students memorized the entire book. Students, this book has over 300 pages."

Tadeusz looks at his professor in amazement, for he expected the professor to punish him. The author wrote this book in verse. Tadeusz decides to memorize the book, too. After about ten pages, he realizes the difficulty of memorizing the book and quits trying to memorize the book.

Tadeusz's second professor teaches mathematics. Before the war, this professor taught at the University of Warsaw and his colleagues considered him a brilliant mathematician. Unfortunately, this professor has become absentminded and easily distracted. Today, he has become a shadow of his former self.

The students, all young boys, play tricks on this professor. Once they barricaded the front entrance to his classroom and he could not teach that day. The boys think of many ways to disturb this professor.

Today the boys put string along the ceiling from which they suspend puppets. When the professor walks into the classroom and sits down at his desk to teach, several of the boys lower the puppets in front of him. The professor tries to grab a puppet and the boys jerk the puppet away from him. In utter frustration and profound fear, the professor runs out of the classroom screaming. The boys do not understand the words the professor screams. The next day the professor did not return to the school.

Instead, the school president comes to the classroom to talk to the students. He severely lectures the boys on their unkind actions toward their teacher. The president praises their professor. He tells the class what a great mathematician their professor is and honors earned in the past. Softly but powerfully the president tells the students what the Germans did to their professor.

He states firmly, "Your professor lost a good part of his mind when the German Gestapo shot your professor's entire family, his wife and two daughters and a baby son, in front of him. The Germans bound your professor's hands and legs firmly so he could not move—he had to watch them murder his family and he could do nothing to help them. Yes, he snapped after this horrific killing and he will never be his former self again. However, you boys must realize, without mental stress, your professor can teach brilliantly. Under pressure, he may suffer a breakdown. You boys are lucky to have such a brilliant professor. I expect you to learn and play no more tricks on your brilliant professor."

The students, contrite after his talk, say to their president that they will not play pranks on the professor. Some of the boys do realize what a great math teacher they have. Unfortunately, after several weeks, a few of the students pull more pranks on their professor and he leaves the school. Now the students must listen to a new professor who is not as good a teacher, but this professor puts up with no nonsense from his students.

The curriculum in Tadeusz' sixth and seventh grades is ambitious. Tadeusz and his classmates learn English, math, writing, and history. The professors also teach the boys Latin, Greek, and algebra, plus some geometry.

Life at Camp Cambridge for Tadeusz becomes pleasant and the food acceptable. All the students eat in a large mess hall that allows every student to sit at a table and eat their food. The staff eats separately but joins the boys to say grace and sing the Polish national anthem and some other patriotic and religious songs. In addition, the boys attend the Catholic Church that has a Polish priest.

The school president has the sixth- and seventh-grade boys isolated from the rest of the camp physically. The boys live in Quonset huts with twelve boys in each hut. Organization in this camp is informal. However, there are elections for hut chief and class president. To Tadeusz's surprise, the students elect him hut chief and president of their class. Tadeusz shows good leadership skills at the young age of eleven. He always tries to help other students who need help.

Tadeusz does not like it when bigger boys bully smaller boys. When this happens, Tadeusz steps in and stops the bullying. One boy in particular is small and meek. The bigger boys love picking on this small boy. When Tadeusz sees what they are doing, he steps in and stops this bullying of the small boy.

Figure 3. Tadeusz

A year later, this boy plays the music of Chopin, a Polish composer, beautifully at their school play. This achievement earns the small boy the respect and a noble status in their little society that the small boy richly deserves.

Often a representative from the Polish government in London comes to talk to the students at their school. Today, the Polish official talks about the lack of funds to run their government. Tadeusz immediately stands up, empties his pockets of about twelve shillings, and gives the money to the government official. Tadeusz has a deep love and profound patriotic feelings for Poland, his native country. The money he gave away is not much, but a small fortune to Tadeusz.

The romance between Jadzia and Frank has grown, and Frank asks Jadzia for her hand in marriage. They plan for their wedding day, for they know they want to be together always.

Jadzia learns from Frank that he was on the same train that she and her family were on that took them to Archangel. Jadzia tells Frank everything that happened to his sister Hanka. She explains to Frank how desperately Michal and Maria tried to get help for Hanka. She tells Frank how devastated Michal was when Hanka died. She tells Frank, "I thought he would die or kill a Russian, he was so distraught and angry at the Russians."

Jadzia and Frank's love grows stronger as they share their stories. Frank tells Jadzia a little of what happened to him and the deaths of his other sisters and his parents. As Frank tells Jadzia his stories, she feels a great gratitude to God that he survived.

The British trained Frank as a radio operator and paratrooper, and he became part of the Polish Independent Parachute Brigade. In 1944, the Allies plan their ill-fated "Operation Market Garden." The soldiers try to take a bridge over the Rhine at Arnhem, Holland. A bloodbath results that later becomes a movie in "The Bridge Too Far."

Frank tells Jadzia one of his experiences in the war. Frank speaks softly and with difficulty at first. He says to Jadzia, "I parachuted into a river with a revolver and a large radio set strapped to my chest in hopes of helping the trapped British solders. I hoped to free the soldiers. I found a little rubber boat, but before I could get to them, the Germans blew the soldiers out of the river. Jadzia, Jadzia, I survived. I still wonder WHY I live."

Jadzia puts her arms around Frank and hugs him. She cannot speak for she feels grateful Frank lives. Tears flow from her eyes as she speaks softly to Frank, "I am so glad you lived. I need you. Frank, I love you." Frank holds Jadzia in a fierce embrace for a long time. He thinks, *Perhaps God wants me to do something more with my life.*

Frank now faces another struggle—learning English. While Jadzia lived in India, she learned English. Jadzia teaches Frank English. Whenever they are together, they speak only in English if possible. Frank learns quickly, and soon Jadzia and Frank speak English with just a slight Polish accent.

Frank and Jadzia marry in August of 1949 in Tetbury, England. They have a real Polish wedding and their Polish priest marries them in their Polish church.

Tadeusz attends the wedding, and adults now regard him as an adult. Tadeusz has grown tall for his age of eleven. He enjoys the wedding because Felicia, a girl he likes, came to the wedding. In fact, Tadeusz feels he loves her. Felicia becomes Tadeusz's first love.

Tadeusz enjoys this wedding even more when the adults allow him to have a few drinks. He feels all grown up drinking alcohol.

In late 1949, Tadeusz meets the young woman who spends a lot of time with his dad.

This woman has a son and feels he needs a father, and Michal feels Tadeusz needs a mother. Michal and this woman realize they care deeply for each other and decide to marry.

Michal considers her to be well educated because she finished high school. She even worked in an office during the war. Michal feels pleased that she has an education.

Tadeusz likes this woman but does not want his dad to marry. Tadeusz thinks he will not have any freedom or independence if his dad remarries. Tadeusz even thinks about stopping the wedding but can think of nothing that would stop his dad from marrying.

They marry in their Catholic Cathedral Church in Cirencester, England, in the spring of 1950. They hold their reception in the community hall in their camp. Tadeusz looks at all the kids at the reception and knows he is the only kid almost thirteen years old. All the other kids look like they are only five or six years old.

In July of 1950, Jadzia gives birth to their first child, a son. Frank and Jadzia know they have no future in England. They think seriously about where they want to live. Frank and Jadzia write to Aniela for help, for they have decided they want to move to America.

Frank and Jadzia know war has begun in Korea for the Americans. They hope this war does not intensify. Michal and his new wife also have concerns about this war. They feel the war will not affect Frank and Jadzia directly or prevent them from going to America, but perhaps it will keep them from going to America.

When Aniela receives Jadzia and Frank's letter, she excitedly opens their letter. As Aniela reads their letter she shouts with joy, "Yes, yes," as she runs to another room where her husband Ed is working. Ed first has to calm Aniela so he can find out just why she is shouting so happily.

Once Ed understands that Aniela's sister and her husband want to come to America, he tells Aniela to write them back and let them know they will be their sponsors. Aniela immediately writes them and tells them that they will be their sponsors and they hope to see them in America soon.

Late 1950, Michal knows they must decide where they want to live. Since the communists of the Soviet Union control Poland, Michal knows they cannot return to Poland. The Russians still own his home, his land, and the brickyard. There is nothing for Michal back in Poland. In England, there are few opportunities to make a good living. Michal and his wife must decide where they want to live.

Many of the Polish displaced people migrate to the United States of America, Canada, Brazil, Australia, and even New Zealand. All of these countries welcome the immigrants. Whatever country the Polish displaced people enter, they enter the country legally.

Michal considers Canada, where he would receive 320 acres of land—free. This sounds great to Michal until he learns the land lies in northern Canada and has few people living there. In addition, the nearest town is almost a hundred miles away from their land. The weather in northern Canada is much colder than Michal likes, and the winter snows could keep them snowed in for a few months every year.

To Michal, the United States of America seems the most desirable place to settle. America has limited quotas for immigration and they must have a sponsor. The sponsor guarantees that the emigrant will have a job and a roof over his or her head when they sleep at night.

Perhaps the biggest reason for Michal to come to America is his sister Aniela, who lives in Vancouver, Washington. Aniela has agreed to sponsor Jadzia and Frank. Aniela cannot sponsor any more members of her family, according to the American immigration laws. Still, Michal decides to apply for permission to enter America with his wife and their children. He applies for all the necessary papers for immigration to America and a sponsor.

In the summer of 1951, Tadeusz's dad decides not to send his son back to his former school, for they should be leaving in a few months for America. Michal believes in education and sends Tadeusz to an English school in a nearby village. This means Tadeusz can now work to improve his knowledge of the English language, thinks Michal.

On Tadeusz's first day at the English school, he learns that he is the only Polish person in the school. At once, he becomes a curiosity to his classmates. Tadeusz quickly applies for a position on the schools soccer team. After the school's first game, Tadeusz is an instant celebrity.

Tadeusz plays the right wing and does well in this position. He scored two out of three goals in one game and won the game. Tadeusz never had any coaching to play soccer, but his technique became excellent and came naturally to him. What he lacked in finesse he made up with his aggressiveness and his strong and young physical body.

In this English school, Tadeusz's classmates have difficulty saying his name, and Tadeusz decides he wants to change his name. He thinks for a long time and considers several names, but the one he likes the best is simply Ted.

After much deliberation, Ted tells his dad he wants to change his name to Ted. Much to his surprise, his dad and stepmom agree the name Ted is fine with them.

At school, he tells his friends to call him Ted. Tadeusz feels pleased at his friends' quick acceptance of his new name. Ted's school friends like his new name, for they can say "Ted" easily. Ted's new friends like Ted for his physical ability playing soccer and his pleasant personality.

Ted's early education in the Polish schools led him to do well scholastically. His skill in math, science, and grammar remains excellent. Ted just needs to concentrate on building up his vocabulary in English. He writes good essays and one time he boldly wrote, "In 50 years, man will land on the moon!" His new English friends said, "Ted, you are a dreamer." Ted received an excellent grade on this paper.

Although Ted has many friends at the English school, there are those children who do not like him. These children are the school bullies who "run the school." These kids feel that Ted does not show them the respect they deserve. They view Ted as a challenge to their authority and start a program to intimidate him. Ted is new at the school and does not want any trouble, so he does not respond to their constant harassments.

During the noon recess, one of the school bullies kicks Ted in front of a dozen witnesses. Ted immediately says, "I will not put up with your antics anymore. You meet me after classes on the football field and we will resolve our differences like men in a boxing match." Ted turns away from him and says to the rest of the boys, "I invite all of you to join us on the football field after classes today."

For the rest of the afternoon, Ted frets a lot because he has no experience in boxing and he knows he must win to save his reputation. He wonders if his friends and the other students will join in this fight. Ted worries what the school authorities will do when they find out about this boxing fight.

After all his classes end, Ted and twenty classmates walk to the football field. The bully and his pals are not on the football field. Ted and the other students wait twenty minutes for this bully to arrive, but he never shows up.

With great relief and dignity, Ted addresses the students, "Gentlemen, it appears that boy will not show up for this fight. I hope some of you will relay to that boy that I, Ted, consider him a coward and a scoundrel. If he ever annoys me again in any fashion, I will beat him on the spot no matter where we are at the time." This episode ends the problem with the bullies, for they never bother Ted again.

Ted's life is great and he has no problems. Ted often babysits for Frank and Jadzia, who both work at a nursing home in Tetbury, England. Ted usually has no trouble with the little boy except one particular time. Their baby will not stop crying. Ted tries everything he knows, but nothing works, the baby keeps crying. Now Ted thinks, *I will give him a little sugar on a spoon.* Ted gives the baby the sugar and almost immediately, he stops crying and falls asleep. When Jadzia came home, Ted tells her what he did and how well it worked. Jadzia, horrified that Ted gave her baby sugar, gives Ted a tongue-lashing. However, Ted feels sugar is a proven cure for a crying baby.

Military planes in large formations fly over Great Britain, and Ted notices these planes. He learns that Great Britain played a limited role in the Korean War. Ted worries there might be another world war and perhaps countries will use atomic bombs. This thought horrifies Ted, as he remembers how WWII affected him and his family. Fortunately for Ted, all thoughts of war pass as he becomes acutely aware of girls his age.

In England, there is no regular dating of boys and girls. Ted's first love has moved away, so he devises unique ways to meet girls. Ted's biggest problem in meeting girls is his timidity. Most of Ted's romances happen when the girl takes the initiative. Ted now hangs out with a different girl whom he likes, and she introduces him to kissing.

Chapter Twenty-Two
America

After months and months of waiting, Frank and Jadzia receive their immigration papers that allow them to move to America. Several days after Jadzia and Frank receive their papers, Michal and his family receive their immigration papers. The American government has given their approval for all of them to migrate to America for "permanent settlement." However, Maria must remain in England.

Michal goes to the Red Cross to inquire about Jan. The person at the Red Cross tells Michal they will investigate Jan's whereabouts. After several days, Michal returns to the Red Cross, but they have no news about Jan. Michal cannot believe Jan has died.

Maria tells Michal, "I will keep going to the Red Cross, and someday we will learn something about Jan. Michal, I feel Jan lives but I cannot explain this feeling." When Maria talks about Jan she stops complaining and speaks quietly but sadly. Maria has every right to complain, for the authorities do not once consider all that Maria has endured.

Michal and his family move first. After Michal pays for all the expenses for his wife and children, he has only fifty dollars left in his pocket. The two adults and two children have only two medium-size suitcases that contain all their possessions between the four of them.

They say their goodbyes to Maria, to Szczepan, Frank and Jadzia, and all their many Polish and English friends.

Everyone goes to the ship's dock to see Michal and his family leave

Figure 4. The Liberté

for America. Again, Michal and his family say "Goodbye" to everyone. As they leave their friends to board the ship, one of Ted's Polish friends slips him a five-dollar bill. Ted feels suddenly rich. Quickly, everyone boards the French ship, the *Liberté*, in Portsmouth, England bound for America.

Michal and his family know nothing about what to expect when they arrive in America. Most of what they do know comes from American movies. They picture America as a mixture of large industrial cities with huge factories and a Wild West country with savage Indians, cowboys, and—nothing else. Of course, they all believe most Americans are millionaires who drive huge expensive automobiles. Until this voyage, Michal and his family have ridden in only trains, trucks, buses or on a bicycle. No one has ever ridden in a privately owned passenger car.

In the past, Michal and his family stood in food lines and carried their sparse plate of food to a table if there was a table available. On this ship, everything is different. The food is delicious and one can eat as much as one wants. There are no food lines; a waiter brings the food to your table. Michal and his wife enjoy the luxury of this ship. Ted and his new half brother have fun exploring the ship. Michal and his family feel a great wonder at all the luxuries on this ship. Their voyage to America seems like a dream. In the past, they rarely received kindness of any sort from anyone.

The ship has games for adults and children to play. Everyone in Michal's family enjoys playing shuffleboard. No one gets sick on this ship. The weather remains warm and the ocean seems calm with only a few days of rough seas. Fortunately for everyone, the ocean crossing in the *Liberté* is uneventful.

Only Ted has an unusual experience. One day Ted finds a small silver coin. First, he thinks it is a ship's coin because on one side, it says LIBERTY and the ship's name is *Liberté*. A passenger overhearing Ted talk about this coin, tells Ted, "That coin is an American coin worth ten cents." This passenger now walks away from Ted with a smile on his face. However, Ted wonders what "ten cents" means.

The ship arrives in New York harbor just before dawn on November 21, 1951. Michal and his family do not see the Statue of Liberty nor do they know the meaning of the Statue of Liberty.

As the ship passes Ellis Island, someone yells out, "This is where all we immigrants get off. Now the Americans make sure our papers are in proper order." Ted just looks at the big buildings all lit up on both sides of the river. Ted cannot believe all the big buildings. It takes a good four hours before the ship finally pulls up to the dock and stops.

It proves easy to check off the ship and go through customs. They have only two suitcases between the four of them. Ted speaks the best English, so he does most of the talking and helps his dad complete the necessary forms.

As the family exits the port, they realize they are on their own. No one yells at them what to do, or where to report, or to whom. While Ted gets instructions on how to get to the railroad station, a Ukrainian family joins them. The Ukrainian family speaks only in French or Ukrainian, for they lived in France after the war began.

The mother speaks in Ukraine to Ted, "Your dad speaks English well." Then she says, "We plan to go to Cleveland, Ohio." Ted does not understand what she said and gets his dad to help her.

Ted's dad translates what they said to Ted in Polish. Ted gets the directions for them to go to Cleveland in English and his dad translates their instruction to them in their Ukrainian language.

As the family exits the port, they feel the impact of being on their own. Ted has the directions for his family to get from New York City to Jeannette, Pennsylvania, about thirty-five miles south of Pittsburgh.

The family walks outside the immigration building into New York City. They all stop in amazement and look up into the tallest buildings they have ever seen. They all just say, "WOW, oh my." Ted can hardly believe his eyes. Without taking his eyes off the buildings, Ted says, "We just have to walk a few blocks to the train station, and Ted points the way without taking his eyes off the buildings. Suddenly they arrive at the train station.

Ted has no trouble finding the right train for them to take to Jeannette, Pennsylvania. They have only a thirty-minute wait when their train arrives. The family sits on benches available for people to wait for their particular train. The train station is big and ornate, thinks Ted and his family. Soon the right train arrives on time and everyone gets on board. Everything seems so different here in America to Michal and his family as they travel through this new land of America.

As the train leaves the city, the new immigrants wonder at the vastness of the land and its wide-open spaces. Ted compares this new land to densely populated England, and he likes this new land with its wide open spaces.

As the train passes through towns, Michal and his family see many cars parked in front of big buildings. At first, they think these buildings are plants that make cars and the plant boss will ship the cars to other cities. As they pass one huge lot after another, Ted decides these cars belong to individual people. He remembers that his professor told his class that in England there might be one car for thirty people, but in the USA, they have one car for every three people.

As the train enters the Allegheny Mountains, a snowstorm develops. It seldom snows in England, and to the Polish immigrants this is an exciting event to see. This white blanket of snow covers the entire mountainside. After passing through the mountain range, the snow disappears. The conductor on the train tells them that the next stop is Jeannette.

When the train arrives in Jeannette, Pennsylvania, it is dusk. Michal worries that their sponsor, Mr. Thomas, might be unable to find them in the dark.

As they exit the train, a young woman approaches them and speaks in broken Polish, "Are you the family Mr. Thomas is sponsoring?"

Michal answers, "Yes. How did you know us?"

The young woman replies, "Well, you all look different, as if you have been traveling for a long time."

Ted finds it interesting to listen to her speak so strangely in Polish. She mixes English words with Polish words, and that is most confusing. She uses a Polish word and puts an English prefix on the beginning of a Polish word or puts it at the end of a Polish word.

The young woman, Gloria Thomas, is the daughter of their sponsor. Ted thinks she must be third-generation Polish, an Americanized female.

After they all introduce themselves to Gloria, she loads them all into her car, a Buick. Ted looks in awe at this car. He has never seen a car so large and luxurious. Ted firmly believes all Americans must be millionaires.

As Gloria drives away from the train station, Ted cannot believe how expertly Gloria handles the car. Ted has never seen a woman drive a car, and Gloria's skillful driving impresses Ted. The drive to the Thomases' farm takes only twenty minutes.

The Thomases have a modest farmhouse, but to Michal and his family their farmhouse looks like a palace. The house has three bedrooms and two bathrooms that are both inside the house. The farmhouse has what Mr. Thomas calls a living room, and that living room has furniture in it. Next, he shows them a beautiful kitchen with a refrigerator and a freezer. Ted cannot believe that refrigerator and that it really keeps food cold. Ted feels numb. He has never seen anything like what Mr. Thomas has just shown them. Next Mr. Thomas shows them the dining room where he says everyone sits down to eat.

Mr. Thomas asks Michal and his family to sit down in his living room. Mr. Thomas explains to Michal that he only expected Michal and his son Ted to arrive. The arrival of Michal with a wife and a stepson has surprised him.

It seems that Michal started the application before he married and later neglected to put his wife and new son's names on the form. Despite Mr. Thomas's first confusion, he welcomes everyone warmly and makes them all feel welcome.

The next day, Gloria and her dad explain to Michal and his family that a special day, Thanksgiving Day, occurs this Thursday. Mr. Thomas invites Michal and his entire family to this Thanksgiving celebration. Gloria explains to them all about this wonderful holiday and says there will be plenty of food and three more children about Ted's age will arrive with their parents.

Thanksgiving Day arrives, and all the cooking and wonderful smells coming from the kitchen amaze Michal's family. Soon other people with their children arrive. Ted immediately likes the boys, and they test each other's skills running and riding bikes.

Ted does well in the sprint, but the bicycle racing wipes him out. These boys have beautiful bikes they call Schwins. The bikes do not have hand brakes, you stop by peddling backwards, and no one told Ted this fact before he got on the bike to race his new friends. He races well but cannot stop the bike and so he just falls off the bike.

Ted does not hurt himself, but the bike suffers some damage. His new friends immediately ask Ted, "Are you hurt?"

Ted answers, "No, I am fine but, I am so sorry I hurt your bike." Ted explains to his new friends that he has never had or seen a bike like these Schwins.

Ted and his family have a wonderful day feasting and getting to know new people. Michal and his family feel welcome and enjoy this special Thanksgiving Day.

Everything is new to Michal and his family. Michal helps around the farm as much as they let him, and then he visits with Mr. Thomas and his relatives. Michal and his family help as much as they can. Michal understands farming, but all their farm equipment puzzles Michal.

Ted cannot believe that parents let kids only sixteen years old drive a car. The kids drive just fine, too. Ted views these new Americans as wealthy. Not only do the families have one or two cars, they have trucks plus a pickup truck.

One day, Mr. Thomas takes the boys into town with him to do some shopping. They look with amazement at the stores. All the stores are huge, and it seems you can buy anything you might wish for or need, think the boys. This is in stark contrast to England, where they still have food rationing because of the war and so many people to feed.

The following week, Michal and Mr. Thomas have a talk and each agree that Michal and his family need to move. Mr. Thomas feels his house is not large enough for two large families. He also believes his farm does not produce enough food for two families. Mr. Thomas offers to help Michal find a job and a place to live.

On December 21, 1951, the manager of one of the two glass factories in Jeannette hires Michal to work in his factory. Most of the employees have an Italian background and speak mainly Italian on and off the job. Michal gets along well with the Italians and speaks enough Italian to talk with them. While fighting in Italy, Michal learned enough of the Italian language to enable him to talk with Italians. Making glass is tough work, but Michal thrives on hard work.

Michal rents a small place for his family. Michal rents two rooms in the basement of an old house on top of a hill on the outskirts of town. Michal and his wife occupy the only bedroom. The kitchen serves as the main living and eating room. Ted and his new brother sleep on a couple of old couches that turn into beds at night. These couches line the wall away from the stove in the kitchen. Outside there is an outhouse!

To get to their rooms in the house on the hill, they must drive up a steep street about a half mile away from their place or walk up 186 steep steps. Since they did not have a car, they all walk up the steps and develop strong leg muscles.

There is no shower or bathtub in their small apartment, so they take a bath every Saturday at one of the homes that several Polish families have invited them to use for bathing purposes. Michal, his wife, and the boys carry towels and a change of clothes down the steps to the home where they take their bath. The two boys have only two sets of underwear and clothes to change into. Therefore, they wear one set of clothes for seven days and change into the clean set after their bath. Ted's new mother always has the dirty clothes washed and ready for the boys to put on the next week when they take their baths.

After they each take a bath, they have dinner with their hosts and spend the evening visiting with them. After the visit ends, they climb up the stairs to their rooms.

In 1951, Jeannette has a population of about 18,000 people. About

6,000 are Italians and 6,000 Polish, and 6,000 of mixed American ancestry. One could walk whole sections of Jeannette where one heard only Polish spoken. The city of Jeannette has a strong Polish minority with a large Polish club where the Polish people often congregate.

Michal and his family join this club, for they feel a strong need to be with people like themselves. The Polish club has a large library full of great Polish literature. In the next eight months, Ted reads nearly 200 books. His stepbrother enjoys the company of other Polish boys his age, and Michal and his wife enjoy the companionship of other Polish adults.

In January of 1952, Michal enrolls Ted in St. James Catholic School. The school principal considers Ted's age to be fourteen and because of his former schooling, she places Ted in the eighth grade.

The school starts with a morning mass and then the teachers move the students by grades to their respective classrooms. As the group moves toward the red brick and one-floor schoolhouse, a young boy approaches Ted and greets him in broken Polish.

He tells Ted his name is Fred. Fred does not speak Polish well. Ted thinks he must be another third-generation Pole. This boy speaking broken Polish to Ted, well, his words are music to Ted's ears. The boys immediately become close friends and their friendship lasts for many years.

On entering the classroom, Ted and Fred realize their teacher is Sister Anita, the school principal. She is short but stern looking as she greets the class. Ted and Fred soon learn that their teacher is a strict disciplinarian who does not hesitate to bang the heads of anyone who disobeys her.

Ted's previous education at Gymnasium puts him ahead of his

American students by at least a year in his academic studies. Sister Anita realizes Ted must speak better English. Although she is a busy person, she takes the time to help Ted adjust to his new environment, and most importantly, she spends many extra hours helping Ted learn the English language. She assigns his new friend, Fred, to work with Ted to help Ted improve his English.

Fred's parents often invite Ted to their home, for they genuinely like him. Fred helps Ted improve his English. Now Fred asks Ted to teach him the Polish language. This arrangement pleases Fred's parents, and especially his grandmother who speaks only Polish.

Fred's parents have a black-and-white television set that fascinates Ted. He has never seen such a TV set in his life, and this TV captivates him. Whenever possible Ted watches this TV for hours, and he even enjoys the commercials. Fred's parents only let Ted watch the TV after he has done his English lesson. Ted needs to make progress in speaking English without his deep Polish accent.

Another treat for Ted is after an evening of learning and watching TV, Fred's parents often drive Ted home in their automobile. The rides in that automobile give Ted a huge thrill. Ted quickly forgets the horrors of war that he and his family endured. Ted wants some of the comforts that Fred's parents provide for Fred and themselves.

Ted tells his dad about Fred's family, their TV, and automobile. Ted wants a TV, and especially a few more clothes. Playing sports gets Ted's clothes dirty by the end of the fourth day, yet he must wait three more days before he can take a bath and change his clothes.

Fred's family also has a telephone. Ted cannot believe that a phone can ring and when you pick it up you can talk to a person on the other end. You can even pick up this phone from the wall, dial certain numbers, and reach a person and talk with that person.

Ted tells his dad about this phone. Michal tells Ted that he cannot afford a telephone, for it costs too much money and he does not make enough money to have a phone. The one item that Michal makes sure his family has is enough food to eat every day. Michal feels grateful he can afford to provide his family with food each day. Michal's family does feel blessed to have enough food to eat every day. Yet, now there are other things to want besides food.

Young Ted wants more than his father can provide. Ted decides he must have some of the items that Fred's family enjoys. Ted looks for a job that he can do after school and finds a job in a shoe store working only two hours a day for six days a week. Ted does not make much money, but the few dollars he earns each week helps his family.

Ted's family has settled into a routine. Michal writes letters to his other family members who remain in Europe. He writes to his oldest son, Josef, still in South Africa. Josef writes back that he works in a diamond mine and is happy living in Africa.

A letter comes to Michal from his brother Szczepan, still in England. Szczepan writes he has married an Englishwoman and they plan to remain in England. He also writes that Maria, Ted's grandmother, is still in England and that Jadzia and her husband hope to bring her with them when they leave for America. He also writes Michal that he has no word about Jan. Michal feels a deep sad pain when he learns no one knows anything about his son Jan. Regardless, Michal continues writing to various agencies and organizations for help in finding Jan. Michal cannot explain the feeling he has that Jan lives. He keeps writing all the agencies and organizations hoping for a miracle. Sometimes miracles do happen, he thinks.

On this particular day in early June, Ted leaves school happy that he has learned he will graduate to the ninth grade. Ted's boss has not scheduled him to work today, so Ted returns to his family's small apartment. As Ted enters their apartment, he sees his dad sitting on a chair with a piece of paper in his hands.

Ted asks his dad, "Dad why are you home, did you lose your job? Are you sick?" Ted notices his dad's jovial manner and wonders what has happened.

Michal gets up off the chair and gives Ted a big hug. Now Michal says to Ted, "Look at this picture." Ted looks at the picture of a group of volleyball players. He does not recognize the players except one. One player looks like him. The others are total strangers.

Ted looks at his dad and says, "Dad, this person looks like me, but I don't understand, the others are strangers, and Dad, I do not play volleyball." Ted's dad gives Ted a big smile. Ted looks at the picture and feels bewildered.

Ted asks his dad, "Why do you have this picture?"

Michal teasingly says, "Ted, I did not know you played on a volleyball team."

Ted becomes more confused and now he feels upset. Ted looks at the picture again and closely. Now Ted notices the players look older than he does, and he points this out to his dad. Michal stops teasing Ted and explains that in this picture, the person that looks like Ted is his brother Jan. Jan sent the picture to Michal in the mail with just a brief note and his return address.

Jan wrote, "Dear Dad, I am fine and here is my picture. I received your address in a strange and mystical way. I do not have time to tell you more about this now, but will write about everything later. Please write to me. Love, Jan"

Ted goes into shock and says not a word for a few moments. Then Ted says, "Gosh, Dad, that person looks just like me only older."

"Yes, Ted, Jan is alive and he looks just like you. I was afraid he was dead, but I had a feeling he was alive. I cannot explain it but, OH GOD, you have answered my prayers," exclaims Michal. "Ted, you and I can write Jan as often as we want. Soon I hope to learn what happened to Jan. How did he find us? This has to be a miracle," says Michal.

"Dad, he looks good and healthy in this picture," says Ted.

Michal replies, "Yes, he does look good. How did he find us? I have tried and tried for so long to find him with NO success. This is a miracle."

Michal and Ted hug each other and continue to look at the picture of the volleyball team with Jan in the picture. They just want to touch and hug Jan.

About an hour later, Michal's wife and her son arrive home. Michal shows them the picture with Jan in it. Michal and his wife hug each other and cry in profound happiness. They all wonder what happened to Jan, and most important, how did Jan get Michal's address? How did this miracle come to be?

The next day Michal goes to the immigration office in Jeannette to learn how to bring Jan to America. Many letters to Jan and Jan to Michal eventually reveal what happened to Jan and how Jan came to know where his dad lives in America.

Michal writes Jan that he has married. He writes, "Jan, you have a new mother and brother." Michal writes Jan the address of his wife's family who still live in Poland. "Perhaps, Jan, you can visit some of her family." Michal gives Jan the addresses of other family members in America, England, and Africa so Jan can write them, also.

Ted graduates from the eighth grade in a ceremony put on by the school. The day after Ted's graduation Michal receives a letter from Aniela telling them that she and her husband, Ed Ledbetter, will visit them in Jeannette. The letter says they will arrive before the end of June. Michal and his wife look at their tiny apartment and wonder where they will put two more people.

Chapter Twenty-Three
Vancouver, Washington

Ed returns from work on June 18 and tells his wife, Aniela, he has two weeks off from work. Aniela, delighted, immediately prepares for their trip to Jeannette, Pennsylvania.

The next day, Ed and Aniela get in their car and drive to Michal's place in Jeannette. This trip takes them only five days, for they are eager to get to Michal's place. They plan to talk Michal and his family into returning with them to Vancouver, Washington.

On June 23, Ed and Aniela arrive in Jeannette. They find Michal's apartment but cannot believe the conditions under which they live. Ed and Aniela walk up the long flight of steps. They look at each other and voice their determination to get Michal and his family out of Jeannette and to move to Vancouver.

Today the whole family stayed in the apartment to wait for Ed and Aniela. Michal greets Ed and Aniela when they knock on his door. Everyone hugs and kisses each other, for they are glad to be together.

Ed and Aniela stay with Michal and his family in their tiny apartment. Aniela feels sad as she looks at Michal's shabby apartment with no indoor bathroom—just an outhouse. How this tiny two-room apartment holds two more people amazes Ted.

Aniela and Ed talk only about Vancouver, Washington. They tell

Michal and his family that Vancouver is wonderful and a little bit like their former home in Poland. They tell Michal that they should move to Vancouver because there are more job opportunities and better schools for the boys.

After listening to their glowing descriptions of beautiful Vancouver, the boys yelled, "Let's move to Vancouver." Both Michal and his wife not only need but want better job opportunities and better schools for their boys. That very evening they tell Ed and Aniela they will join them on the trip back to Vancouver.

Ed and Aniela feel a great relief after they learn Michal and his family will go back with them to Vancouver. The next day Michal tells his boss he plans to move to Vancouver and that his last day of work will be the end of this workweek. His boss just says "OK."

Michal sends a letter to Jan telling him of their plans to move to Vancouver and gives Jan Aniela's address. Michal even mentions his hope that Jan can join them soon in Vancouver. More important to Michal, he asks Jan how he found them. Michal writes telling Jan how he searched and searched asking every organization that helps families find lost family members without any success. He also writes Jan, that he asked every Polish person who came to England if that person knew about Jan—all without success.

When Michal finishes writing this long letter to Jan, he tells Ted to take this letter to the nearest mailbox. Ted takes the letter down the 186 steps to the nearest mailbox and puts the letter in the mailbox. Ted wonders if he will ever see his brother Jan since they are moving so far away.

The next day Ted knows he must tell his good friend Fred about their move to Vancouver, Washington. After telling Fred about the move,

Fred asks, "Why are you moving to Canada?"

Ted explains, "No, we are not moving to Canada, Fred. We are moving to the state of Washington."

Fred replies, "Oh, Washington, D.C."

Ted replies, "No, Fred, we are moving to Vancouver, Washington, in the western part of America."

Ted grabs the map he has of the United States and shows Fred the route they will take to Vancouver, Washington.

Fred looks at Ted and says, "Oh, Ted, that is far from here. Gosh, Ted, I miss you already. Can't you tell your dad you want to stay here with me?"

Ted tells Fred, "Fred, I wish I could, but my dad wants to move and be near his sister and I have to go with him." Ted feels a deep excitement about this move to Vancouver and wants to move.

Ted and Fred promise to write to each other forever. Fred now tells Ted he wants to become a priest and Ted tells Fred he wants to become a doctor. The boys make a pledge that Ted will take care of Fred when he gets ill and Fred will bury all of Ted's mistakes. However, both Fred and Ted follow different paths but these were their plans as young teenagers.

After just a few years their writing dwindles to just a Christmas card and soon they both stop writing.

Ed's car is a Henry J. and can carry only four adults. However, Ed gets all four adults, two boys, three suitcases, and several bags into and on top of his car. The car cannot hold another piece of anything inside or on top. They look like a pile of Gypsies traveling across America. Ed has the only driver's license and must do all the driving.

Ed wants to get back to Vancouver as quickly as possible as he has now been gone for ten days. To get back to Vancouver more quickly, Ed decides to drive continually for forty-eight hours, day and night.

The first day of driving goes without any problems. Ed makes good time driving. They travel on Highway 30, the main east-and-west highway in America. This highway has only a two-lane road—one lane goes east and the other goes west. This highway is in good condition, and Ed feels confident he can drive straight through without any problems.

Ed drives from Jeannette into Ohio and then into Indiana without any problems. It is late in the evening, about 9:00 p.m., when Ed drives into Illinois and must stop and get more gas. This stop gives everyone a chance to get out of the car and stretch his or her legs while Ed fills the gas tank. When the gas tank is full, everyone gets back into the car.

After Ed turns the car on and drives to Highway 30, everyone but Ed and Ted falls asleep, for it is past 9: 00 p.m. Ted talks to Ed and gives him coffee from the thermos to help keep Ed awake. Again, they are making good time and Ed is wide awake. Everything is fine when Ted sees a sign that says "Welcome to Ohio." Ted yells at Ed to stop the car. Now Ted tells Ed he just saw a "Welcome to Ohio" sign.

Immediately Ed checks his map and sure enough, they have been driving in the wrong direction after stopping for gas. Ed cannot believe he has wasted so much time traveling in the wrong direction. He is glad Ted saw the Ohio sign before they traveled any further in the wrong direction. Ed turns the car around and now heads west. He thanks Ted for being alert and telling him about this error before he drove back to Pennsylvania.

The trip across America turns into an education for Michal and his two sons. In 1952, there are no interstate roads or freeways. All highways pass through every town or city, whether the place is big or small. It takes almost four hours to go across Chicago.

Michal and Ted find the changes in the geography interesting. Ted notices the cities have many people but the countryside has few people. Ed explains the cities have many people but in America, there are long stretches of land without a single building and no people either.

As Ed drives into Iowa and then Nebraska, the terrain is flat with many acres of corn growing in the fields. The highway is straight and one can see, it seems, forever. In fact, the driving is so monotonous that Ed dozes off on several occasions and once ran off the highway. Fortunately, no damage occurs to the car or the family.

As Ed drives into and across Wyoming, he tells Ted, "You will not see cornfields here but you will see big ranches, the big ranches of the West."

Ted often sees men riding on horses. Ed tells Ted, "Those men are cowhands called cowboys."

Ted cannot believe his eyes and can say nothing. It is one awesome sight after another for the Polish immigrants. Ed now drives through the Grand Teton Mountains, part of the Rocky Mountains. Ed stops the car and sleeps for only an hour and a half.

While Ed slept, the passengers get out of the car and stretch their legs. When he awakens, their journey continues. Ed will stop the car and doze briefly a few more times before they reach Ed's home.

Michal and his family become speechless as they view huge mountains that seem to touch the heavens. These mountains touch the heavens, thinks Ted. They all wonder what Vancouver, Washington, will be like.

Everyone falls asleep for long periods except for Ted and Ed. Ted cannot shut his eyes. Ed tells Ted to watch for Indians, and Ted keeps looking for Indians but never sees any during the trip. Ted does see many of what he thinks could be cows. Ed tells Ted those big animals are cattle not cows.

Ted falls asleep for just brief periods. He awakens suddenly to see more ranches and then the Cascade Mountain Range. Michal becomes concerned they will live on a mountain and he prefers flat land like the land they had in Poland. He expresses his feelings to Ed.

Ed tells Michal, "Do not worry, for the land will change as we are just fifty miles away from Vancouver." Michal looks at the mountains and feels worried.

A few miles later Michal feels relieved as they leave the mountains and enter a beautiful valley with huge forests and a big river—the Columbia River. Ed tells Michal, "This road will take us around The Dalles and all the way to Vancouver, Washington."

Initially the forests are of Ponderosa pines. As they cross the Cascades summit, the forest changes to huge Douglas firs, many of them a hundred feet tall and over a hundred years old. Ted, amazed at everything he sees, feels a real thrill to be here. For Michal the big trees remind him of their imprisonment in Russia. Michal gets hold of his emotions with difficulty as he looks at the trees. Upon close inspection of the trees, he realizes these trees do not look like the trees in Russia.

Shortly after noontime, Ed drives into Vancouver, Washington. The entire family is immediately impressed and pleased with Vancouver. Vancouver has a population of about 30,000 people. The streets are wide and the homes are far apart on large lots. The homes appear new and not like the homes in Jeannette. In Jeannette, the homes were often fifty or more years old.

Ed tells Michal, Vancouver has become a booming city and last year a prominent man announced that Vancouver is the "All-American City." The homes appear magical to Michal and his family with their large lawns and huge trees lining the streets.

Ed drives to his and Aniela's home, in the "Heights" area. Their home looks lovely. Not as big as some of the homes they saw on the way to Ed and Aniela's home. Comparing Ed and Aniela's home to their two rooms in Jeannette, Aniela and Ed's home looks like a palace.

Their home has three bedrooms, a big indoor bathroom, a kitchen plus an eating area, and a sitting room. Michal and his family are speechless. Aniela's house looks so beautiful and comfortable.

Ted asks, "Mom, where is the outhouse?"

Aunt Aniela laughingly says, "Ted, there is no outhouse here. You use this bathroom to take a bath and the toilette to pee in."

"OK," says Ted, still unsure about this bathroom, for he has never seen anything like this bathroom before in his life.

Aniela bought all new furniture for her home. The boys do not want to sit on her furniture, for the furniture looks beautiful and expensive. Suddenly, Ted notices the telephone and cannot believe his eyes. His aunt has a telephone. Ed sees the stunned look on Ted's face. He says, "Ted, are you looking at our telephone?"

Ted says, "Yes."

Ed proudly tells Michal and his wife, "We own our home." He does not tell them they have a loan at the bank and the bank owns their home.

In the early fifties, no one uses credit cards. People pay cash for all the items they buy. So far, Michal and his family have only bought food. During the trip to Vancouver, Michal helped Ed pay for his gas with cash. Michal knows he must learn to pay for items he needs with American money.

The first week in Vancouver, Michal and his family live with Ed and Aniela while they search for their own place to live. Ted notices how much Aniela has forgotten of her native language, for Aniela speaks in English all the time. As the days pass, Aniela improves speaking the Polish language simply because Michal and his family speak in Polish all the time. Michal's new wife and her son speak English when they are alone. She wants to be an American and not a foreigner.

During the first week in Vancouver, Ed starts teaching Michal how to drive a car. This proves easy. While Michal served in the Polish army, he learned to drive a truck. Now he quickly becomes a skillful driver after just a few tries. Within ten days of arriving in Vancouver, Michal takes the driving test and passes the first time.

Quickly Ed and Michal find an apartment in an old large house the owner converted into an apartment building. The apartment is inexpensive, and Michal likes it. On each floor of this three-story building is one bathroom and two apartments. More work needs to be done on their apartment building, but it is a huge improvement compared to their place in Jeannette.

Their apartment consists of two bedrooms, a kitchen, and a small living area. The owner has provided the furniture in the apartment. The apartment also has an electric stove and a refrigerator. Michal immediately talks to the owner and pays for the first two months of rent. Michal is glad he does not have to buy this apartment, as his money funds are low. Michal's wife likes this place with the indoor bathroom and real refrigerator. She thinks this place is a huge improvement over their place in Jeannette.

The next day, Michal looks for a job to support his family. Finding a job proves difficult, for Michal speaks limited English. In Jeannette, many workers spoke Polish and some broken English, but here in Vancouver almost everyone speaks only English.

After three weeks of searching for work, Michal gets a temporary job in a cannery. Michal has only a half mile to walk to work, so he does not have to buy a car.

Michal and his family settle quickly into their new home. The entire family likes their new apartment—they love their refrigerator and bathroom.

The boys have a lot of time with nothing to do because it is still summertime. School does not start until early September. Ted's brother meets some boys his age and quickly starts speaking in the English language and begins to lose his Polish accent. Ted and his dad continue to speak in their Polish language most of the time.

Ted's new mom tells Michal that they should all speak English at home. She feels if they all speak English at home then their English would improve faster and perhaps the English-speaking people would accept them and their children sooner. Of course, Michal feels she is right, but Michal and Ted do not want to give up talking in their Polish language.

Now that Ted's stepbrother has friends, Ted is alone, for he has not found anyone his age that speaks Polish. Ted becomes lonelier and wants a friend. Ed senses Ted's loneliness and introduces Ted to his younger sister, Betty.

Betty is seventeen years old, and Ted is almost fifteen. Their age difference and the fact that Betty speaks only English keep them from becoming close friends. However, Betty does provide Ted with hundreds of comic books that Ted reads repeatedly.

On weekends, Michal and his family visit the Polish Hall in

Portland, Oregon. The family meets people there that share their culture and speak their Polish language. Two different groups come to the Polish Hall. One group is from the generation of WWI and they are mostly in their sixties or older. This group built the Polish Hall and the Polish Catholic Church, St. Stanislaus.

The second group consists of the more recent and younger immigrants. Michal and his family have more in common with the recent immigrants. However, they respect and cherish the older people, for they give the new immigrants the best support when they need help. The Polish Hall also has a Polish library that Ted uses extensively.

There are three theaters in Vancouver, and Ted sees each movie at the theater at least once. The price is only ten cents to see a movie and five cents for popcorn or a drink. Ted gets either a drink or popcorn, as he cannot afford both.

Summer ends, and the boys must go back to school. Michal enrolls Ted in Shumway Junior High School and Ted enters the ninth grade.

Michal's wife walks her son to school on his first day. He immediately sees some of his friends and enters the school happily. She feels a huge relief, for she does worry how the other children might treat him. Now Michal's wife looks for a job and finds one in a restaurant as a dishwasher.

Ted leaves home early and walks to his school. He does not want to be late and arrives before he can enter the school. Ted sees hundreds of kids. All the kids are greeting one another happily. These kids have obviously known one another most of their lives and perhaps since first grade. Ted feels like an outsider, different from the other kids. Suddenly he feels lonely and sad. This sad, lonely feeling is a new experience for Ted.

In the past, Ted started school in different places and countries. However, back then, Ted and the other students came from different areas and few students knew one another. Now, Ted realizes he is in a strange situation—he is an outsider. He sees other students glance at him with that look that says, "Who the hell is that stranger." Suddenly Ted has a huge need to cry for he feels lonely and scared.

Despite these feelings, Ted firmly walks into the school and enters the principal's office. Immediately the principal notices Ted with that scared look on his face. He greets Ted as if Ted is an important person. He asks Ted a little bit about himself. Ted explains that he is new to this school and he speaks in broken English. The principal smiles at Ted and takes him to a classroom where he introduces Ted to Miss French, his new teacher. The principal talks briefly to Miss French and then leaves. Miss French introduces Ted to the class and gives the class a brief history about Ted.

At the end of the school day, Miss French tells Ted to return to the principal's office. Ted, a little worried, does what his teacher tells him to do. The principal sees Ted enter his office and tells Ted he has assigned two boys, David and Chuck, to show Ted around and explain to Ted how the school works. These three boys become instant friends, and their friendship lasts for many years.

The three boys walk together to school each morning. The walk to school for Ted is nearly a mile and a little further for Chuck and Dave. Ted meets them at the designated street each morning, and it feels so good to Ted to have friends. Having friends is important to Ted, yet there are those times when he wonders about his brother Jan and why has he not written to them. *What has happened to Jan?* wonders Ted.

Michal also wonders why he has not heard from Jan. Michal wrote

Jan about their move and gave him Aniela's address. So far, Aniela has not received a letter from Jan. This concerns Michal, for he fears for Jan's life while he lives in Poland—behind the Iron Curtain. It just might be a problem for Jan having a family in America, thinks Michal. Each day and night, Michal prays for Jan's safety.

A week after the boys started school, Aniela comes running to their apartment in the early evening. She has a letter in her hand and says breathlessly, "Hey, everyone, I have a letter from Jan."

Michal takes the letter from Aniela and reads aloud Jan's letter to everyone, for Jan has written the letter in Polish.

Jan's letter reveals how happy he is to have found his family. He writes how he found their address in Jeannette. Michal talks slowly as he reads Jan's letter.

Dear Dad and Tadeusz,

Dad, I never gave up trying to find you and I talked to all my friends about how to find you. My friend, Alexander, he told me to advertise in England about my need to find my family. Dad, I did just that. I wrote to Alexander's brother who lives in London, England; he advertised my need to find my family in the London newspaper.

Dad, you are not going to believe this. Two weeks before I learned you were alive, I am waiting at my bus stop to go to work. This Gypsy woman comes up to me and asks for some money to tell me my future. I, of course, told her NO, but she insisted that I listen to her. She told me, "You will not regret what it will cost you and it will not cost much." I gave her some money and she laid out her cards and started talking. She tells me, "You will be very joyful in a couple of weeks. You are going to get joyful news from overseas and you will find the family you have tried so long to find." Dad, I thought, how could she know this? I started to ask her questions but she did not listen to me. Instead, she said, "You are going to get two letters in about two or three weeks." Then this gypsy woman just walked away from me. I could not believe her. How could she know I was trying to find my family? She did not even know my name. Was this ESP? Dad, I never saw her before and never since that day.

Dad, two weeks later, the director of the dormitory where I live calls my name and gives me a letter from Grandma and then another letter from Tadeusz's English girlfriend, Felicia. They both said they had seen my volleyball picture in a Polish newspaper at the displaced Polish camp. Felicia wrote the paper and got my address. She wrote Grandma's letter to me, also.

Grandma's letter said you and Tadeusz live in Jeannette, Pa., USA. She also wrote that Tadeusz has changed his name to Ted. This is when I wrote to you and put the picture of my winning Polish volleyball team in my letter.

Dad, I cannot go to the Polish immigration office right now because that would be a dangerous thing for me to do. Since I have a family in a western country such as the USA, my government might consider me an enemy of Poland. Dad, we live under Russian rule. I will try as soon as I can to get to America, Dad. Oh, Dad, I am so happy to have found my family. I am ecstatic, for now I have my family back and I am not alone anymore.

Love Jan

Michal finishes reading Jan's letter as the tears flow from his eyes. Michal tells his family, "I am so grateful to hear from Jan and to know he is alive and well."

Immediately, Michal looks for his writing supplies and finding them, writes a long letter to Jan. Michal puts his new address on the outside envelope and inside the letter. Now Jan can write directly to his family.

Ted feels a great relief that his brother Jan is alive, but sad that he cannot get to America immediately. Ted wonders again if he will ever see his brother. He especially wonders what happened to Jan after the family left him in the hospital in Uzbekistan.

Ted returns to his studies, for he must write a paper to present in his class tomorrow. The paper must be in English. Writing in English is difficult for Ted. Sometimes Ted thinks, *Why must I learn English, it is too hard to learn. It would be so easy for my teachers and friends to learn Polish.* Ted knows he must learn English since he lives in America and his dad demands that Ted learn English. Michal tells Ted often, “We are now Americans and we speak English.” Michal is having difficulty learning English and tells his wife, “We can do this, we must learn this English. We are Americans and this is our country and we speak English.”

Michal does not realize that his wife already speaks English quite well. Nor does he realize that his wife and stepson speak only English when they are together. Michal continues to speak in Polish at home. Learning English is a struggle for Michal, but he does learn English and speaks English properly but never loses his Polish accent.

Ted does well in all his studies at his new school. Ted reads and prepares reports on about forty books. Ted’s many reports set a record at his school. Ted’s English has improved, and he speaks English with his new friends at school. However, Ted prefers to speak in Polish.

At home, Ted speaks Polish and whenever he speaks English, he speaks with a Polish accent. Toward the end of his ninth grade, Ted's vocabulary has improved. Ted knows many words but not the words' real meanings.

For example, during an outside gym class, Ted is goofing off. The gym coach tells Ted to "take a lap." Ted feels confused, and his puzzled look tells the coach that Ted does not understand his command. The coach explains what Ted is to do and Ted looks as if he understands. Ted believes he must run this lap as punishment for goofing off but does not understand how far he must run.

Ted spots two high hurdles about fifty yard apart, he runs from one to the other and returns to his gym class. The coach, surprised to see Ted back so soon, says nothing to Ted. Therefore, Ted believes a lap is the distance between two hurdles.

Other confusing expressions for Ted are "throwing a curve" and "thrown for a loop."

Ted enjoys his gym class but he has problems with the coach's many expressions.

After Ted's school day ends, he and his friends walk home together. The three boys often go to Dave's house and play cards with his mother and her boyfriend or they simply watch television. Ted likes Dave's mother and considers her a great lady. She often provides the boys with cake, ice cream, and sodas. Ted is fond of Dave's mother and believes she likes him.

Sometimes the boys go to Chuck's home, where they play with his BB gun. The boys shoot at targets and sometimes birds that get in their field of vision. The three boys become good shooters and decide to shoot at a match held in the hand of one boy. Chuck shoots at the match that Ted holds in his hand, but the pellet lodges in the fleshy part of

Ted's thumb. Ted manages to get the pellet out of his thumb, puts a small dressing on his thumb, and hopes his dad does not notice the dressing. This pellet hurt Ted's thumb a lot, but Ted does not cry. That pellet gun now frightens Ted.

Ted returns home. Michal does not notice Ted or the dressing on his thumb. Michal looks for another letter from Jan. Michal worries that something bad has happened to Jan; perhaps the Polish government learned about his family in America and considers Jan a traitor. Jan's first letter arrived in early September and it is now late November of 1952.

Michal's temporary job at the cannery ends, and Michal looks for another job. Fortunately, his wife still has her job as a dishwasher at the nearby restaurant. Her earnings help the family but are not enough for all their expenses.

A week after Michal lost his job, he finds a job that looks good. The local paper mill hires Michal to do clean-up tasks. Michal tells his wife, "This job looks good and I think it will last a long time."

Before 1952 ends, Frank (Hanka's brother) and his wife Jadzia (Michal's youngest sister) arrive in Vancouver with their young son. Michal helps them find a place to live. Michal tells Frank about the vacant apartment in his building. Frank rents this apartment, and their apartment is on the same floor as Michal's apartment. Michal feels proud to help his younger sister and her husband.

Frank immediately gets a job in a furniture store that he does not like. Just two months later, he gets a great job at the Alcoa Aluminum Company. Frank's pay and benefits are great, and he works there until he retires many years later.

Jadzia often asks Ted to babysit her son. Ted and the boy do not get along. The minute Jadzia leaves the apartment he starts crying and does not stop until Jadzia returns. This time sugar does not work. When Jadzia stops asking Ted to care for the little boy, Ted feels deep relief.

Just before Christmas of 1952, another long letter arrives from Jan. He writes what happened to him when he awoke from his illness and his feelings of despair.

Chapter Twenty-Four
Jan Tells His Story

Jan remained unconscious for many days in the hospital in Uzbekistan. The doctor believes Jan must live because Jan knows how to love. The doctor feels the world needs people who know how to love. Now the doctor uses all his skills and saves Jan's life.

The doctor is thrilled the day Jan awakens and asks, "Where am I? Where is my dad?" The nurses and doctor cannot answer Jan's questions. The doctor feels wonderful that Jan can ask questions about his family. The doctor does not answer Jan's question today. He wonders how to tell Jan that he does not know where his dad has gone except to say his dad fights for his country.

When no family members come to visit him, Jan becomes scared, for he feels lonely and lost. When the doctor comes to see Jan, he asks the doctor, "Why doesn't my dad, my grandma, and my brothers and aunt come to see me? Do you know where they have gone?"

The doctor feels great pleasure that Jan remembers his family. Now the doctor takes a deep breath and tells Jan, "I have no idea where your family lives today. I know your dad had to leave with the army when he received orders to fight in Italy. Your brothers, grandmother, and your aunt Aniela and Jadzia received orders, too. The military moved them somewhere, but the military refuses to tell me where they sent them.

Jan, I am so pleased to see that you are back with us. You were unconscious for so long, I wondered if you would ever wake up and remember your family. The nurses and I are immensely gratified you awoke and remember your family."

Jan just looks at the doctor. Jan feels instant fear, a fear he cannot explain or comprehend. Jan thinks, *I am alone. How do I survive?* Jan wonders if any of his family is alive or could they all be dead. He shivers with fear and hugs himself.

The doctor continues talking to Jan and tells him, "A young soldier has come to visit you once or twice recently. I do not know his name. I hope he comes to see you again and soon."

A soldier in uniform does come to see Jan. When he arrives, Jan looks at the soldier and asks him, "Do you know if my dad is alive?"

The soldier replies, "Jan, I trained with your dad and met your family. They were all well when they left here, but I do not know any more. Your dad left to fight in the war. Jan, I had orders to stay behind to protect the people here. I told your dad I would check on you. I am so sorry; I have no idea how to reach him."

Jan looks so lost the soldier stays a little longer with him. Now the soldier knows he must tell Jan his new orders. Slowly and hesitantly, he tells Jan he must leave to fight in the war.

"Jan, I leave tomorrow for Italy. Someday you will find your family; I just feel strongly that you will."

Jan looks at the soldier and grabs the soldier's hand. "Thank you for coming to see me and telling me about my family. I will pray for you." The soldier sadly leaves Jan.

Jan wonders how his family could just leave him. Jan feels fear being alone. Each day Jan gets stronger as his health improves. He remembers the Russian trooper forcing him and his family out of their home onto that hideous cattle car already full of people.

As Jan remembers everything that happened to him and his family, he cries many tears for several days. Remembering the past events hardens Jan, now just nine and a half years old. He does not expect anything good to happen to him. He fears his entire family is dead and knows he is alone in a world at war. Jan feels a profound gratitude toward the doctor for saving his life but wonders how he can survive alone in this world at war.

The day comes when the doctor tells Jan, "Jan, you are better and now I must dismiss you from the hospital. The authorities told me they will put you in the orphanage here in Uzbekistan." Jan looks sadly at the doctor as he leaves Jan's bedside.

Three days later, the doctor discharges Jan from the hospital. A stranger in an official-looking uniform takes Jan to the orphanage in Uzbekistan.

At the orphanage an older-looking woman greets Jan and takes him to a large room with many cots. She tells him in Polish that this is his bed and he must remember how to find it. Jan looks around at the many small beds and hopes he will remember his bed.

Kids are from everywhere in this orphanage, and many speak Polish, but many do not. Some of the kids are from the Ukraine and many from Stalingrad, a German-occupied area. *Just kids like me, no parents,* thinks Jan. The children range in ages from six to sixteen years old. Fights often break out among these children, especially the older kids. Jan decides he must avoid the older and bigger kids.

Lack of food has become the biggest problem in the orphanage. The smaller and youngest children get little food because the older kids grab their food off their plates. Older kids attack the smaller children and force the smaller children to give up whatever food they have to receive protection from other groups of rough older kids.

Little children die like flies because of lack of food and water. The adults supervising the orphanage are no better than the gangs are, for they too are hungry. Everyone feels hungry. There is little food for all the people, and that includes the children.. Outside the orphanage, there are no cats, dogs, or rats anywhere—the people have killed and eaten them all.

Fortunately for Jan, the authorities decide to send him to another orphanage after just one week at the Uzbekistan orphanage. The next day Jan traveled with a nice woman to the new orphanage. He remains in this new orphanage for about a year. Here a teacher notices that Jan speaks differently. She asks Jan many questions and realizes that Jan is Polish. By coincidence, the teacher married a Polish man also named Jan.

Jan wonders why this teacher is so kind to him, for he trusts no one anymore. He thinks she feels sorry for him. The teacher tells Jan that she knows of a Polish orphanage in another city and will try to get him into that orphanage. However, it takes her almost a full year before she gets him into the Polish orphanage.

Polish teachers founded this Polish orphanage for Polish children without parents. This orphanage is located in Kokanda, Uzbekistan.

Jan's teacher finally receives permission to take Jan to the orphanage on a train. Immediately after walking into this orphanage, Jan realizes this is a good orphanage. The place is clean and Jan sees no fights on his arrival. Soon after introducing Jan to his new teacher, his former teacher leaves. Jan immediately feels lost and fearful.

Jan looks at his new teacher in a state of shock and absolute fear. The new teacher says "hello" to Jan in Polish. Her voice sounds kind and Jan begins to relax.

A bell rings and Jan jumps, turning around. His new teacher sees Jan's fear. She puts her hand on Jan's shoulder and tells him, "Jan, that bell announces our dinnertime. Our cook wants all of us to sit down to eat in our dining hall. Follow me, Jan. I will show you where we eat in our dining hall." Jan likes the sound of his teacher's voice, and slowly he turns and follows her into a large room with a long table. Many children are entering the room and sitting down at the table. The children are not fighting or hitting other kids. Instead, the children are just talking quietly and no one is fighting as they enter the dining room.

This orphanage does have a shortage of food and clothing, but the teachers have taught the children to be kind, and they do not allow fighting. Jan immediately notices that no one fights for food. Every child here sits at the table; a woman puts a plate of food on the table in front of each child. The children eat their food without anyone stealing their food. Jan sits down at the table; a smiling woman puts a plate of food in front of him. Jan eats and enjoys his meager plate of food.

After a few days, Jan realizes many of the children here are Jewish children from Poland. Polish and Jewish does not matter; most of the kids are Polish kids from Poland. Yes, there are still some bullies, but they came from outside the orphanage, and the children call them "Uzbeks," meaning bullies to them.

These bullies do not live at the orphanage. They attack the Polish kids only when the kids leave the orphanage to go to school, visit a doctor, or a dentist. The bullies do beat Jan up a few times, but the Polish kids in the orphanage never beat him.

Again, Jan has bleeding gums. He must leave the orphanage and visit the dentist. The lack of fruit has contributed to Jan's bleeding gums.

The next day, his teacher tells Jan he must visit the dentist. To get to the dentist, Jan must walk through a large farmer's market. Jan's teacher draws him a map and shows him how to get to the dentist and back to the orphanage. The orphanage feels Jan is old enough to visit the dentist alone.

Jan leaves the orphanage and walks around the side of the market. A big man grabs him. Jan becomes instantly terrified and cries out, "What! You get away from me!"

This man looks like a Russian man. He says to Jan in broken Polish, "You will come with me." Jan looks at this huge Russian and thinks, *Gosh, what a big bully he is.*

The Russian has a firm grip on Jan's arm. This Russian pushes and carries Jan for a short distance. Suddenly he throws Jan into a one-room house with several other kids. Some of the kids look like they are only eight or nine years old, *The same as me,* thinks Jan. One kid looked older, perhaps sixteen. All the kids look terrible, thinks Jan, for they have scars on their faces and terrible-looking sores on their faces and arms.

Jan feels absolute terror. He knows he is going to die. He thinks, *I will never see my family again.* Jan forces himself to stop thinking about death. He says to himself, "I want to live. I must get out of here. This Russian wants to do something horrible to me." Jan's brain tells him he must get out of this place now. Jan wonders, *How do I get out of here?*

Jan calms himself and looks this place over for a way to escape. He sees three adults and about thirty kids all in this one room. Two adults are standing by the door as if they are guarding the door so no one can get out. Jan wonders if the Russian has the door locked. Jan wonders if these kids did something wrong—did they steal something?

Terror grips Jan's body, and yet he does calm himself. Slowly he plans a way to get out of this awful place. *If I stay here,* he thinks, *they will make sausage of me—I know I want to live.* Jan feels petrified with fear but realizes—he must get out of this place.

Slowly Jan inches his body closer to the door. Jan notices the man at the door often looks away from the door. Jan moves a few feet closer to the door each time the man looks away. Jan's heart beats faster and faster. Suddenly the door opens and a different man throws another kid into the room. Slowly but firmly, Jan moves closer to the door. Now he waits for the moment the adult at the door looks away. He feels certain the door has no lock on it.

The moment comes; the man starts talking to another man and does not look at Jan. Jan stands up and runs, hitting the door at full speed; the door bursts open, and Jan runs fast like a bullet—probably the fastest he ever ran in his life. Jan glances back and sees the man running after him. Jan screams his prayer, "God, don't let that man catch me."

Jan runs into another section of the market with many people. He senses the man getting close to him. Jan spots an official-looking man standing on crutches. Jan screams in Polish to this man, "Save me, I will tell you everything, please save me." Today Jan does not know why he said those words, but he did say them. Jan never forgot this incident.

The man does not understand anything Jan says but he sees a big man chasing this small boy. The official-looking man stepped out on his crutches in front of the Russian and said, "Stop! You leave this boy alone!" The man stops chasing Jan stops and says nothing, but he turns and walks away from Jan.

Jan cannot stop shaking as he tries to explain to the official-looking man why that man chased him. The man does not understand what Jan says. This man felt that the man chasing the boy did not have any good intentions towards the boy. He tries to calm Jan with some success. Jan keeps talking in Polish. The man knows some Polish words but very few. He speaks the few Polish words he knows to Jan. His Polish words help Jan calm down.

The man suspects Jan came from the orphanage and walks with Jan a few blocks that take them close to the orphanage. The man cannot walk fast because the injuries to his leg were so severe he must use crutches. He asks Jan in broken Polish, "Do you live in that orphanage?" Jan nods his head yes.

He tells Jan, "Go to your orphanage and do not be afraid. I will watch you until you are safe inside." Jan makes it safely back to the orphanage but before going inside the gate, he turns and waves his hand at the man. The man gives Jan a salute and watches as Jan enters the orphanage.

Jan missed his dentist appointment. He tells the teacher at the orphanage what happened to him on the way to the dentist. The next day a teacher accompanies Jan to the dentist. The dentist smears his gums with some medicine that stops his bleeding gums. Most of the children visit the dentist several times a year because of their bleeding gums.

When Jan turns twelve years of age, he learns he must help with the work on the farm outside the city that provides food to the orphanage.

The orphanage gets almost all of their food from this farm. Jan does not want to leave the orphanage, for he remains terrified of the outside world. Jan has no choice; he must take his turn working on the farm.

Jan learns from another boy at the orphanage who has worked on the farm that a big Georgian guy runs the farm. The boy tells Jan, "This guy, he lives on the farm with his wife and he has built himself a small shack on the farm. The boys from our orphanage help him with the farm chores and he needs the help we give him. Jan, we have fun working on the farm." Jan does not believe this boy, for Jan feels something bad will happen to him.

Today Jan and his friend must leave the orphanage to work on the farm. Early in the morning, the boys pick up their buckets of food for their lunch and leave for the farm. To get to the farm, the boys must walk into the orchard that lies next to the farm.

Several wild boys about seventeen and eighteen years old live within this orchard. These boys like to cause trouble, and they create problems for anyone walking through or near the orchard. The town merchants know the boys are of Chechnya origin and call the boys "hooligans."

As Jan and his friend, Abram, walk into the orchard, suddenly without any warning, a huge guy jumps in front of Jan and yells, "Give me your matches."

Jan and Abram have no matches and they tell the guy in scared barely audible voices, "We have no matches."

The big guy grabs Jan and says throatily, "You come with me." Another big guy grabs Abram in a tight grip.

Both Jan and Abram feel terror. The boys remember hearing the tales about these big guys that drown little boys just for the fun of it.

Jan thinks this cannot get any worse and wonders where these guys plan to take them. *Do they plan to kill us?* wonders Jan. A few minutes pass. Jan feels the big guy's grip on his hand slacken. At this precise moment, Jan jerks his hand away and runs as fast as he can toward the river. Abram gets away from his captor and runs with Jan toward the river. The boys run as fast as they can and when they reach the river, they jump in and swim frantically. They never let go of their lunch buckets.

Jan and Abram, now just a short distance from the farm, get out of the river. As the boys leave the river behind them, they start screaming for the Georgian while running as fast as they can toward the farm. The Georgian hears the boys' screams and walks quickly toward the boys. The hooligans are almost on top of the boys. They see the Georgian come at them. The big boys quickly turn and run back into the orchard.

The Georgian, seeing the fear on the boys' faces, explains to the boys that those big bullies are stealing the fruit from the orchard and taking the fruit to the farmer's market for money. He tells the boys, "People are stealing and killing for food and money. These times remain hideous, especially for you children and any honest adults here in Uzbekistan."

After the boys complete their work, the Georgian walks Jan and Abram to the other end of the orchard and watches as the boys head for the orphanage. When the Georgian returns to his shack, he tells his wife, "These are horrible times for children to grow up."

America now fights in this war, and people in Europe think the end of the war will be soon. When finally the war ends, people say, "Hell has ended. Now, perhaps, we can become civilized people again."

In Europe, WWII ends on May 8, 1945. On September 2, 1945,

Japan signs the surrender agreement. The United Nations becomes officially born on October 24, 1945.

Once the war ended, the authorities arrange to return all the children of Polish origin to an orphanage in Poland. This task will take several years to carry out. The authorities finally send Jan to the Polish orphanage in Poland in late 1946. Jan stays in this orphanage until he becomes eighteen years old.

Jan studies in the gymnasium (high school) and starts technical school (junior college) while living in the orphanage. Living in the orphanage, he learns to play volleyball and soccer even though he has no shoes to wear.

The orphanage, always short of shoes, tries in vain to get shoes for the children. Sometimes they get lucky and receive shoes. When the shoes get holes, the boys tape the holes, so they can play volleyball and soccer. Jan loves playing volleyball and soccer, with or without shoes, and he plays the games like a professional.

At the age of eighteen, Jan must leave the orphanage and provide food and shelter for himself. The munitions plant making fuses for antiaircraft has hired Jan to work for them. After work, he continues to play volleyball and soccer, with or without shoes. Most important to Jan, he wants to find his family.

At the age of twenty, Jan learns his family lives in America and they are alive. Now, he must find a way to get to America.

Chapter Twenty-Five
Politics Versus Immigration

In the final stages of World War II, the Polish army fought with the Russian troops until they captured Berlin. The bond of hatred for the Germans unites the Russian and Polish troops as they fight the Germans. As the war ends, many political changes occur in Poland.

In early 1945, the Allied Powers set Poland's eastern border along the so-called Curzon line (see map). This puts the town of Lwow (or Lviv) and the area where Michal and his family lived inside the Russian border. Many Polish people living in Russia move back inside the Polish border. Russian leaders continue to rule and dominate Poland. The Allied Powers placed Poland under the protection of Stalin of Russia even though Poland protested. Polish leaders want Poland to be a nation run by Polish leaders.

The western border of Poland extends to the Oder and Lusatian Neisse rivers. August of 1945, in Potsdam, President Truman of the USA, Stalin, and Clement Attlee settle Poland's western border. The three leaders also turn Gdansk on the Baltic Sea over to Poland. The leaders in Potsdam decrease Poland's land in the east and increase Polish land in the west and north.

In early 1948, Gomulka (a Russian) rose to power as secretary-general of Poland. In September of 1948, the PPR (Polish Workers'

Party) removes Gomulka from his position of power and puts Boleslaw Bierut in Gomulka's position.

In early 1952, it is not as difficult to migrate to America as it has been in the past. Bierut, now Poland's secretary-general, is instrumental in getting a new constitution passed. The death of Stalin and Poland's new political course leads to changes in Polish political life. It becomes easier for a Polish citizen to migrate to America than it was in the past.

Jan immediately goes to the immigration office to get permission to move to America. The immigration people refuse Jan's request to move to America. Several times Jan goes to the Polish immigration office seeking permission to migrate to America, and each time the immigration people refuse Jan's request. Jan wonders why the immigration office keeps refusing his request.

Jan talks to his friends about why the immigration office refusals to let him migrate to America. Jan's friends tell him, "It is your work at the munitions plant making fuses for anti-aircraft." Jan, stunned, thinks his friends are right. To find another job and not in munitions will not be easy for Jan.

After WWII ended, Poland had huge losses of population; the Germans destroyed their industry and agriculture. Warsaw barely exists. The war and politics divide the Polish people, and the Russians continue to rule Poland.

In 1956, Gomulka returns to power and Poland's dealings with the Soviets become stable. Still, Jan cannot get permission to migrate to America.

Two more years pass and Jan remains at the munitions factory. Jan does deal with sensitive secretive material. Jan, now twenty-two years old, meets a young woman named Gabriela.

Gabriela is a young and beautiful woman. She knocks Jan off his feet, and he is speechless. All he can say to this lovely young woman is "WOW, OH I am pleased to meet you." Jan realizes his heart beats much too fast.

Jan immediately starts to court Gabriela. They get along well and enjoy each other's company. Jan tells Gabriela about his family in America and his need to travel to America. Gabriela understands his wish to visit his family after so many years of separation.

After only a few months of courtship, Jan proposes to Gabriela and she hesitates for just a few seconds before saying "YES." With her word of "yes," Jan feels like a king who has won the hand of his queen.

Jan and Gabriela marry in their Catholic church in Poland. Their Catholic priest presides over their wedding, a traditional Polish wedding ceremony. Gabriela's parents and siblings plus all their friends come to their wedding. Jan and Gabriela feel deeply blessed.

After a few months of marriage, Gabriela tells Jan, "Jan, we will have a son or daughter in several months." Soon after their first wedding anniversary, they welcome a baby boy into their family. Two years later, a baby daughter arrives. Jan and Gabriela feel a deep happiness.

Jan and Gabriela continue to live in Poland, and Jan goes to the immigration office every month and tries to get permission to migrate to America. Jan has been looking for a different job but unsuccessfully. Then one of his close friends tells Jan of a position available in a business that does not deal in munitions. Jan immediately applies for this position and the company hires him. Jan gives his notice to the munitions company he works for and a few weeks later, he works at his new business.

Jan and Gabriela are hopeful they will be able to come to America soon.

Chapter Twenty-Six

Life in America

In the early spring of 1953, Frank and Jadzia buy an older home on ten acres. They love their new home and the land that has many big beautiful trees. The most important fact to Frank and Jadzia is this home and the land is now all theirs. Of course, they do have a mortgage, but they know they can meet the payments for they have not overextended themselves financially.

Michal and his family visit Frank and Jadzia often on weekends, and they all enjoy their roomy home and the freedom to roam their ten acres. The boys love the big beautiful trees and enjoy sitting under one particular tree that has wide sweeping branches that shade them from the sun. They all enjoy sitting under the big trees during a gentle rain.

Summer is fast approaching, and Ted looks forward to the end of the school year so he can find work and have a little money for himself. Ted finds work picking strawberries. When strawberry season ends, he gets work picking beans, peaches, and then apples. Ted makes enough money to buy all his school clothes and has enough money left over just to spend on whatever he wants.

In September, Ted starts his sophomore year in high school and resumes his friendship with Dave and Chuck. The boys continue doing many sports not sponsored by their school.

At the end of a school day, the three boys enjoy swimming in the Columbia River and playing on Hayden Island. They swim in the Columbia River almost every day after school. It is now almost the end of September, and the boys are swimming in the Columbia when Chuck, floating on a log, calls out to Dave and Ted for help. The current is taking Chuck out beyond the safe area. Immediately, Dave and Ted start to swim towards Chuck.

Unfortunately, Dave and Ted are not good swimmers and they have a difficult time reaching Chuck. When Dave and Ted reach Chuck they are out of breath. Now the boys must use every ounce of strength they have to bring the log and Chuck back to safety.

When they are all safe, the boys realize they have had a narrow escape from death and that their wonderful Columbia River is a dangerous place to swim. They continue to play on Hayden Island but stay out of the water except to swim to the island.

Frank and Jadzia have continued trying tirelessly to bring Maria, Jadzia's mother and Ted's grandmother, to America. Today they receive a letter from Szczepan that Maria will arrive in America soon. Maria has been in England for a long time; Ted did not think the authorities would ever allow Maria to come to America.

Jadzia and Frank tell Michal they want Maria to live with them and help them with their children. Michal feels relief and sadness, for he does not have room in his home for his mother.

Six weeks later, in mid October, Maria arrives in Vancouver, Washington. Jadzia and Frank meet her at the train station, where they hug and kiss her repeatedly. Maria never learned any English; therefore Jadzia and Frank greet her in Polish.

Maria does not want to learn any English and refuses to try to learn

English. However, she does love to watch two English-speaking TV programs and she watches them faithfully. One is the *I Love Lucy* show and the other is *Portland Wrestling*. Ted cannot believe his grandmother's choice of TV programs.

Maria does involve herself with her grandchildren; she helps Jadzia and Frank with their children as much as possible. Maria enjoys watching TV. Maria sometimes feels bitter toward her family for the rough times she has lived through, but she knows it was the Russians that forcibly took her and her family from their home. America is alright, but Maria hungers for her home and farmland in eastern Poland. Maria has always hoped and prayed she would someday return to her own home and farmland that she loved so very much.

Maria enjoys her grandchildren and shows them much love. In spite of Maria's poor attitude toward all her moves, Jadzia, Frank, and Maria have a pleasant relationship. Maria does help Jadzia with her children and teaches Jadzia to bake bread and cook. Maria's faith in God helps her adjust to life in America, and she even learns a little English.

Ted does not see his grandmother often, for he prefers being with his friends .Since the boys do not swim anymore, they play in the woods and build forts. They also build fires and trap rabbits without any luck. Since they cannot catch rabbits, they settle for fresh fish they catch and cook to feed themselves. When the boys tire of fish, they bring hot dogs, roast them over their fires, and eat the hot dogs without buns or seasoning. Ted hopes and prays every night that nothing will ever happen to change his happiness.

Ted becomes interested in wrestling when he visits Dave during his sophomore year at school. Millie (Dave's mother) takes the boys to see live wrestling three or four times a month. Ted's grandmother, Maria, loves to watch wrestling too, but this common interest does not bring Ted and Maria closer. Of course, the boys have to test their skills against one another. Dave and Ted are equal in their wrestling skills, but Dave is heavier and stronger than Ted, yet Ted is quicker and can usually outmaneuver Dave and win. Ted always feels great when he wins.

In late October, Chuck tells Ted and Dave, "I am going to move to Colorado with my dad."

Chuck's words stun Dave and Ted speechless for a full minute. Suddenly both boys say in unison, "No, no, you can't move away, we love you. You cannot leave us."

Chuck tells his friends, "You guys, I love you both, but my dad arrives next week to take me to Colorado. I am going to live with my dad on his ranch, about fifty miles south of Denver. Perhaps, one or both of you could visit me in Colorado," says Chuck.

Dave and Ted cannot grasp the news that Chuck will move away. They do not believe what they hear Chuck say. The boys just hug one another and wish Chuck much happiness. All too soon, Chuck leaves for Colorado. Ted and Dave spend their spare time together. They both miss Chuck more than they can describe.

Ted's sophomore year ends in June of 1954, and Ted learns he has made the honor roll. He feels proud and can hardly wait for his dad to come home so he can tell him the great news.

When Ted's dad walks into their home after work, Ted tells him his news. His dad simply replies, "You could have done better." Then he walks away from Ted and says nothing more. Ted cannot believe his dad's words and he feels a profound disappointment.

Years later a more mature Ted realized his dad was proud of his achievements but some code he learned years ago would not let him show pride or joy. Ted's dad never knew how much young Ted needed praise and reinforcement from his dad. Ted notices that his stepmom always praised her son even when he did nothing. Ted hungers for the praise and encouragement that would show him that his dad does love him.

Although Michal did not make a lot of money, he has managed to save enough money to purchase and be the owner of his own home. In 1954, he buys an old three-bedroom house. This house offers more than their apartment, but not a lot.

The house has a master bedroom and small bathroom on the main floor. In addition, a small living room, dining room, and large kitchen with an eating area are on the main floor. On the second floor, there are two bedrooms and a small bathroom. The house has a large front yard and even bigger backyard. The big backyard has room for a garden, and Michal tells Ted he has the responsibility for the garden.

Upstairs, Ted gets the larger bedroom. At night, Ted can see the large well-lit sign "RED LAGER BEER" that shines through his window into his room and onto his bed. Ted's stepbrother gets the smaller bedroom. The builder did not finish the basement. In fact, the basement has no concrete foundation under the house. The house simply rests a few feet above bare ground, and the first (main) floor that consists of wood suffers water damage over the next two years. Michal and Ted spend many hours working on this house over the next few years.

Michal continues working at the paper mill, and his wife continues with her job as a dishwasher. Together they do not make much money but enough to buy their own home. They feel thrilled to have their own home. Michal continues trying to bring Jan and his family to America. Michal does not understand why it is taking so long or it is so difficult to bring Jan and his family to America.

The summer of 1954 arrives and Ted works picking strawberries, beans, peaches, and apples for money. This summer Ted is a more skillful worker and makes more money than he did in the summer of 1953. This time, no fruit enters Ted's stomach and the boys do not throw any fruit at each other, as they had been prone to do in the past.

While picking fruit, Ted sometimes thinks of Jan and wonders if he will ever see his brother again. Ted remembers that once when he was little and hungry, Jan gave him food off his plate.

Summer soon ends, and Ted returns to school, a junior, at Vancouver High School. Ted's gym teacher, Mr. Poe, tells Ted he should try out for the football team. Ted decides to try out for the football team and makes the team.

The first two weeks of school consist of the usual studies and now "daily doubles." Ted must practice football every morning and every afternoon. At first, Mr. Poe concentrates on physical conditioning but all too soon football training starts.

Ted prides himself on being in good physical shape, but this coach finds muscles in Ted that he did not know he had. By the end of the first week, Ted is so sore it hurts to touch any part of his body. During the second week, they practice tackling and blocking. This means you hurl your body into the air (an unnatural act for a person to do). It does take Ted a while to master this technique.

During the third week, the boys learn football plays. This game is new to Ted and all those X's and O's are unfamiliar to him. However, he does eventually memorize the plays and properly executes the plays.

Ted wants to play the end position, but the coaches decide he would be best as a tackle.

During the fourth week of football practice, Ted's uncle Ed Ledbetter invites Ted to go deer hunting with him. The weekend before they leave, Ed takes Ted to an old quarry where they practice with a rifle they will use when they go deer hunting. Ed cannot believe that Ted can shoot so accurately. Ed does not know that Ted used to shoot a BB gun and was an accurate shooter.

The morning before they leave to hunt deer, Ted develops a terrible right lower abdominal pain. Michal calls the doctor and when he comes to see Ted (back then doctors made house calls), he immediately diagnoses Ted with acute appendicitis and rushes Ted to the hospital. At the hospital, the doctor performs an appendectomy. After his appendectomy when Ted becomes fully conscious, the doctor tells Ted, "Your appendix was about to burst and had you been in the woods deer hunting you might not have lived."

Ted's appendectomy not only canceled the hunting trip, it also ended Ted's football career. Ted remained in the hospital for ten whole days. This was a normal hospital stay for an appendectomy in 1954.

The money Ted made picking fruit is gone and he needs more money. Ted gets a job working in the high school kitchen. He works the early lunch and receives his lunch free. Ted does not like this job, but it does help with his finances. Ted also becomes good friends with three other students that work in the school kitchen. Their names are Mick, Dick, and Allan.

Mick works with Ted in the school kitchen. Mick has a tendency to get sick often and miss work. Still, he plays a good game of chess and can play pinochle.

Dick plays on the football team, and he plays well. Dick has a great sense of humor.

The third boy Ted works with is Allan. Ted believes Allan is the smartest of all his friends. However, Allan sometimes forgets important facts or so thinks Ted.

During Ted's junior year, he becomes involved in more and different school clubs. Some of the clubs are the chess club, French club, and the international club. The international club consists of students from different nationalities and exchange students from other countries. Ted's life becomes unusually busy with his clubs and studies. Still, he decides to run for the junior class vice president.

Three other students are running for the class vice president's position, making four students competing for this position. Ted knows nothing about campaigning, but he comes in second. Later in the school year, Ted's classmates elect him to the student senate. This group meets once a month, and Ted enjoys all the other students in the student senate.

Ted is a friendly person, and most of his classmates are friendly to him except for a few other students. Some students resent Ted because of his Polish accent and his good grades. These unfriendly students make snide remarks to Ted and call him a "Pollock" or "foreigner." Ted tries to ignore these remarks, but they hurt just the same.

One day, an annoying boy walking behind Ted as they both climbs a flight of stairs, yells at Ted, "You get out of my way or I will kick the shit out of you."

Ted snaps and whirls around, grabs the boy by his jacket and lifts him off his feet so the boy's face is level with his face. Ted snarls at the boy in a deep voice, "Just you try it."

Ted holds the boy off his feet for about fifteen seconds. Then suddenly Ted forcibly sets him down. This boy never gave Ted trouble again. However, some students continue to make unkind remarks to Ted.

Ted's half brother does well in school. He gets good grades and has many friends and he now speaks almost perfect English and rarely speaks Polish even at home. His mother speaks only English to her son and she speaks English with just a slight accent. Ted feels they should all speak in Polish when they are home.

Ted never dates during his junior year. He likes girls but hesitates asking a girl for a date. He goes to several dances but always alone. He considers himself a poor dancer, yet he is able to get around a dance floor with a girl rather smoothly. He goes to dances at his local church, St. James Catholic Church. He meets girls at church but no romances develop for Ted. He thinks of the first girl he fell in love with back in England and wonders if he will ever have those feelings again.

The international club consists of exchange students, immigrants from other countries, and anyone who has an interest in foreign countries. Ted joins the international club and thoroughly enjoys their movies, games, and speakers that talk on different topics. At each meeting one or two of the members talk about their country. It could be anything from geography, history, customs, or traditions of their particular country. Each semester the members have an international potluck that everyone enjoys.

Chapter Twenty-Seven
Michal's House

The first house that Michal buys in Vancouver, Washington, is old and has only a dirt basement. The ceilings of their home are high and the house is hard to heat in the wintertime. The house next door to Michal has a new owner, and he has the same style house. This man raises his house up a few feet. Now Michal decides he must raise his house up a few feet. Michal wants storage space below the main floor. Raising the house will provide more storage space underneath the house and reduce the dampness in his house.

To raise a house up several feet is not an easy task. However, Michal decides he must renovate his whole house from the bottom to the top, and he tells his son Ted he must help him after school every day and weekends until they complete the work.

First, Michal puts in a concrete floor in the basement of his house. He had this done by the cement company. Next, he borrowed massive jacks from his neighbor to raise the house.

Michal leaves work about 3:00 p.m., and Ted arrives home about 3:30 p.m. Michal demands that Ted get home promptly and not waste time talking to his friends. Today, Michal and Ted work together putting four massive jacks under each side of the house. The space under the house is only a few feet in height.

The first day they work is a school day, Friday, Michal and Ted put only six jacks in place. The second day, Saturday, they put in the rest of the jacks. They put sixteen jacks under the house. On Sunday, both

Figure 5. Michal's House

Michal and Ted go around and around the house, moving each jack up a few inches at a time. They do this until they have moved the house up high enough for Ted and Michal to stand erect in the basement.

Now each day after school Michal and Ted work putting in a foundation of cement blocks under the raised house until the blocks touch the underside of the house. Next, they carefully remove each jack and replace the removed jack with concrete blocks.

Ted feels thrilled that he has finished his work. Quickly, Michal tells

Ted he must help him knock out some interior walls and lower their ceilings. Ted cannot believe what his father has just said to him.

Michal and Ted cut carefully into the wall between the living room and dining room. They make sure they avoid the electrical wires. Next, they reroute the wires. Now, they add support to the ceiling because the upper floor begins to sag.

Michal likes his much larger living room. The next task is to put in a new ceiling at least eighteen inches lower than the original twelve-foot ceiling. When Michal and Ted complete the work on the ceiling, Michal tells Ted they must now replace most of the floors that now cave inwardly. Ted says nothing to his dad, but inwardly he feels deep anger toward his dad because of the continual series of tasks to be done.

Michal and Ted replaced the downstairs floors with new plank flooring from the lumberyard. When they finish putting in the new floors, Michal says to Ted, "Now we must do the walls." Ted looks in shock at his dad.

The work on this house has taken a good six months. Ted and his dad do all the work themselves. They set up a routine for getting the work done in a satisfactory manner. Michal does not have good math skills, so Ted does all the figuring for the amount and sizes of the materials they need to complete each task. Michal and Ted do not have the abilities of skilled builders and make many mistakes. Michal and Ted cut their wood with a handsaw; everything they do is by human sweat, for they have no power tools. Often, they work until late in the evening, sometimes as late as 10:00 p.m. When they complete their work, Ted does his homework.

After six months of working on this house, Ted rebels. Rather than getting the tasks started when he gets home from school, Ted goes to a movie and stays out until ten o'clock.

Over the years, Ted received several beatings from his dad when he did something his dad did not like. Tonight, Ted decides that he will not let his father beat him.

When Ted arrives home, Michal screams at Ted for not being available to work when he came home. Michal takes a broomstick from behind his back and swings it at Ted as hard as he can. Ted automatically lifts his left forearm to block this blow and breaks the broomstick into two pieces. Michal reaches to pick up the bigger piece of the broomstick, but Ted forcibly stomps on the piece of broomstick and makes a fist of both his hands. Ted is ready for anything.

Michal sees in Ted's eyes anger and a determination to fight to win. Michal backs away, keeping his eyes on Ted. Ted walks past his dad and hisses, "NEVER AGAIN, NEVER."

Ted walks away from his dad, goes to his room, and locks his door. He stays awake and alert for hours, for he does not know what his dad might do to him. Nothing happens that night. However, father and son do complete all their projects but at a slower pace.

Michal and Ted attend the events at the Polish Hall. Ted enjoys talking with Polish people in his Polish language. Ted meets a young woman his age at the Polish Hall, and they develop a friendship. Ted wants to fall in love but feels no connection to this woman. Ted feels he will never fall in love.

In the spring of 1955, Oregon State University hosts a model of the United Nations. Ted takes part in this event, as he is the chairperson for the international relations club in his high school. Ted and three other students from Vancouver High School and their faculty adviser join in this event.

The boys and their faculty adviser stay at the OSU dormitory, for the students at OSU are on spring break. Two hundred and fifty students, all from many high schools, came to this event. The students represent different countries in the General Assembly.

The Assembly chooses Ted to represent the country of Panama. Ted must research the issues facing Panama and then present a resolution to the General Assembly. The Assembly does not debate Ted's resolution because of a lack of time. However, this is an excellent experience for Ted and whets his appetite for diplomacy and politics.

After this General Assembly experience, Ted, now almost seventeen, can take the test for his driver's license. Ted's dad rarely lets Ted drive his car. Occasionally, Ted borrows a car from one of his friends and once from a teacher. Ted has the reputation for taking good care of cars lent to him. He always makes sure that when he returns a car it is clean and has more gas in the tank than when he received the car.

Ted goes to the motor vehicle licensing place, takes his driver's license test, and passes. Thrilled that he passed his driver's test, Ted goes over to his friend Dave's house. Ted learns that Dave is serious about a woman that Ted does not like. Even Dave's mother prefers that her son find a different woman.

Dave tells Ted they plan to marry and he wants Ted to be his best man. Ted agrees to be Dave's best man but hopes something happens to stop his wedding.

The summer of 1955 begins like all the rest. Ted gets a job picking strawberries. This farmer hires only the best pickers, and he pays a premium wage. Most of the workers are high school students, and they do not engage in horseplay.

After several days of work, Ted meets a young woman who intrigues him. Her name is Charity, and she is the same age as Ted. Ted believes she is intelligent and has good taste in young men. Charity and Ted talk constantly while picking strawberries and despite their constant talking, they pick more strawberries than if they did not talk to each other.

Charity has a sister, Pam, and Pam has a boyfriend. Ted, Charity, Pam, and her boyfriend, Roy, begin dating and often go to the movies. The two couples continue seeing each other even after Ted's senior year begins.

Ted continues to see Charity and hang out with her sister and her boyfriend. The four of them date for the next six months. Roy has his own car so he drives most of the time. They go to the movies, dances, roller-skating, picnicking, swimming, or just watch TV. One time they went to see Elvis at Jantzen Beach in Portland. Elvis is famous but not the star he becomes later.

As Ted and Charity's friendship grows, Charity brings up the subject of marriage. However, Ted remains determined to go to college and further his education. Charity and Ted have different objectives, and this creates a rift in their romance. Suddenly and without any warning, Charity states she does not want to see Ted again. This is a blow to Ted, and he tries to get an explanation from Charity, but she gives him none.

The rest of Ted's senior year passes uneventfully. He continues to plan for college. Ted knows his dad has no money to pay for college, so Ted decides to find a way to pay for his college education.

Ted's plan is to work at the paper mill during the summer and attend Clark Junior College in Vancouver for the first year. By living at home and working evenings and weekends, he can build up a reserve of money for the next three years.

Shortly before his senior year ends, Ted applies for work at the Crown Zellerback paper mill in Camas. The boss at the paper mill hires Ted immediately, and he starts work the day after his senior prom. Ted feels thrilled as his plan begins to work.

Vancouver High School holds the senior class graduation party and dance at the Vancouver Elks Lodge in early June of 1956. This is an impressive occasion for Ted, for he is proud to have achieved a high school education and the right to enter college in the fall.

Ted has always felt impressed by the Elks Lodge building, as it is a splendid building. The Elk members cover all the costs of the senior prom. In addition, the Elk president says the Elks will give out ten scholarships.

Ted does not know what a scholarship means or how it might benefit him. Ted does not even know that he can apply for a full scholarship. Although Ted believes himself fully Americanized, he knows nothing about many American privileges that other students take for granted.

Ted arrives at his senior prom at 9:00 p.m. He dances with many young women and talks with his friends. To Ted's surprise, he receives a scholarship for one hundred dollars from the Elks at an achievement award ceremony that evening. This is the only scholarship he ever receives. Ted never applies for a scholarship because he knows nothing about scholarships or that he could apply for one.

At the prom, someone brings out several bottles of alcohol. Now alcohol flows freely to those at the prom. Ted drinks a whole bottle of the alcohol and goes home drunk at 1:30 a.m.

Ted finds Michal waiting for him in the kitchen when he arrives home. In shock, Ted asks his dad, "Why have you waited up for me?"

Ted's dad tells him the paper mill supervisor called and wants Ted to report for work immediately. The mill supervisor knows that Ted is at his senior prom but wants him to come to work as soon as he returns home.

Ted refuses to tell his dad or the mill supervisor that he cannot work because of his drunken condition. Instead, Ted quickly changes into his work clothes, gulps down a cup of coffee, grabs the lunch bucket his stepmother prepared for him, and leaves for work.

Chapter Twenty-Eight
The Paper Mill

Oregon and Washington state experience heavy flooding of the Columbia River during the spring of 1956. The paper mill put up many dikes and levies to protect the paper plant. In doing this, the men working at the paper mill used heavy timber and tens of thousands of sandbags to keep the water away from the paper mill. It is now early June; the Columbia River has receded to a normal level.

The order from the mill to their labor gang is to demolish all those dikes and levies, empty all the sandbags, and haul all the debris to a huge pit on the paper mill property.

For Ted, this first day of work at the Crown Zellerback paper mill proves to be a hideous day.

Ted's fist assignment is to the labor gang department. This department does all the heavy clean-up and repairs of equipment. This is a tough job, but for Ted this night is the worst he will ever have.

Ted's supervisor is an old-fashioned slave driver who pushes everyone to the limit. The only breaks the laborers receive are "smoking breaks" required by the labor agreement with the paper mill. The breaks are fifteen minutes every four hours. The way the supervisor read this clause is if you do not smoke, you do not get a break. The laborers learn to light a cigarette in their hands when on a break even if they do not smoke.

Working during the night hours, Ted suffers scratches and bruises that cover his entire body. Every muscle in his body aches and his hangover is killing him, he thinks. Yet, he keeps on working.

At 8:00 a.m. the morning work shift arrives, but the supervisor expects the night shift to keep working. The only good news is their slave-driving night supervisor leaves. From eight in the morning until noon, the work is hard but done at a more normal pace. Now the workers receive an unexpected break. There are no more trucks to load.

The supervisor grants the men a ten-minute break that turns into half an hour. Ted sits with his back against a wall and closes his eyes.

Suddenly the supervisor rudely awakens Ted and says, "Get those empty trucks filled with this debris."

All the workers including the night shift work until mid afternoon. At 3:00 p.m., the supervisor tells Ted to go home and return at midnight. Ted simply returns home to his room and falls asleep before his head hits his pillow. Michal wakens Ted at 10:30 p.m. Ted eats some supper and leaves for work. Ted must be at work by midnight.

During the summer of 1956, work at the paper mill consumes almost all of Ted's time. Ted and his dad continue to visit the Polish Hall, where Ted reads all the Polish books available. Ted and Michal's contact with other Polish people continues to be important to both father and son. While visiting with other Polish people, Ted and his dad feel at home and subordinate to no one.

Ted continues to see Dave and his family, but less often. Several weeks pass before Dave talks to Ted. He tells Ted that he plans to marry his girlfriend on August 1, 1956. Dave asks Ted to be his best man and Ted says reluctantly, "Yes."

Dave's family is poor, and Ted lends Dave his sport jacket that looks fine for the wedding ceremony. The bride wears a modest dress. The wedding ceremony inspires Ted, and he thinks, *Someday I will marry.* Ted felt good being Dave's best man. After the ceremony, Dave told Ted he had an interview at Alcoa Aluminum Company this coming Wednesday. Dave hopes to get a position with Alcoa Aluminum, as their benefits are great and the pay good.

The Alcoa Aluminum Company hires Dave, and now Dave's work schedule conflicts with Ted's school schedule. Unfortunately Dave and Ted now rarely see each other. Ted feels he has lost a good friend and feels sad that he and Dave are so far apart. First Chuck moved away, and now Ted rarely sees Dave since his marriage. Ted feels lonely without his best friends.

When Ted receives his first paycheck from Crown Zellerback paper mill, he immediately buys an old Chrysler. Now, Ted does not have to rely on others to transport him to work or to college. His car burns oil but serves Ted well for over a year.

Ted's car burns so much oil that when Ted has the gas tank filled he asks the attendant to first fill the car up with oil and then fill the gas tank. In 1956, workers at the gas stations always filled a person's car with gas or oil and washed their cars' windshields too.

The few times that Ted and his dad work the same shift at the paper mill, his dad insists on going to work nearly an hour before their shift starts. If their shift starts at 8:00 a.m., the paper mill's rule is you cannot clock in until after 7:30. This fact does not matter to Ted's dad; he insists that they get to work before 7:00 a.m. Ted's dad is never late for anything.

In Poland, Jan continues asking for permission to come to America with his family.

October 20, 1956, Mr. Gomulka convinces Khrushchev and other Soviet leaders that they must respect the independence of Poland as a people's democracy. On October 21, by a secret ballot, Gomulka becomes first secretary of the Polish Communist Party.

Secretary Gomulka, a revolutionary, is more pro-western than any communist ruler has ever been behind the Iron Curtain. Mr. Gomulka announces his plan to grant more freedom and allow travel to the Western countries such as America. This is wonderful news for Ted and his dad, and they hope Jan can bring himself and his family to the United States soon.

Michal quickly contacts the American State Department and gets all the information to carry out the goal of bringing Jan and his family to the United States. Again, this will not be easy. Many obstacles keep Jan and his family from coming to America.

Chapter Twenty-Nine

Citizenship, College, Return to the Paper Mill

By November 21, 1956, Michal and his family have lived in the United States as legal residents for five years. They are now eligible for citizenship in the USA. Michal and his wife decide to take night classes to study American government and history so they can apply for their citizenship.

Ted's half brother, now ten years old, will automatically receive his citizenship when he becomes sixteen years old if his mother receives her citizenship. Ted is eighteen years old, so he must take the tests and receive citizenship in his name.

Ted takes the citizenship tests without a single problem. He always enjoyed studying history and government and read many books on those subjects. Ted breezes through the battery of tests and passes the entire test for citizenship in the United States of America on his first attempt.

Michal and his wife study hard too, to pass their tests. Ted gave them as much help as he could, and they all pass their citizenship tests. The entire family plans to take their oath of allegiance to America in a special ceremony in 1957.

In the fall of 1956, Ted begins his first year at Clark Junior College.

He finds college life exciting and interesting. The campus is on federal property, and the classrooms are old military barracks, but the atmosphere remains exhilarating. The professors do not consider their

Figure 6. Ted at Age 18

students to be “school brats,” instead, the professors consider their students as “ladies and gentlemen.” The college lets their students make their own choices and shape their own lives within reason.

Ted decides to major in civil engineering. He bases this choice on the fact that while in high school he had good grades in math and science.

Ted must also take chemistry. His chemistry professor knows and enjoys teaching chemistry. He imparts his knowledge to his students without difficulty. He carries a wooden yardstick in his hand and does not hesitate to break the yardstick over a desk to wake up a dozing student or to stress an important point.

Ted’s political science professor is different from his chemistry professor. This professor speaks softly. This professor instills in Ted a deep interest in political science and helps Ted realize that he prefers political science to civil engineering. Ted enjoys all his professors and does quite well in his first year of college.

After the first year of college ends in the spring of 1957, Ted, Michal, and his wife take the oath of allegiance to America. All the people who passed the citizenship test take the pledge of allegiance to the United States of America in a special ceremony.

As Ted takes the oath of allegiance, he realizes what a momentous occasion this has become for him. He has a great love for his native land, Poland, and he feels a loyalty to Poland. Ted often dreams of returning to Poland.

Ted does not hesitate to speak the pledge of allegiance to America. However, he feels a deep sadness when he gives up his allegiance to Poland. Ted fully understands the outcome of his pledge to the United States of America. He feels a deep pride becoming a citizen. He tells himself, *I am now an American citizen. It is all right for me to have a special affection for Poland, but in a case of conflict between my old country and my new country, America, my loyalty is to the United States of America.*

After the ceremony, Ted and Michal return to work at the Crown Zellerback paper mill. Ted continues working at the paper mill during the summer of 1957. He works weekends and some nights during the week, for he needs the money to pay for his college tuition in September of 1957. Ted has applied at Washington State University, and the university has accepted him. It costs a lot more money to attend Washington State University than Clark Junior College.

The paper mill is a pulp and sulfite mill. Every day the paper mill spews out of the plant's chimneys hundreds of tons of chemicals that corrode cars and roofs of houses and anything that is outdoors. The odors from this paper mill are awful to smell. The toxic fumes can and do cause some people, including Ted, to become ill and to vomit. The paper mill pollutes the water, and polluted water is a health hazard for all the people living near the mill.

The ground wood shop is where the workers grind the wood into pulp. During the next process, the workers process the pulp into paper. Most of the building, where everything to make paper occurs, lies underground. At the covered end of the building are the grinding machines. Steam and hot water make these machines work. It is always hot around these machines because they release large volumes of steam. During the summer months, the heat is unbearable as there is no air-conditioning.

At the other end of the building is an open pit. Trucks come and go around the clock seven days a week dumping loads of wood into a large open pit. A worker has to be on the lookout for the trucks when they dump their loads. The truck drivers are supposed to blow their horns before dumping the wood into the pit where workers are picking up the wood to put into the carts. However, the workers seldom hear the horn, for the grinding machines are making a hideous loud noise all the time. Some workers had narrow escapes when the trucks dump their load of wood. The falling wood could bury or seriously hurt a worker. The only thing that prevents serious accidents is the workers' agility.

Ted and other new workers load the wood into large carts and deliver the carts to the machines. Each cart holds two cords of wood. Each piece of wood is about eighteen inches long and a foot to sixteen inches in diameter, weighing fifty to seventy pounds. The wood is usually wet, and this makes it difficult to handle the wood. Doing this type of work is extremely difficult, especially during the winter months when it is bitter cold and perhaps raining.

It is backbreaking work for all who work at the Crown Zellerback Mill. Most jobs require the employee to be in excellent physical condition in order to survive the hardships of work at the mill.

Ted knows he does not want to work at Crown Zellerback Mill for the rest of his life. Ted wonders how his dad can endure the extreme physically hard labor at the paper mill and for so many years.

Ted works every summer at the mill to pay for the following college year. This plan worked until the summer of 1959. This summer Crown Zellerback cuts back and does not hire Ted until after five weeks of summer have passed.

Now Ted does not have enough money to pay for his junior year of college at Washington State. Michal, Ted's dad, learns of Ted's lack of money for college. His dad goes to his bank and withdraws enough money for Ted to complete his junior year of college. Michal gives this money to Ted. Ted is grateful but worries that his dad will have problems meeting his needs.

Michal tells Ted, "You take this money and get a college education because education is important. Ted, it is more important than you can ever imagine."

Ted graduates from Washington State University with an excellent grade point average. Both Ted's dad and stepmother came for his graduation. Ted's dad is very proud of Ted's college degree. Until Ted's graduation from college, no member of their family graduated from more than grade school. Ted managed to graduate not only from high school but also from the university. On top of this, the Marine Corps invites Ted to go to officer training school and become a Marine lieutenant.

Epilogue

Many years later, the Polish government is successful in its demands that the Russian government compensate the owners of the land and homes Russia so brutally took from their Polish citizens. Russia does agree to pay those owners for their land, but the owner must request the compensation. Michal is eligible for compensation but never requests anything from Russia because he does not trust the Russian government.

Russia rules Poland until 1990, when finally the Polish United Workers' (Communist) Party dissolves itself in January of 1990, creating in its place the Social Democracy of the Republic of Poland. The former Communist Party turns over most of their property to Poland. In May of 1990, Polish elections are entirely free.

In November of 1990, the people elect Lech Walesa president of Poland for a five-year term in a free election. Lech Walesa becomes the first popularly elected president of Poland.

After 1990, Poland makes great progress toward achieving a fully democratic government and a thriving economy. Forty-five years after WWII ended, Poland becomes a free country with free elections. Finally, the Polish people have their country back.

What happens to Jan and his desire to bring his family to America?

Does he bring his family to America? Michal wants Josef, his oldest son, to come to America. Does Josef ever change his mind, leave Africa, and come to America? Does Ted accept the Marine Corps offer to go into officer's training? Perhaps this is another story for another time.